PERSISTENT EVIL
The Demon Slayer

Diogenes Ruiz

This is a work of fiction. Names, characters, businesses, places, events and incidents are either the products of the author's imagination or used in a fictitious manner. Any resemblance to actual persons, living or dead, or actual events is purely coincidental.

ISBN:0976312638
ISBN-13: 978-0-9763126-3-5

This book is dedicated to Fr. William McConville.

"The most interesting man in the world"

TABLE OF CONTENTS

1

It's Over

He lay dead on the damp black asphalt. The smell of burnt rubber and hot metal emanated from the bowels of the truck. The set of skid marks left by the metal behemoth were freshly pressed onto the asphalt canvas, like two strokes from death's paint brush.

Two out-of-breath policemen approached the spot where the body lay. The paramedics would arrive soon. There was nothing they would be able to do. The impact of the Mantis Moving Company truck tossed the body like a rag doll, slamming it against a parked pickup truck filled with landscaping equipment. The front of the victim's scalp had been torn off. The left arm was dislocated and tucked behind his back. His eyes were still open.

Officers Hernandez and McNally had been chasing Monty McPride without any chance of catching him. The man seemed to have sprouted wings on his feet. He was running so fast that they had started to give up the chase. Then, they heard the painful screeching of brakes and a loud thud as the truck pummeled the body.

~~~

The ambulance arrived. Two paramedics made their way to where the victim lay. Carl, the lead paramedic, knelt beside the body and felt for a pulse. "Not much we can do here."

His assistant, Jake, prepared the gurney. Carl looked up at Jake. "Poor bastard took quite a hit. All we can do is take him to
~~~

the hospital and process him for storage in the morgue until someone comes to claim the body." Carl then turned to Officer Hernandez. "Was this simply an accident or was something else going on?"

Carl listened as Officer Hernandez explained how Monty was wanted for the attempted murder of his father, Blake McPride. The murder attempt was foiled by the miraculous recovery of the old man who had summoned the police before his son could arrive to finish the job. Monty's plan was to blow the old man's brains out. After all, the ungrateful old buzzard had selected someone else to run McPride Industries. In Monty's mind, the promotion should have gone to the handsome, brilliant son.

But, in a sting operation, the police staked out the nursing home where Blake McPride was living. Monty thought he had successfully snuck in the back entrance by threatening one of the facility's attendants, an undercover policewoman who pretended to be out on a smoke break. She surrendered a set of keys to him when he threatened to kill her. He locked her in the facility's storage shed. Then he entered the nursing home, intent on finally getting rid of the old man. The police confronted him as he was about to put a hole in Blake McPride's head. Monty made a run for it and nearly made it.

With red lights flashing and a crowd looking on, Monty McPride was pronounced dead at 6:19 pm.

As Carl was about to close the corpse's eyes, Officer Hernandez yelled, "Wait!" He pointed at the man who was approaching. "That's the guy's father."

The old man, now the picture of perfect health, approached Monty's body.

Carl closed Monty's eyes. Then he turned to Blake McPride. "I'm sorry, sir. There was nothing we could do. He was already dead when we arrived.

Blake did not respond. He looked down at his son's mangled body and muttered in a low voice, "God help you Monty. May He have mercy on your soul, and may He have mercy on me for being such a lousy father." Hot tears pooled in Blake's eyes.

Time slowed to a near halt. Sounds became dull murmurs. His peripheral vision faded to a blur as he stared at his son's lifeless body. He surrendered to the flood of memories that rushed in and held him in a trance.

~~~

Monty's life has been full of trouble. Blake loved his son, but he also felt that the boy had an unusual tendency to make trouble. He seemed to enjoy it. Blake never fully admitted it to himself while Monty was alive, but after almost being killed by him, he knew that there had been an evil side to his son that he could not explain. As a young father, Blake had hoped his gut feeling was wrong hoping his son was going through a phase. But one phase led to another, each with its own brand of evil.

His thoughts turned to his wife and how much he missed her. Both were independent, logical thinkers. Neither was religious. Any relationship with God was private and distant. Unfortunately, keeping God at arm's-length meant that other forces could work their way into the space that would otherwise be occupied by Him. Their son would develop a special relationship with evil.

Shortly after Shelly McPride learned that she was pregnant, she and Blake went on a cruise. One of their stops was Jamaica. After climbing the waterfall at Ocho Rios, Shelly was approached by several natives who owned souvenir shops along the route back down to the bus. She didn't want to buy a souvenir, so politely continued on her way down the path. More pushy vendors approached her. Some were children, some adults. After being approached by so many pushy merchants, she simply ignored them and walked hastily down the hill to reach the bus waiting to take them back to the ship. As Shelly made her way through the crowd, an old woman approached and grabbed her by the arm.

"Here, dear, just for you. It's only ten dollars." The scrawny old woman, with a weird tattoo in the middle of her forehead shoved a bracelet onto Shelly's wrist. It was the type that easily fit onto any wrist. Shelly looked at her with fear and disgust. She removed the bracelet with her free hand and shoved it back into the old woman's bony hand. She tried to break free of the woman's grip, but she would not let go. "Go ahead, it's only ten dollars. It looks good on you. Put it on. Put it on!"

Shelly was in tears, as she yelled, "LET ME GO, YOU WITCH!"
~~~

Blake caught up to his wife after buying a souvenir from one of the pushy vendors. "What's going on?"

"This old woman is harassing me to buy a stupid bracelet. I tried to be polite, but she grabbed me and would not let go. I just want to get out of here!"

The old woman looked at Blake McPride and held out the bracelet. "Only ten dollars, buy for your pretty wife."

Blake smiled politely. "No, thank you."

"Buy for your pretty wife," the old woman persisted. She let go of Shelly's wrist, and wrapped her bony hands around Blake's.

Shelly screamed, "Stop it, you old witch! Can't you see we don't want the stupid thing? She turned and marched away, leaving Blake in the clutches of the old woman. Blake reached into his pocket and gave the woman ten dollars. He was about to leave to catch up to Shelly, but the old woman still gripped his wrist. He looked at her and tried to pull away, a second time.

She smiled exposing her rotten teeth. "Here, bracelet for your pretty wife."

Blake put up his hand. "No, you keep it."

The old crow's smile took a serious turn. "Here, you take the bracelet, you pay for it, you take it." She still had not let go of him.

Blake grabbed the bracelet and ran after his wife.

Later that night Shelly became sick to her stomach. She spent the rest of the cruise in her cabin.

A few weeks later she began suffering recurring nightmares of the pushy old woman. She dreamt that she was in the hospital delivery room. Instead of Dr. Langley delivering her child, the old woman was delivering the baby. She would awaken in a cold sweat, breathing heavily.

When it was almost time to deliver the baby, Blake had to promise he would not allow any old women near her. Shelly didn't care if they were real nurses or not. Blake promised.

Monty was born at exactly 9:19 pm on June 19. Shelly was relieved that no old woman showed up at the hospital and her baby was born normal and healthy. After giving birth, Shelly was more herself and stopped obsessing about the cruise incident. Aside from telling Blake that she was done with cruises, she was pretty much her normal, joyful self.

Blake and Shelly loved their son and tried to encourage him to be gentle. They noticed he had a way of destroying his toys, unlike typical children who might wreck them from overuse and playing hard. Monty seemed to take more pleasure in destroying the toy than playing with it. It was the deliberate destruction which seemed to thrill him. Blake thought it was a developmental phase and was sure that he would outgrow it once Monty went to school and played with other children.

On Monty's sixth birthday, he became upset because he did not get the red bicycle he wanted. Blake had been all right with it, but Shelly thought that Monty was too young for a two wheeler and told him they would reconsider getting him a bike next year. Blake agreed to comply with his wife's wish.

The birthday party was a disaster. Monty acted like a brat the whole afternoon. Blake and Shelly reprimanded their son by taking away his play privileges. He was not allowed to watch television or play any video games until he apologized for his behavior.

Blake left on business the following morning. Shelly spent the day trying to help her son see the error of his behavior. She even promised to bake an apple pie for desert after supper. Monty spent the day in the garage pretending to organize some of his toys and other items stored there. Shelly was relieved that her son was at least doing something positive.

After spending most of the day in the garage, Monty came into the house to ask his mother what time she would be starting dinner.

"I'll be starting in about half an hour after I finish folding the laundry. Would you like to help me?"

Monty stood at the entrance to the kitchen. "No, I'm busy fixing stuff in the garage."

"It's good to fix things, Monty. You'll have to show me what you've been working on after dinner."

"OK," he said as he turned to head back to the garage.

While Shelly was in the laundry room, Monty closed all the kitchen windows and opened all the burners on the gas oven. He set his little remote-controlled car in the corner of the kitchen floor. He had observed that it always gave off a tiny spark in the little battery operated motor when he toggled the remote control to move the little race car forward. Twenty minutes later, Monty saw Shelly enter the kitchen to start dinner. He was across the street but still within range of his remote-controlled toy.

When Shelly entered the kitchen, Monty did not delay in toggling his remote-controlled car to move forward. Nothing happened. He tried it again, this time hitting reverse. In an instant, the kitchen exploded killing his mother and destroying three quarters of the house. The debris flew high into the sky and landed all over the street and on some of the nearby houses.

Neighbors came out to see what happened. They stood silently covering their mouths in disbelief. In the distance, the fire engine's siren could be heard approaching the scene of the blast.

"Are you all right son?" cried Mrs. Schultz. She was a widow who lived across the street. Some of her windows were shattered by the explosion. She rushed toward Monty, frantically feeling his head and sides, searching for any sign of injury.

Monty brushed her hands away. "I'm OK." "What happened, Monty?"

He looked on, fascinated by the debris and the amount of damage he had successfully engineered. "I was playing with my remote-controlled car. Then there was a big boom."

Mrs. Schultz looked over at what remained of Monty's house and asked "And your mother, child, where is she?"

Monty pointed to the destroyed house.

Mrs. Schultz pulled Monty to her and hugged him tight. "Come on, child, you'll stay with me until your Pa can come home. I saw him leave this morning. He needs to be informed."

Blake McPride cut his business trip short and rushed home to the devastation. He was beside himself at the death of his wife but relieved that Monty had been spared. He spent the next few days making arrangements and situating what was left of his family into a temporary home. Blake's heart was broken, as he thought his son's must be, over the death of his mother. The day she was buried, Blake hugged his little boy and asked, "Is there anything I can do for you, son?"

Monty looked at his father, "A red bicycle would be nice."

Now, almost thirty years later, Blake still missed his wife. He never remarried. Now his son was dead. His business was his only family. In spite of Blake McPride's sadness over the misguided life, and now death, of his son, he felt great physically. Having just come out of a comatose state, induced by an attack from Monty, he was eager to put these past few weeks behind him. He would immerse himself in work. No doubt, there would be a lot of work to be done repairing the damage Monty had caused while running McPride Industries for the short while he acted as CEO. Monty had forged an executive order that made him CEO in Blake's absence. Blake was absent as a result of a stroke that left him in a vegetative state. It happened when Monty intentionally withheld his father's medicine with the intent to kill him. Blake's stroke was an unfortunate delay in Monty's scheme to get rid of the old buzzard.

The first order of business would be making arrangements for the body's cremation. Blake was eager for morning. He wanted to take his mind off his loneliness and apply it to something constructive. He couldn't wait to be back to work again.

~~~

"...Sir? Excuse me, Sir?"

Blake snapped out of his trance and turned to Carl. "I'm sorry, Sir but we are ready to proceed."

"Blake stood silently for a moment, took a deep breath, then wiped his tears. "Go ahead, take him. It's over."

Carl nodded. "We'll take the body to the morgue at Raleigh Central. You can come down tomorrow and sign the necessary paperwork. I'm very sorry for your loss."

Blake nodded, turned and walked toward the chauffeured limo now waiting for him in front of the nursing home.

~~~

The ambulance began its six mile journey to Raleigh Central. The night was settling over the city. Their route took them through downtown. They approached the Moore Square Park area. As they passed the park, which was known to be a regular hangout for some homeless wine enthusiasts, one inebriated friend pointed at the ambulance and asked the other, "What's so special about that one?"

His buddy, reeling with booze, replied: "He has caused an ungodly amount of hurt and suffering. This one's a keeper." They both smiled at each other revealing a few assorted rotten teeth. Their bottles clicked together in a congratulatory fashion, and they drank their wine as the ambulance passed.

~~~

Arriving at the hospital, Carl and Jake unloaded the gurney and rolled the body down the corridor to the elevator. Reaching the lower level, the doors opened, and they proceeded down the hall past the large silver double doors that led to the morgue.

"Geez, can you believe it, Carl? The guy tried to kill his father. Did you see him crying as he stood there looking at his dead son? Man, that was so sad."

Carl had been on many "Dead On Arrival" calls, but on this one he felt worse for the old man than for the dead son. Carl shook his head. "Yeah, I know. It's a crazy world."

They entered the large room with shiny metal tables. Carl pulled the sheet off the body. "Here, give me a hand with this. Let's get him onto the table."

Jake scratched his head. "Hey Carl, didn't you close his eyes?" They both looked at the corpse. The eyes were open.

Carl examined the eyes. "Yeah, I did. Sometimes they pop open on their own. It's rigor mortis, nothing spooky about it. Come here and look at the retina. See how the whites of the eyes have yellowed?"

Jake stepped to the other side of the table and looked closely at the yellowish eyes. "Yeah, they look like the eyes of a drug user. Was this guy on drugs?"

"I don't know," replied Carl. "See the tiny vessels running along the edges of the cornea?"

As they leaned in to look at the tiny blood vessels, Monty's eyes turned and looked at Carl.
~~~

2

Oliver

She couldn't help noticing his extraordinary physique as he sat quietly waiting to get his hair cut. He was muscular but not overbuilt. His biceps were well sculpted. He reminded her of a modern day Viking. She did not remember ever seeing him come into the salon before. She definitely would have remembered. When it was finally his turn, she gestured to him to come and have a seat in her chair. All of the five other hair stylists were working with customers. He gave her a quick smile and took seat number three. Regina was no spring chicken, but she still looked great at 40. He must be in his mid-forties, maybe early fifties, she thought as she smiled at him.

"What's your name, handsome?"

"Oliver." He smiled at her question. "And what's yours?" His voice had a rough quality to it.

"Regina." She didn't see a wedding ring, but wondered whether or not he was married. No wedding ring? But that meant nothing. Maybe he was a regular Don Juan able to juggle a wife and several mistresses. He looked like he had the stamina for it. "You new here? I don't remember seeing you come in before."

"Yeah, this is my first visit." He looked at her with piercing blue eyes. "A friend recommended I come here. My last hair cut was a disaster, so I decided to try out the place."

Regina smiled. "Well, I'm glad you did" She looked at his hair. "How do you want me to do you?" She caught herself. "I mean, how would you like me to cut your hair?"

"Just a trim."

A few moments later she paused to wipe some of the hair clippings from his eyebrows. "So, Oliver, you got a girlfriend, wife, space alien DNA, or vampire marks that would make you a poor choice for a girl to hit on?"

He smiled and looked at her reflection in the large mirror as she continued trimming his hair. "No, I don't have a girlfriend, wife, space born bacteria or vampire marks." Then he chuckled. "Say, Regina, are you coming on to me?"

"Don't tell me you're gay." She said half-jokingly.

"No, I'm not gay." She continued to work on his hair.

"Well, that's good. It would be a waste if you were." She was feeling better about her prospects with her interesting new customer.

Bonnie and Carla, two of the other hairdressers, were following Regina's conversation with Oliver. In fact, all of the female hairdressers were carrying on with their little bit of chatter while keeping an ear on what was going on at Regina's station. The one male hair dresser just rolled his eyes and lost interest when Oliver told Regina he wasn't gay.

Regina took her time trimming his hair. "So, where you from, Oliver?"

"Upstate New York. I lived in the city for a while then moved to Raleigh about five years ago."

"And what brought you down here? What do you do?"

He glanced at her as she snipped away. "I'm a priest."

She stopped cutting his hair and stepped back for a moment to look at him as though to say, "Are you kidding?" She continued to stare at him. He remained silent. Everyone in the salon stopped talking. You could hear a pin drop. After a moment of silence, Regina stepped forward and continued trimming his hair. The shop was still quiet. All you could hear was the sound of her scissors.. The chatter was absent. "What kind of priest are you?"

"I'm a Catholic priest."

After several minutes, her handiwork was complete. She handed him a mirror. He took it, gave a look. "Nice work. Thanks." He handed the mirror back to her.

She dusted the remaining hair clippings off his shirt. "What are you doing tonight, Oliver? We could get together later if you're not too busy?"

"Thank you, Regina, that sure sounds tempting, but I'm the presider at tonight's Mass."

"Well, if you change your mind, you know where to find me."

Oliver smiled. "Thanks for the haircut." He walked to the front, paid his bill, and a generous tip. As Oliver was about to exit the salon, another customer came in. He looked at the woman and knew immediately something was wrong.

She brushed by him and marched to the receptionist at the counter. "I need to be out of here in half an hour. Don't tell me I have to wait."

The young attendant kept her cool. "Bonnie is finishing up. She'll be with you shortly."

The woman rolled her eyes and slammed her hand on the desk. "Damn it, if I'm not in that chair in two minutes I'll find another place that actually keeps to their schedule!" She crossed her arms and huffed.

Oliver turned to the woman. "Is there a special event you're getting ready to attend?"

She looked him over from top to bottom. "It's just a stupid baptism. Why do you ask?"

"Stupid baptism you say? Did you know, when someone receives the sacrament of baptism they are also anointed priest, prophet, and king?"

She laughed. "You're kidding me, right? Besides, it's a girl. What are you, some kind of religious freak?"

"Religious, yeah. Freak? I wouldn't necessarily describe myself as a freak. Overzealous, maybe just a little." He smiled. She did not. He continued. "Have you been to a baptism before?"

"Not since grade school. Idiotic ritual. Give the kid a few bucks and be done with it."

Oliver nodded as though in agreement. "Yes, but you would miss the best part of the baptism. Do you know what it is?"

"What?" Her tone was full of anger and sarcasm.

Oliver grabbed her by the arm and stepped in close.

Her eyes opened wide as she tried to break free of his grip. "Let me go, you jerk!"

Everyone in the salon looked to the front to see why all the commotion, Regina turned to look and thought, *"Oh no, my hunk of a client is a crazy person."*

Oliver continued. "The best part of baptism is when the priest traces the sign of the cross on your forehead and says, I claim you for our Lord and Savior, Jesus Christ, in the name of the Father, and of the Son, and of the Holy Spirit. Amen." As he said these words, he traced the sign of the cross on her forehead.

Her frightened eyes changed. They went from hateful to grateful. Her body became less tense as she stopped resisting his grip. She immediately became quiet and stopped trying to get away. He released his grip on her arm slowly, making sure she would be able to stand on her own. She looked up at him, covered her face with her hands, and began sobbing.

"Call 911, the guy's a loon!" yelled one of the hair dressers.

Regina grabbed her purse and reached for the pepper spray. She carried it for protection against crazies like Oliver.

The woman sat down in one of the waiting chairs. She was still sobbing. Oliver sat next to her and put his arm around her. "Are you all right, Miss? Is there anything I can do? Is there anything you want to say?"

By now, several of the staff were closing in on Oliver. One had a gun. Regina held out her pepper spray. She pointed it toward him. "Get away from her you pervert. We've called 911, and they'll be here any minute."

The woman stopped sobbing then looked at Oliver. "Thank you," she said in a low voice.

Everyone in the room paused and looked at each other, not sure what was going on.

Oliver got down on one knee and looked into her eyes. "I knew something was troubling you. I just wanted to help."

"How did you know? What did you do? I feel like the weight of the world has been lifted from my shoulders."

Regina lowered her pepper spray. The other hairdresser lowered her gun.

"I'm so sorry," the woman continued. "But somehow, I know it's going to be all right." She continued to cry. "This is weird. I don't usually cry like this."

Oliver looked at Regina. "Is there someplace she can be

alone quietly for a few moments? I think it might help."

"Sure." Regina helped the woman get up. "Come on, honey. You can rest for a few moments in the staff lounge." The hairdressers and customers headed back to their stations. Oliver slipped out the front door.

3

Finding Paul

Both men jumped in terror as the eyes of the corpse focused on Carl.

"Oh crap!" Jake backed away in a panic. He shot backward and bumped into a cart full of surgical tools causing them to crash to the floor. He tripped again, fell backward and scrambled to get as far away as possible from the not-quite-so-dead corpse.

The instant the dead man's eyes looked at Carl, the left hand reached out, grabbed him by the neck and pulled him in close. Now nose to nose with the corpse, Carl struggled to pull away, but the dead man's grip was too strong. Carl tried to stiff arm himself with his right arm so he would not be pulled any closer. With his left hand he beat the corpse frantically to get free. The corpse pulled him in. The wretched disfigured jaw and twisted lips connected with Carl in what seemed to be a long farewell kiss. The next instant the corpse was limp, its arms fell away, then dangled off both sides of the table. The eyes were closed again.

Jake stood in horror as he watched Carl struggle against the romantic overtures of the dead man. Now that it seemed to be dead again, both men stood quietly in shock. Neither dared move. It's as though they expected someone to open a hidden door and say, "Gotcha, you're on Scared-to-Death!" But no one stepped forward to lighten the mood or provide relief from this reality.

Finally, Jake slowly approached Carl, keeping his distance from the corpse. "Hey man, are you OK? Is that thing dead? What the hell just happened?"

Carl was silent for a moment. He looked at the corpse, then at Jake. He reached down, picked up one of the tools from the floor, the one with the long handle, and hit the corpse with it. After several whacks, he approached it maintaining a high alert, just in case it should try to kiss him again. He wiped his mouth with his shirt sleeve, as he approached to examine the body. It was limp. The eyes were closed.

"I don't know what the hell that was. I've been doing this job for ten years, Jake, and never saw rigor mortis like that. Its grip was a vise. I couldn't break free. It wanted to pull me down. Geez, I'm going to need therapy after this!" He threw a blanket over the body. "Let's finish putting this guy in the icebox, but first I got to pee."

"Me too. I haven't pissed in my pants since I was five, but I sure came close."

"OK, then we'll finish up and get out of here."

Both men went down the hall to the restroom. The trip made them feel a little better. Jake joked about the romantic rigor mortis. "Maybe the dead guy thought he would reach out and touch someone before moving to the great beyond. You probably were just his type."

"I'm sure there's a rational explanation for all of this," Carl replied.

As both men entered the morgue to finish storing the body, they were surprised to see Paul Herodias standing over the corpse, examining it.

"I wouldn't do that if I were you," Jake warned. "He's liable to take a liking to you the way he took to Carl." Paul squinted at them through his thick glasses causing wrinkles on his forehead to form a series of parallel lines. His hair was receding. His expression resembled someone experiencing stomach discomfort, the spokesman in a laxative commercial. He looked down and continued his examination.

Carl noticed some of the surgical tools were still on the floor. "We were just about to put him on ice but we had a little accident. The corpse had some wild rig. Scared the crap out of us."

Paul poked and prodded at the corpse with his instrument. He raised the eyelids and looked in each eye. Then he checked the jaw by moving it around. "He took quite a beating. How did it happen?"

"A truck slammed into him," Jake replied.

Paul walked around the body and was particularly interested in the bruising. "Excellent, this body will be a great exhibit for my lecture. You guys can go. I'll finish up here. I just want to finish examining it. I think I'll show this one to my morning class."

Carl was relieved that Paul volunteered to finish up. "That's fine with me, Paul. To be honest, this one gives me the creeps, and I don't creep out easily. I need a blood test to make sure I haven't caught anything." He shook his head as he replayed the incident in his mind. "Paul, the rigor mortis was like nothing I've ever seen. It literally pulled me down. My face was right up against it. Then it just went limp."

Paul looked up. "No problem. If he tries that on me, I'll kill him." He held Carl's gaze for a moment, then smiled. "That was a joke, Carl. He's already dead." Paul stepped away from the body and picked up the surgical tools off the floor.

Jake looked surprised and amused. "Why, Paul, I do believe you have a sense of humor. That almost tops being French kissed by a corpse."

Carl turned to exit the room. "Thanks for finishing up, Paul." He gave a wave and was gone.

Jake hung back for a moment. "Now, Paul, if our buddy gets fresh with you, just let him know that you don't kiss on the first date." Before Paul could look up, Jake was gone.

Jake caught up with Carl headed down the corridor toward the elevator. When they reached it, Carl turned to him. "I hope the lab isn't too busy." He paused to press the button. "I have a bad feeling about this, Jake."

As he pressed the button, a chilling scream came from the other end of the corridor. It was followed by the crash of metallic objects on a hard surface. Both men ran back to the morgue. They gasped at the foul stench. Something was burning. They covered their noses with their hands and entered the large room. The corpse was engulfed in flames. The sprinkler system was on. The fire continued to burn. It seemed to ignore the water, consuming the body at an alarming rate. Paul was nowhere to be seen.

Carl looked around the room. "Paul! Where are you?"

Jake called from the other side of the room. "Over here!"

Carl ran to Jake, being careful not to slip on the wet floor. Jake pointed to the metal desk in the corner. Below it was a man curled up in a fetal position. His face was buried in his knees, and his arms were wrapped together with tightly closed fists.

Carl got down on his knees. "Paul, what happened? Are you all right?"

Paul did not move.

"Jake, get the doctor on duty."

"Paul, look at me. What happened?"

Paul stirred, his arms dropping to his side. He slowly raised his head and turned to Carl. In a low voice he whispered, "Where am I? Who am I?"

"What are you talking about? Are you hurt?"

"Hurt? Why did you call me Paul?"

"That's your name. Come on. Let's get you up to see a doctor. Where are you hurt?"

Carl reached out and put his arm around the distraught man. He felt Paul's soaking wet weight tug on his left side as he began trying to stand. Paul's other hand, the one Carl could not see, the one holding the long surgical blade swung toward Carl. As Carl helped Paul stand, he felt the cold stab from the surgical knife as it penetrated his chest. It was cold, silent, and instantaneous. At first, Carl didn't know what happened. He didn't really feel anything. *It couldn't have happened. My senses must have miss-registered something.* Both men were now standing, facing each other. Carl looked down at the surgical knife stuck in his chest. Then he looked up at Paul, whose sick grin confirmed that something had gone terribly wrong. Carl felt the energy begin leaving his legs. He clutched his chest, began running toward the exit, then collided with a chair. He grabbed it with his other hand to try to steady himself. The chair tilted. Carl collapsed onto the floor, still clutching his chest. The blood stain spread rapidly across his shirt.

Paul stepped over Carl's body, now gasping for air. He looked at the dying man and said "My name's not Paul. It's Monty." He paused, turned his head as if trying to remember something and whispered, "I'm pretty sure that's my name."

Jake hurried down the corridor with Dr. Carson, the doctor on duty that evening. They failed to notice the man leaning against the side corridor wall. After they passed, Monty walked to the stairs and exited the hospital.

As Jake and Dr. Carson entered the morgue, they found Carl's body on the cold floor in a pool of blood. Dr. Carson lunged to reach Carl. "I'm barely getting a pulse. He's lost a lot of blood. Help me stop the bleeding, Jake, and help me get him to the operating room. We don't have much time."

Jake's face turned pale, but he did as the doctor instructed. They lifted Carl onto the rolling metal table and wheeled him to the emergency operating room. Jake worked to keep pressure on the wound as they arrived at the OR. Doctor Carson was joined by several nurses and Dr. Jones, the lead surgeon on duty.

As the team of doctors prepared to operate on Carl, Dr. Carson turned to Jake. "Thanks, Jake. We'll take it from here. I know he's your partner as well as your friend. We'll do everything we can. I think you know he is in pretty serious shape, but we'll do our best."

"Thanks Doc. I'd better contact his wife, and we need to find Paul. My guess is he's the one who stabbed Carl. No one else was here. I wasn't gone very long. He couldn't have gotten far."

Once outside, as Jake and Dr. Carson's team scrambled to try to save Carl's life, Monty noticed the two large parking garages on either side of the hospital. Instinctively he headed for parking area B. He entered the garage just as Nurse Mitchell was walking toward the exit. She was on her way in for her shift. As he approached her, she greeted him. "Hi Paul, I thought you were on duty tonight."

"I am, I have to run out for a minute, but I can't remember where I parked my car."

She smiled. "It's where you always park, right there." She pointed to the row of cars. "I park there too, just like always, and your car is there, just like always." Say, are you feeling all right? You look a little confused and you're soaking wet."

"What kind of car do I drive?"

She gave him a concerned look. "Paul, are you all right?"

"Just answer me women. What do I drive?"

Nurse Mitchell became frazzled. "Paul, are you drunk or something? You are being rude."

Monty grabbed Nurse Mitchell by the hair, pulling her face close to his as he whispered in a controlled rage. "My name is not Paul, you cow! Now tell me what I drive or I will slit your fat ugly throat."

Nurse Mitchell tried to answer, but all she could do was stutter. "It, it, it is is is a blue Dodge minivan"

Monty tightened the grip on her hair. "I'd rather be dead than be caught driving a minivan. What do you drive, my sweet little bovine?"

She trembled, "a, a, a, BMW convertible."

"He again yanked her head. "Give me the keys."

She immediately handed them over.

"Now, you and I are going to take a short stroll. If you scream I'll have to run, but will come back and kill you. I may just kill you before I run. Either way, I promise I'll give you a mega chin tuck." He grabbed her by her meaty arm and walked her to the row of cars, next to a sign that read, "On-Duty Staff Parking." She climbed into the back of the minivan. "Go to the rear. Lie down and stay down for fifteen minutes. If you move, you die." He shut the sliding door and casually walked toward her car. He got in and started the engine. "Who am I supposed to be?" he wondered as he reached into his pocket and pulled out his wallet. He examined the license. "Paul H. Herodias? What a stupid name." He found three credit cards and sixty three dollars in cash inside the wallet. He looked at himself in the rearview mirror. "You're not much to look at." He released the emergency brake and was about to pull out when a large black Mercedes pulled up and stopped in front of him, blocking his way.

Monty sat up, surprised to see what appeared to be two winos getting out of the car. They both gave him a friendly wave, as though they were his pals. Each had a bottle in one hand. They approached him on either side. Monty rolled down his window.

"Hello, friend," said one of the drunken men. "We're supposed to take you to a safe house."

Monty glanced at each of the men. "What safe house? What for?"

"Keep you safe, of course." The second wino replied.

The first wino said "C'mon, Monty, we need to get you out of here."

Monty's curiosity was peaked. "You know my name. At least, I think that's what it is. I can't remember a damned thing."

"We know. C'mon. It'll all be explained to you. You're very important. You can't stay here. We need you to come with us for your own safety."

Both drunks waved at the same time, signaling Monty to come with them. Both exhibited friendly smiles and waved again.

Monty opened the door and got out. One of the winos opened the back door of the Mercedes as though he was Monty's personal butler. The other climbed into the driver's seat. The Mercedes pulled out of the parking deck heading southbound.

The wino driving turned to him. "It's unfortunate your works were cut short, but now they'll have a chance to flourish."

The wino butler turned to him. "She is looking forward to seeing you."

"What work?" Monty asked. "Who sent you to pick me up?"

"Perpetuating evil," said wino chauffeur.

"Mama Crossbones," said wino butler.

4

Uncle Ned and the Boy in the Quicksand

Oliver hurried out of the salon. He didn't want to get caught up having to explain what just happened. The day was warm. It was beginning to get dark, a beautiful evening for a walk, but tonight he was going to relax and read his book over a cup of coffee.

Oliver enjoyed taking long walks, especially on nature trails, the fewer people the better. He had learned to ignore the out of place shadows most of the times. Sometimes, however, it wasn't possible and he was forced into the inevitable confrontation. Even as a child, Oliver could see them. It started on his 5th birthday.

The day was full of fun, cake, and toys. Janice McShane had invited friends. Most had children the same age. His Aunt Cheryl and Uncle Ned came later. Janice's husband, Paul Bravard McShane, was a successful Irish folk singer. He toured frequently, and was killed in a plane crash when Oliver was just two years old. Janice had not remarried. She worked as a teacher. She was very close to Cheryl, her older sister. Cheryl and her husband, Ned, lived in Virginia. They would not miss Oliver's 5th birthday. It had been almost nine months since they last visited.

Later that afternoon, after the party guests had gone home, Cheryl and Ned arrived. Janice hugged both of them after opening the door. Oliver was busy playing with his new toys. He didn't notice that his aunt and uncle had arrived. They would spend the night in the guest room and head back to Virginia in the morning, where Ned had important business.

After the hugs, Janice called to Oliver. "Look, Oliver, it's Aunt Cheryl and Uncle Ned!"

Oliver looked up from his game to see his aunt and uncle in the foyer. Aunt Cheryl looked the same as he remembered, with her pretty red hair and rosy cheeks. Uncle Ned looked different. Oliver felt a chill travel up his spine. There was something wrong, terribly wrong. When he got a good look at his uncle, he gasped. Oliver stood up and backed away slowly, continuing to examine his uncle. His mother called to him again.

"Come here, Oliver. Say hello to your aunt and uncle." Oliver didn't want to come near them. He was terrified of the thing claiming to be his uncle. There was no way he would get near it.

Janice, Cheryl, and Ned entered the living room. Janice was about to call Oliver again to come greet their guests when she noticed the fear on her son's face. "What's the matter, Oliver? She approached him. "Are you feeling all right, honey?"

Oliver did not respond. His gaze was fixed on a demon head shifting in and out of focus. One minute it was uncle Ned's face, the next minute it was the face of a demon.

Janice reached her son and got down to examine him closely. "Oliver, what's wrong?" Beads of sweat had formed on Oliver's forehead. His mother checked him for fever.

Cheryl stepped forward. "Hi sweetie, I sure hope you're OK. We brought you something special for your birthday."

Ned stepped forward with the gift. Oliver screamed "Don't come near me!" He broke free of his mother's grip and backed up against the living room wall. He was still fixated on the thing that was supposedly his uncle.

"Hey, what's wrong, buddy? It's me, your uncle Ned." The demon thing stepped forward with the gift and knelt down next to Janice. Oliver's eyes widened with terror. He opened his mouth to scream, but nothing came out. Sweat ran down his forehead. Ned reached out to touch his nephew's cheek in an attempt to comfort him. Oliver was frozen with terror as the beast reached out for him. All of a sudden, everything started to move in slow motion. Oliver saw Aunt Cheryl's and his mother's concerned look. He saw his uncle's demonic eyes peering at him, reaching for him.

He didn't want to be touched by it. It was bad; really, bad.

It wasn't just the way it looked. It was the feeling of deep, hungry malice oozing from the hideous demon that was his uncle. As it reached for him, Oliver felt as though he was sinking in quicksand. He dreaded feeling its touch. Time seemed to trap him in this instant for what seemed like several long, terrible minutes. He noticed the creature had a strong pulse, which he could feel as its hand approached. The closer it got, the more he could feel its throbbing pulse. Oliver knew he would die if the creature touched him. *Why didn't mom and aunt Cheryl listen to me? Why are they letting the monster get me? What's wrong with them?*

Oliver was frozen, sinking further into the quicksand. Then the terrible instant occurred. He felt its horrific touch. The dull immense throb was now upon him with the force of a sledgehammer. Oliver closed his eyes and started to suffocate. He felt the quicksand engulfing him. He was fully immersed. The throbbing continued. The quicksand solidified all around him. There was a burst of white light inside Oliver's mind, as though someone snapped a picture with a powerful flash. The five year old boy collapsed into his mother's arms.

Oliver was trapped in the quicksand. He could not move any part of his body. The demon's constant pulse was holding him there. He tried to wake himself out of the quicksand, but every time he was about to wake up, the pulse knocked him back into it. His very being was one with the suffocating quicksand. He would be stuck there forever, never again able to wake up.

After what seemed like hours of being overpowered by the throbbing pulse, Oliver heard a faint and familiar sound. It was the voice of his mother calling his name. He focused on the sound. It was gentle, and it was filled with love. Although it was faint, he was comforted hearing her voice. He heard it again, a little louder. Each time it was getting closer. He could feel it trying to reach him. But he was paralyzed with fear and could not move.

The next moment, Oliver could see himself lying on his bed with his mother sitting beside him calling his name. He understood her words. He could hear them clearly now. "Oliver, it's me your mother. Don't be afraid. She kept repeating it. Each time, it drew him closer to her. The quicksand's grip loosened. His body lunged into a state of semi-consciousness, but his mind was still trapped. Oliver knew that he had a very fragile connection with the outside world and, if he lost it, there would be no coming out of the quicksand.

"Don't touch me." He said to his mother. His body was sitting up. "Don't touch me," he repeated, fearful that even the slightest touch might sever his connection to reality.

Janice withdrew her hand and continued to speak softly. "Oliver, it's me your mother. Don't be afraid." With each repetition, he felt his mind slowly rejoin his body. He was no longer looking at himself from outside his body. He was sitting up in his bed looking through his own eyes. His mother's voice was clear now. The throbbing pulse which paralyzed him was gone. He recognized her face as he looked at her from within his own eyes.

An exhausted Oliver lay back down in his bed. "Where are they, mom?"

"Aunt Cheryl and Uncle Ned went home. They left a birthday present for you. Would you like me to get it?"

Oliver shook his head "No." He looked into his mother's eyes. "Something is wrong with Uncle Ned. He's turning into a monster. I didn't want him to touch me."

The next day Janice took Oliver to the doctor to have him checked for anything which might help them figure out what caused this seizure-like behavior. The doctor ran a series of tests and found nothing physically wrong with the boy.

The following week, Uncle Ned was arrested in Virginia on child pornography charges.

5

Mama Crossbones

The Mercedes rolled into the driveway of a small house on the southeast end of Raleigh. The place was in need of extensive repair. It was in a neighborhood known for its heavy drug activity. A few male teens roamed the streets with their baggy pants hanging so low you could see half their underwear hanging out. They strolled down the street, strutting from side to side with an occasional jock grab thrown in for effect. It was ghetto fashion at its finest. They stopped and stared at the Mercedes as it cruised past them. This seemed to elicit several crotch grabs followed by nose wipes from the saggy bottom boys.

As they watched the vehicle pull into the driveway of the little house, they looked at each other and murmured. When wino chauffeur and wino butler got out of the car, the boys gave them a ghetto salute, raising a hand with index finger and pinky finger extended while the rest of the fingers remained in a fist.

They stood by as wino butler opened the door for their special guest. As Monty got out of the car, the boys elbowed each other as they gestured their ghetto salute to Monty.

Monty ignored them and followed his tour guides up the short set of steps to the front door of the house. The steps were cracked, the door frame was badly warped, the small wooden porch had several missing slats and there were strange symbols painted on the floor. Even with the small amount of light cast by the single bare bulb hanging from the porch ceiling, Monty recognized the symbols. He had dreamed about them long ago. Seeing them now brought back the dream. It was a beautiful woman dressed in black. She was cradling a small child and the child's eyes were solid black. It was dressed in a black gown as well. The symbols emblazed on the woman's robe and on the baby's forehead were the same symbols he now saw on the porch.

Wino butler proceeded to knock on the door.

A moment later the door opened. A slender green eyed young woman stood at the entrance. She gestured them to enter. In stark contrast, the interior was exquisitely decorated with antique furniture, the kind one might expect in the lounge of an exclusive country club. There were antique books, swords, and a collection of ancient artifacts.

Monty looked around the ornate room. There were weapon collections everywhere, all different types. One section of wall held what appeared to be throwing knives. Another section held fencing swords. Yet another held samurai swords. One wall was empty except what appeared to be a poorly drawn illustration of a Roman arch. His eyes came to rest on an old woman sitting in the corner. She was holding a glass of brandy, smoking a cigar. The same symbol decorating the porch was tattooed on her forehead.

She held his gaze. "Come here, my child. I have longed for this moment."

Monty approached her slowly. "Who are you?"

"I'm your mother."

"My mother?" Monty thought of the kitchen explosion that killed Shelly. "My mother is dead."

"Your surrogate mother is dead. You did a fine job getting rid of her the way you did. I always knew you had great potential. I am your real mother."

Monty opened his mouth to speak, but the old woman held up her hand in a stop gesture. She continued: "Your surrogate father may have planted his seed in her, but he was devoid of heart and so was she. You would have been empty, too, with no one to guide you. I could see these things as a waste. It was I who gave you the gift of passion for evil. It was I who helped you return to this world. You had been outsmarted by fools who claim to know the man Jesus. An unfortunate accident cut your career short. I am seeing to it that you continue your work, even if you must use an inferior human body specimen as host to accomplish it."

Monty looked down at his hands, arms, and feet.

"No matter. Mama Crossbones always knows what to do. Now, you are back. I am pleased." She paused and studied him for a moment. "Now come to me and let me purge you of the other one."

Monty slowly stepped forward and stopped in front of the old woman. "Kneel before me," she said, gesturing to the floor directly in front of her.

Monty kneeled as instructed. She leaned forward, placing her bony hands on the top of his head. She closed her eyes and murmured. Monty stiffened. She clasped his head tightly. A moment later, she let him go. He was thrown backward several feet. He opened his eyes and looked around slowly. Then he rose and brushed himself off.

"Well, that was refreshing," he said in a sarcastic tone.

"Good." She said. "The one known as Paul is dead. You are the owner of this body now."

Monty picked up a silver pitcher on a nearby table to look closely at himself. "Geez, couldn't you have picked a better looking specimen for my comeback? This one looks like crap."

"I tried to give you the body of the one called Carl, but it did not take. He was already filled with the man Jesus. It is good you killed him. Now that you are back, my task here is done. I must return to Jamaica to continue my work."

"What work?"

Mama Crossbones got a fire in her eye "My work is to recruit and populate the world with disciples of evil. We choose popular getaway places where many wealthy people visit. They come from all over the world to have fun and spend their money. Then they go home and continue to live their hollow lives, embracing nothing but themselves. They are perfect for recruiting to our cause. I choose the fertile ones who are with child. I make it my child, a child of darkness. There are many whom I have helped come into the world this way. They have bombed, poisoned, stolen, tortured, and inflicted pain. Whenever a lover of the man Jesus dies, it is a bonus. But ultimate success is attained when we convert a lover of the man Jesus over to our cause. This is especially rewarding."

Monty put down the pitcher. "So do you take over their free will?"

"No, I merely highjack their souls to make sure their taste for evil flourishes." She squinted as she looked at him. "I highjacked yours for your ultimate liberation."

"How can you have liberated me from something I was never free to decide?"

"You were always free to decide. I blessed you with a predisposition to do my will, all things in the way of evil. It was planted in you when I met your hollow mother. She refused to wear my amulet. Her husband purchased it nonetheless. Since they were married, his consent provided me with her consent as well. You see, evil must be invited in or it is powerless. She eventually threw the bracelet away, but it was too late. I had cast my spell and placed the master's mark on the growing fetus in her belly. You were mine before you were born. All the fun you experienced in your past life was through my help and intervention. Don't forget that. Without me, you would have been a miserable, hollow pathetic worm of a man without the extensive pleasure that comes from a blackened heart.

Fortunately, you never allowed the idiotic advances of those who follow the man Jesus to affect your thinking." She spat on the floor. "That's one of the dangers we face. When one of our kind turns to him, we are cast out of their hearts. But the same rule applies to Him. He must be invited in. That is why I select my recruits carefully. With wealthy and spiritually hollow surrogates there is no chance they will seek the man Jesus. Why should they, when their money takes such good care of them? They are ideal hollows."

She paused and peered at Monty. "You have been gifted in our cause, so you must continue your work of personal gratification at the expense and suffering of others. You must also hone your skills and become more selective. Although they are harder to attain, converting lovers of the man Jesus is your ultimate destiny. First, you must spread more evil and chaos to inspire those on the fringe. These are ripe times. Our numbers are increasing. Eventually, the world will be consumed by our cause. Evil takes what it wants. It spreads like a fungus in the dark. An invitation by way of apathetic indulgence is all we need to enter a person's heart. Those who follow the man Jesus must willingly seek him. For those unable to decide, we decide for them.

"You will play a key role in taking down those arrogant God lovers.. You will know when the time is right to harvest lovers of the man Jesus. Your rewards will be great indeed as the power of darkness continues to grow within you."

"Why is it so important we take down Jesus freaks? There are plenty of unbelievers, hollows to go around, and plenty of kinky things I could think of doing."

She looked at Monty and raised a finger. "You don't understand, my little manflesh. It's simple math. For every lover of the man Jesus we convert, especially those of the cloth, we gain a hundredfold as their followers leave the church to rebel against their God. They are too stupid to see it is not their God who has abandoned them. It is their man flesh which has allowed itself to be corrupted. It is a grand prize."

Monty glanced over at the two winos who escorted him. "What about Howdy and Doody, are they my personal servants? What's up with them?"

She glanced at the winos. "They are not what they appear to be. Those fools are merely tools made pliable and easy-to-control by their lack of self-control. The alcohol coursing through their veins surrenders them to any who would take charge of their faculties. They make excellent hosts."

"So are you controlling them?"

"No," she replied. "But I will let you meet two of your brothers in order to explain." She looked at the winos and spoke. "Come, alas, forward into my sphere, for this I allow, though not allowed as I claim the dark power to heed my command."

The two winos stood where they were for a moment. Their eyes rolled back into their heads, and they collapsed onto the floor. The two shadow demons inhabiting the winos remained. Each resembled a cross between a bat and a bull. They were evil manifested in all of its hideousness.

"These are your brothers, Monty. They hated once, as you hate. Their bodily term on this sphere has ended. They now carry out their tasks on a different sphere. Their work continues. You have the advantage of the physical rewards that evil in our sphere can attain. It is filled with self-serving and grotesque pleasure.

Enjoy them while you are here. Their sphere has different rewards, such as staying out of the eternal fire. As long as they are fruitful in their endeavors in the name of darkness, they are free to roam and not be cast into the pit. That is their reward. It is a different kind of reward, one you will eventually learn to appreciate. For now, enjoy the pleasures of this sphere; they are many indeed."

She took a sip of her brandy and puffed the cigar. "There is much to do. We will get into those details tomorrow. But before we go any further, let us be one. This old woman longs for the pleasures of the flesh."

Monty flinched. "Excuse me?"

6

Demon Vision

Oliver walked briskly after leaving the salon. He ignored the approaching sirens and made his way into Cup-a-Hoot, a coffee bar a couple of blocks away. Today was his day off. When not out for a long walk, he would frequent his favorite coffee houses. This locally owned little hole in the wall was one of his favorites. He ordered a plain black coffee and a cup of Turkish coffee. He was not a Cappuccino kind of guy. Turkish coffee was his favorite. It was like drinking hot sand. He loved it. He would wash it down with a cup of black coffee. After paying for his order, he sat down pulling a book out of his jacket and got lost in reading.

Almost an hour later he checked his watch and his phone, miraculously no calls or text messages. Perhaps the wave of death, despair, divorce, disease and the demented was on the decline today. The five D's is how he half-jokingly referred to the lives of many of his church's parishioners. There actually were six D's, but he purposely omitted "demonic" when talking about it, although it was one of the growing D's, as far as he could tell. It happened over time, but he noticed a definite increase.

Oliver's relaxing hour came to an abrupt end when someone ripped the book out of his hands and put it down next to his coffee. "Care to explain what that was all about? You disappeared before the police showed up. I for one would like to know what you did to that woman." Regina was on her way home when she happened to see the familiar head.

"I just stopped in here for a take-out Frappuccino when I saw your head. I couldn't see your face, but I knew it was you. Hair dressers can identify their work in a crowd. I would have spotted that haircut handiwork anywhere. It's like a signature left on each customer's head. Over time it grows away, but yours is still very fresh. Now, start talking or I will cause a scene and call the police."

Oliver was not sure what to make of her threat. "You wouldn't really do that, would you?"

"Just try me, Father Funny Bone." She looked serious and he didn't want to risk her making a scene.

After a moment, Oliver chuckled. "Wow! You should have been a reporter or a lawyer or something instead of a hair dresser. Man, you are tough."

She gave him a look of acknowledgment. "I was a reporter for my small town newspaper in my previous life, before I moved to the big city. The job sucked. But, had I been a lawyer it probably would have sucked even more. I don't like bureaucracy, especially people who don't speak the truth. Being a hair dresser, I listen to a lot of crap, but it's usually true and I still enjoy uncovering a good story, though I no longer have any interest in reporting."

"I'm not sure what to tell you, Regina. The woman came in. I just talked to her, that's all."

Regina began dialing her cell phone.

Oliver sat straight up. "What are you doing?"

"Calling 911, I told you I would cause a scene or call the police. I've decided to do both since you are being uncooperative. Hello? Yes, this is…"

He grabbed the phone out of her hand, ending the call. "All right, I'll tell you what I know, but you're not going to believe me."

Her phone rang. She answered it. "Hello, 911?" She glanced at Oliver. He nodded as if to say he would comply and tell her what she wanted to know. "I'm sorry. I must have dialed by accident. Yes, everything is all right. I'm sorry – Thanks – Bye."

Oliver rolled his eyes. "You really shouldn't be this pushy you know."

She gave him a look.

He began. "Yes, I am a priest and my name is Oliver. But before I continue, you must promise me you will not repeat our conversation or any portion of it to anyone. If you can't agree to those terms, then you're welcome to call the police, the pope, or anybody else you'd like."

She looked into his serious eyes. "I can accept those terms. I just want the truth."

"The woman who entered your establishment was not alone."

Regina looked puzzled. "What do you mean? I didn't see anyone else with her."

Oliver continued. "She had a demon residing inside her."

Regina looked away, shook her head, then looked back at him.

"I told you that you wouldn't believe me."

She sighed. "It's OK. I'll reserve judgment and let you continue. I promise not to interrupt. If I think you're crazy, I'll just get up and leave, and you better not follow me."

"Agreed." He continued. "Since I was five years old, I have been able to see what can best be described as evil imprints on people. These imprints are of two types. The first is a record of your un-forgiven evil. It appears as a shadowy rash on your skin, dark blotches that seem to intensify as a person does more evil, things not acceptable to God. The second types of shadows are demons. They are evil manifested in our world. They become part of the person who lets them in. It just so happens they are visible to me.

A demon without a host will appear as an extra shadow without an object to claim it. They are stalking, waiting for someone they can inhabit. Once they inhabit a host, that person's face takes on the appearance of the demon. Their real face and the demon face share the same space. The one that dominates will be seen more often. I've had to learn to ignore the shifting of a person's face when speaking to them. It is not an easy thing to do."

Regina listened. Oliver found her hard to read. She just sat looking at him without much of an expression.

"The woman who came into your hair salon was demon inhabited. It was as clear as day to me. Sometimes, I follow the person and try to figure out a way to make their goodness come forth. This works every once in a while if the person takes time to listen and talk with me. Their demon hates this. It knows what I am attempting to do, so it fights hard to keep the person in darkness. It is very difficult for someone who has attracted a demon to get rid of it. Typically, this can happen if the person has a near death experience, turns to God and begins re-evaluating their life. At other times they are strong enough to do it by finding God without having a near death experience. Purging evil is not easy. It totally depends on what path the person chooses. Free will is a wonderful and dangerous thing.

Regina listened without revealing much expression one way or the other.

Oliver continued. "Our culture has enabled the spread of evil. For many people, what I might consider a second chance at salvation is seen either as luck or coincidence. They fail to see the Divine in anything or simply choose to ignore it. They have hardened hearts.

The woman today was very sad, perhaps even suicidal. That's a big score for evil. Lately, I am seeing more and more of them. Perhaps I've gotten better at spotting them. When she told me she was going to attend a baptism I took that as an opportunity to try to expel the evil. In her case, I traced the sign of the cross on her forehead and claimed her in the name of Jesus Christ. She was tense and wanted to get away. The demon inhabiting her was a bully demon. Most of them are. They pick easy targets and intimidate them into evil through guilt and a number of logical and seemingly justifiable emotions.

When I claimed her for Jesus, the demon took a hike. Rather, I should say it was evicted. In that moment, all the emotions and reasoning justifying suicide were gone. I think she was able to think clearly for the first time in a long time about her choices. Nothing can ever be so bad as to drive someone to throw away God's precious gift of life. I think you would agree with that."

Regina nodded.

"I know I could be arrested for doing something like that, which is why I act only when I'm sure it will have a positive effect. On several occasions I've seen a demon expelled by the power of the Holy Spirit. It descends on that person, sometimes as a butterfly, a bird or some harmless harbinger. The landing is ever so gentle. The expulsion is quick and violent. It's as though the demon was caught completely off guard. It explodes from within into a shower of ashes that gently float to the ground. I've seen this happen only twice. It's like nothing I might have imagined.

The second time I witnessed this was not too far from here. Greg, one of the parishioners at my church, had attracted a demon while living a wretched life of drugs, gambling, beating his wife for the first time and quitting his job. I saw him walking down Hargett St. and recognized him. He had a terrible dark aura around him, so I followed him into a local bar. As he turned to sit at the counter, I noticed he had a gun stuck in the side of his pants. No one else saw it. I caught sight of it for a brief second as his jacket flapped to the side.

He ordered a beer and looked around. He didn't seem to notice me. His beer came. He took a sip and was about to reach for his gun when something caught his eye. An inchworm floated a few inches above the counter. He sat there studying the inchworm, wondering how it came to be hanging around inside a bar. Surely, someone would have seen it and knocked it down. Yet, the little green worm just floated, hanging from its single strand of silk. He reached for the inchworm. A moment later the most remarkable explosion took place. There was a burst of light and a silent explosion, all emanating from Greg. I felt the force where I was sitting. It was the force one might feel standing in front of a ten foot speaker blasting a bass note. The force packed a wallop. It went right through me, though it seemed to have had enough force to shatter the windows. There were ashes everywhere. Flakes were floating down. As each touched a surface, it emitted a red glow and disappeared. I was the only one who saw it, and probably experienced only a fraction of the intensity of what transpired. No one else in the bar seemed to see, hear, or feel anything.

Regina put up her hand. "Oliver, do you use any hallucinogens for fun or for "religious" purposes?"

Oliver shook his head. "No, I don't do drugs of any kind and I drink in moderation."

She looked into his eyes, as though she was searching for evidence to the contrary. "OK, go on."

"I later heard that a group of parishioners started a prayer circle to try to help Greg and his wife Amanda. They had a two year old son. Greg was becoming irritable after Amanda found him shooting up in the bathroom. His drug addiction started on his last business trip to Vegas. He later told me that he had planned to rob the bar that night for the cash, to buy drugs. When he saw the inch worm hanging there, he thought of flicking it with his finger just to see how far it would travel. Maybe he would aim it at the bartender. Then he decided he wanted to watch it crawl on his finger instead. As soon as the little worm started to crawl on his finger, he said his world changed. Prayer is a powerful thing.

He described it as being overcome with a sense of grandness and insignificance simultaneously. He saw himself as God holding the inchworm. At the same time, he was the insignificant inchworm on God's mighty finger. In that instant Greg was flooded with an understanding that his destiny was held in a precarious balance by each of his actions. His next actions would be critically important to his life.

He knew the inchworm on God's finger would never be harmed. He felt it would be cared for, loved in a manner disproportionate to what it deserved. He also knew the inchworm on his selfish human finger could die easily from a whim of self-entertainment to see how far it could fly with the flick of his finger.

Greg was disgusted with himself and overcome with remorse for what he was thinking of doing, and for what he had become. He got up from the bar stool, paid for his beer and left without taking another sip. All the while, he carefully kept the inchworm on his finger and placed it on a tree a short distance from the bar.

It's dangerous to underestimate the power of demons. They are evil and cunning. They seek empty vessels, people with no beliefs or with hardened hearts – people devoid of faith and full of pride. These folks are easily acquired. Pride does not satisfactorily fill your heart; it only hardens it. As powerful as these demons are, however, the power of God is a power of unimaginable capacity and love, often delivered with a soft touch or a whisper."

Oliver looked at Regina, unsure whether she might simply get up and leave, whereupon he would not follow her as promised. She glanced down at his book. "What are you reading?"

"*My Little Big Life* by Dean Koontz. It's a memoir about

his dog, an autographed copy given to me by a dear friend." He showed her the inscription. *Not all angels have wings, some have fur.* "It's a great book." He then sat back and looked at her in silence.

She looked up from his book. "I believe you."

"You know, for some reason, I'm relieved you do. You're the only person I've ever told this to."

"You mean, the other priests in your church don't know?"

He laughed in a rough, masculine way that made her laugh too. "Are you kidding? They'd lock me up in a white room with padded walls. Ha! I can just imagine the bishop writing a letter to the pope. Dear Pontiff, our very own Oliver is loony, so sorry."

By now, Regina was laughing her own hearty laugh. She paused. "How can you keep this to yourself for so long?"

He couldn't help laughing. "It's called survival, honey. There would be no end to the embarrassment and ridicule I would bring to my parish and the Catholic Church as a whole. This is not something you can talk about in a group, like AA. There are no Demons Anonymous groups for people like me who see these things and, as I mentioned, without consuming a drop of alcohol or other hallucinatory substance. The closest thing some people see as a real demon is their mother in law. Our culture doesn't respond well to things that cannot be recorded, photographed, or otherwise posted on Facebook. I do what I can with the tools I've been given. Trying my best, as the apostle Paul put it, 'to fight the good fight.'"

She looked at him, and her smile fell away. "Is there anything inhabiting me? I'm not religious. Do I have dark blotches all over me or a nasty demonic face?"

"No, no," He replied. "You look fine. Don't get freaked out by this. There are many strange things under heaven we can't see or have the capacity to understand. As long as you are sincere in your faith and do the best you can, you have nothing to worry about. It's people who have no faith and think science is the answer to everything. To them, science and faith are mutually exclusive, but this is not the case. Human pride is something that gets people into all sorts of trouble. In the minds of many, we invented technology so we are in complete control of our own destiny. Therefore, we can only look to human intellect and scientific fact for explanations. I worry about those people. They tend to be more concerned with eliminating wrinkles from their face, than with eliminating sin from their hearts. Hey, but I'm just a priest. I have a bias toward the truth. I'm a follower of Jesus, who is the truth and the way."

"Does being a priest require you use a lot of muscle?" She pointed to his biceps. "I've never seen a beefier priest. You look like a bouncer, for crying out loud. The women in your parish must love you. I bet nobody dares to leave Mass early when you're up there."

Oliver laughed and blushed a bit at her comment. "Don't be too sure. There's a race out the door and out of the parking lot most Sundays."

"You know, I was ready to take you home. Still am." She winked. "Just think, I could take you home. The next morning you could do confession. It would be the best of both worlds with such a shortage of good men." She paused and waved her arms. "I know, I know, you can't. Well anyway, your secret is safe with me. I've had my share of meeting unusual characters, but you take the cake, Oliver." She smiled and added, "In a good sort of way. Besides with that black hair and those blue eyes, you're easy on the eyes and I could stand a bit of crazy."

Oliver sat quietly and smiled. "You are a spirited lady. I hope we can be friends. I'm afraid that's all we can be."

"You need to write to the pope. They need to change the rules so priests can have girlfriends. That's what I think." Regina sighed. "Sure, I understand, but listen, if you ever get tired of being a priest, I get first dibs. Promise?"

"Ha!" He couldn't help but blurt out a bit of laughter. "Sure, but don't hold your breath."

"So, what's next? Do you feel any better now that you've shared your secret with your hair dresser?"

He took a deep breath and exhaled slowly. "You know, as a matter of fact I do. I spend most of my day listening and dealing with other people's problems. It is refreshing to talk to another person about my issues. Yes, I do feel better. Thank you, Regina."

She stood up to leave. "OK, Oliver. Or should I call you, Father Oliver?"

"Oliver is fine."

She put a finger to her temple. Her eyes opened wide as if

she had a revelation. "The next time you come in for a haircut, I want you to check out Irene. Tell me if she has a demon or just PMS. She can be a bitch."

"You got it." Oliver smiled giving a small wave goodbye.

She turned to leave. "Take care of yourself."

"You too." He replied as he watched the voluptuous hair dresser walk out of the coffee shop.

7

The Black Lamia

Mama Crossbones gazed at Monty as he stood looking perplexed. She repeated. "I said, I long for pleasure of the flesh which you shall provide. You haven't forgotten how, have you?"

Monty pretended to be distracted as he looked around the room at all of the artifacts. He was particularly fascinated with her collection of knives and assorted blades. The collections hung on the walls to the left and to the right of the old woman's large seat. "That's quite a collection." He admired the beautiful display.

"Yes, I have a weakness for weapons of all kinds. They are beautiful, are they not?" Monty nodded. The old woman stood up and signaled him to come closer. "Which one do you fancy?"

Monty pointed to one of the blades. It was roughly half the size of a typical samurai sword. The case was a deep black finish with no markings. "That is a beauty."

The old woman took the sword down from its display. "You have good taste. I call this one Black Lamia." She snickered. "I'm sure you can put this to good use. She held it out in front of him. Take it. It's yours. You will use it to kill Juan Arias, that miserable little man who got you killed. Then you will use it to mow down those religious fools who will not join us."

Monty took the weapon. He removed the blade from its sleek black case to examine it. The ultra-sharp edge glistened as it reflected the light in the room. "Yes, I remember my loser friend, Juan. He and I go way back to our early school days. He showed up a few days ago. I thought I had gotten rid of the little maggot."

"No, he is still alive. It seems he had a little help from the man Jesus. He will make a good prize. He is unlikely to convert to our side. You will just have to kill him. That's the least we can do for his meddling in our affairs."

"Now, Come here and give Mama Crossbones a big kiss, why don't you. Then you can stick your tongue in my ear and whisper sweet perversions." Her creepy smile caused Monty to freeze where he stood. He did not know what to say.

"So, you don't find Mama Crossbones attractive?" She twirled her hair with her bony finger. A strand came off as she smiled at him. Monty looked to see where the nearest window was located so he could jump through it in case she was serious about any hanky-panky. He watched as she continued to twirl her hair and more of it came off. Monty's face made an involuntary contortion, much like discovering he had just bitten into a moldy sandwich. She noticed the look on his face. At first, she giggled. Then she erupted into a weird combination of choking and coughing laughter. She cleared her throat and spat on the floor. "Is there no stirring in your pants when you look at me, manflesh?"

"That's an understatement," Monty thought, *"I would rather go to hell, than lay down with the old hag. She has to be at least 150 years old. Wow, that would be hell."* Just looking at her was enough to make a man religious.

After her bout of laughter, she looked over at the wino's two demons still present in the room. "Continue as you were in those two pieces of trash and wait outside. When he is ready, you will escort Monty to his new apartment." In a moment the demons disappeared, as they re-inhabited the winos. They stood up and walked out of the house.

She turned her attention to Monty. "Now, it is time to partake of physical delight." As she said this, the beautiful woman who opened the door earlier approached and took Monty's hand. Mama Crossbones nodded to Monty, signaling him to comply. He took the young woman's hand then looked over at Mama Crossbones with surprise. "So, you really want me to make love to this woman?"

In an instant, Mama Crossbones ripped one of the Samurai swords from the display wall. She lunged forward in less time than he could blink. Monty let the young woman's hand go as he was knocked back against the wall. The old woman had the strength of a sumo wrestler and the agility of a well-trained ninja. He was up against the wall before he realized what happened.

She held the sharp blade against his throat. Monty never experienced anything like this, not in this life or his past life. "Love has nothing to do with it." He looked into the old woman's fiery eyes and felt one of her bony hands lock around his wrist as the other held the sword with perfect precision a hair's length from his throat. For the first time, he was afraid.

"That wretched emotion has no place within those who are truly free. Why, I'd just as easily kill you as sleep with you. You serve my purpose, and I help you serve yours. Each of us serves the greater evil. It's quite simple. Don't you forget it, my little manflesh. Speak to me of love again and I will disembowel you. You can be cast into the pit well ahead of schedule. I have others who would gladly take your place."

She released him, then returned to her seat. Monty remained motionless, still in shock. He stood against the wall wondering, *"How could this feeble old woman almost take my head off so easily?"*

Once seated in her chair, she continued. "We serve ourselves at the cost of everyone else, as you have done so brilliantly in your past life. Now it's time to begin your life anew. This time you will be more powerful and cunning, but you will need Mama's guidance.

"Now let us enjoy each other's flesh."

Monty looked up wondering how to decline the offer without getting his head cut off. The old woman chuckled again. "Worry not, manflesh, for you will physically be with her." She pointed to the woman. "She and I are one. She was hollow, so I use her as my second self, for the exploits of physical pleasure. We feel as one. She might be more to your liking than this old woman."

"Actually, I'm gay." Monty blurted out.

Mama Crossbones squinted at Monty and started to wheeze with laughter. She slapped her knee several times as her laughter bellowed. "You don't say, my little manflesh. Gay you say? Well, happy is as happy does. So be it. We won't let that stop us." She pointed to the young women standing beside Monty. When he turned to look at her, he saw a handsome young man in her place.

Monty gasped, "Hernando?" He turned to the old woman. "How do you know him? Can you read my mind? What happened to the woman?"

"I can see many things, as I saw you in the belly of your surrogate mother. It is a power you will acquire with time as my designee."

Monty looked at Hernando then back at Mama Crossbones. "What exactly is a designee?"

"You are the chosen one. I am sure of it. You will help lead the Christian church into ruin as was prophesied long ago. Millions of Christians will abandon their faith as a result of the exploits of their fallen clergy. A plan you will help lead. Most importantly, we must prevent the one called Francis from becoming pope. You will play a key role in the implosion of Catholicism. You are gifted. I have seen your capabilities, and I am very proud of your past life accomplishments. I chose well when I planted my gift of evil in your surrogate mother's belly."

Monty thought for a moment. "What would have become of me if you hadn't cast your spell on me while I was still in my mother's womb?"

She waved her hand in a dismissive gesture. "You would have grown up like the rest of those pathetic fools claiming to have a conscience. It is such a dreadful waste. A conscience serves no purpose, except to prevent the experience of full enjoyment. You probably would not have gotten everything you wanted, including that red bicycle as a young boy. You might have grown up to make the dreadful mistake of following the man Jesus. Who knows, you might even have become a lawyer, dentist, juggler, or even a wretched priest. Fortunately for you, I knew that was almost impossible. My power always guided you toward darkness. You are one of the privileged who attracted Mama Crossbones' eye. Your wretched surrogate parents should have thanked me if they had any sense. They never knew, of course."

Monty wondered how he could have lived his entire life without knowing this old woman's role in it. "So, for as long as I lived I was never truly myself?"

"You always had the advantage." She replied. "That's

right. You always had me. But, more accurately, I always had you. Yet, even under my guidance there was always the risk you might be brainwashed by followers of the man Jesus. Fortunately, that never happened. Then you died much too early, so I brought you back. Once dead, it is no longer possible to turn to the man Jesus. So, of that I am glad but it is a mere technicality. I know you would never entertain such an absurd notion. Significant power and glory await you. As my designee, you will live in luxury and perverted bliss. Money is not an issue."

"So, you mean I can do whatever I want, have whatever I want with money to burn?"

"That is correct. As the chosen one, you will be powerful indeed. I look forward to bringing you before the Council so they might see Mama Crossbones' prize. We will go tomorrow.

Later, we will talk about important matters of which your first order of business will be to kill Juan Arias. Now, that's enough talk. My loins are on fire. Take my hollow's hand and have your way with him. It will give me great pleasure."

Monty smiled. "Could we wait until I have more strength? I'm trying to adjust to this new body. I would be a very poor partner right now. I'm feeling tired and I have a headache. Dying and coming back to life kind of took it out of me. But I'll feel better in the next day or two. I just need a little time to adjust. Then we can indulge."

Mama Crossbones looked at him with a strange expression Monty hoped he interpreted correctly as disappointment, not execution. She waved her hand. "Very well." She summoned the two winos. "Take manflesh to his new home."

8

Where's Paul?

Nurse Mitchell sat in the office after her terrifying ordeal with Paul Herodias in the parking garage. Detective Lopez asked her to describe her encounter. After telling him everything she could remember, he asked, "What can you tell me about him?"

"He's worked here for approximately two years. He was always soft spoken, polite and friendly enough. But tonight it was as though I was talking with a different person. He didn't even know what model car he drove. Maybe he was on drugs."

"We've dispatched a patrol car to his home address. Do you know if he's married?"

"I don't think so. He's a single guy whose vehicle of choice is a minivan. I think that's a little weird."

Lopez jotted down more notes and was ready to finish his questioning. "Is there anything else you would like to report?"

She thought for a moment. "If I didn't know any better, I'd say he was suffering from schizophrenia."

Detective Lopez thanked Nurse Mitchell for her cooperation then headed to the waiting room to speak with Jake. He had taken his statement previously but he had a few more questions.

Jake sat in the waiting room with Carl's wife as they waited for news from Dr. Carson. He rose to excuse himself when he saw the detective summon him from the doorway.

"I have a few more questions, if you don't mind, Jake."

"Not at all, Detective."

"You went to get help for Paul since you thought he was traumatized somehow. Has he ever exhibited signs of schizophrenia?"

Jake thought about his encounters with Paul. "No, he was always consistent in his behavior, kind of nerdy and quiet."

Detective Lopez tapped his pen against his pad. "Do you have any idea why he set fire to the body?"

Jake shook his head. "I don't think he set fire to it. Carl and I were down the hall when we heard the cart crash when all the surgical tools hit the floor. It couldn't have taken us more than a few seconds to get back. By the time we re-entered the morgue, the fire was fully ablaze as though burning continuously. I found Paul under the desk. I think something spooked him. Something happened that I can't explain."

Lopez took additional notes. He looked up from his pad and continued his questioning. "You said you and Carl were spooked by the corpse's rigor mortis. Do you think that's what happened to spook Paul into hiding under the desk? Can a corpse have rigor-mortis twice?"

Jake recalled the horrific scene and how spooked he and Carl had been. "Yeah, that could have happened. It's highly unlikely though to have such severe rig twice, such a long time after death. The fire was strange. The sprinkler system came on but with no effect. The corpse kept burning. It was an intense fire that quickly consumed the body. I've never seen fire so completely unaffected by water. It died down after the body was burned to a char."

The Detective tapped his pen on his pad in triplet beats. "There must have been someone else present to set fire to the body. Unless, of course, the body combusted spontaneously, which is absurd."

Dr. Carson entered the waiting room at that moment. Carl's wife ran over to him. The Doctor took her hand. "He is going to be all right. The surgery went well. He lost a lot of blood but I think we will see rapid improvement, although he'll be sore from the puncture wound. He is resting now. We have him on strong medication. He is out of danger, so my recommendation to you, Mrs. Petterson, is to go home and get some rest. You can see him in the morning. We'll take good care of him.

Carl's wife burst into tears of joy after hearing her husband would live. She thanked Dr. Carson then sat down to contact other family members.

Detective Lopez approached Dr. Carson. "When would it be all right to question him?"

"Give him twenty-four hours, Detective. He won't be doing much talking before then."

9

Monty's Dream

Monty sat in the back of the Mercedes on his way to his new home at Collingwood Manor, a luxurious condo development in midtown Raleigh. Mama Crossbones had it all arranged.

Monty was tired. He thought about the past twenty-four hours, how much had happened and how much had changed. He tried to make sense of it all. *"One moment I'm ready to finish off my old man, the next minute I'm dead. Now I'm alive again in an inferior body that used to belong to some guy named Paul, who is slightly overweight and has a receding hairline. I've discovered more about myself in the past few hours than I ever knew in my previous lifetime. I don't know if I should thank the old wench or curse her. But she did say money was no object, so I get to play and play hard without a care in the world. Not a bad deal."*

As the Mercedes pulled up to Collingwood Manor, another vehicle came to a stop just ahead of them, a Rolls-Royce. The driver got out and opened the door for two passengers, a man and his pregnant wife. Monty watched as she slowly made her way out of the vehicle with the help of her husband. *"From the looks of her, she must be almost ready give birth."* He wondered what Mama Crossbones would think of the child this woman was carrying. *"Is it a good recruit? What kind of person will it turn out to be? Will it choose to be a pilot or a drug dealer? Will it find pleasure in the suffering of others or will it be a fool becoming part of some religious group? Has its fate been predetermined by something or someone? Will it get to know itself?"*

"Monty," came the voice from one of the winos. "Are you OK?" Wino butler had stepped out of the car to open the door for him. Monty was so caught up in watching the couple he had not noticed the excellent wino butler service he was receiving.

Monty got out of the car and went inside. He had no bags. The lobby was decorated in a Rococo style with ornately curved furniture and green Italian marble. Renaissance painting masterpieces adorned the walls. There was a mahogany service counter to one side. He spotted the husband and wife speaking to the female attendant. As he approached, the couple turned and gave him a polite smile, then returned to the business of checking in.

Monty didn't know these people but he knew, the moment they turned to smile at him, he hated them. The hatred bubbled inside him. Then he realized it was not them he hated; it was what they represented – that which he would never know. As his hatred surged, he hated the wretched creature who claimed to be his real mother.

The couple finished at the counter, Monty's mind was a whirl of confusion and rage. At last, his daze was broken by the woman behind the counter. "Yes sir, how may I help you?" She looked at Monty with a friendly smile.

He approached the counter, cleared his throat. "Lovely couple."

The young woman smiled revealing dimples on each cheek. "Yes, Mr. and Mrs. Fairchild. Are you friends with them?

"No, I'm new here."

She hit a button on her computer. "Your name, sir?"

"'Monty. I was told my first name is all you needed."

She scanned her screen. "Yes, so I see. You are with The Council. They own several condos. Here is the key to your suite. It's located on the 6th floor, unit 619."

Monty entered the beautifully appointed suite. It was large and overlooked a small lake, nicer than the place he had shared with Hernando, his lover in a former life. *"No doubt, Hernando knows by now that I've been killed."* He thought of calling, but wouldn't know what to say. *"Hi Hernando, I was dead, but I'm*

OK now, thanks to the old bat who brought me back in this Paul Herodias meat suit." Maybe this whole thing was just a bad dream and he would wake up in his bed with his life back to normal. He would have breakfast, then do his workout routine with Hernando to the beat of his favorite song, YMCA.

He sat down on the bed with an amusing thought. Would a suite owned by the Council have a bible in the nightstand drawer, as is typically found in a motel? He opened the top drawer and there it was. *"This is too damned funny. I'll have to tell the old witch, to get rid of the religious propaganda in their Council rooms."* He picked up the Bible and flipped through the pages without reading a word. It was just something to do as he stretched out in bed against a stack of pillows, gazing at his reflection in the dresser's mirror. The man looking back was a stranger. Who was this person, Paul, whose body he now inhabited? He sat staring at the stranger for a long time. Thoughts kept intruding on his mind. *"What would have happened to me if I had been free to be myself? What would have become of me? How would I know if I was ever really me? How could someone have the power to violate a soul?"* Question after question kept coming into his mind, and his fatigue continued to mount. A few moments later, Monty's hand stop flipping pages and he fell asleep.

He dreamt of his mother. He was sitting in the kitchen eating a chocolate chip cookie and drinking a glass of cold milk. The chocolate chips were warm and soft. She was wearing a blue polka dot dress, her cheeks were flushed from the heat of the oven.

"We were going to name you Mark, after my dad, or Luke, after Blake's dad. Seek them out. They can help you now." Your father was insistent upon naming you Monty, after his grandfather, a very special man. You never met your grandfather. He died before you were born. He was a scientist and loved your father deeply. The doctor was sure you would be born June 15th, but you were a stubborn baby, deciding that June 19 suited you better."

The next instant, Monty was standing across the street from his house. He could see his mom in the kitchen. He noticed the front door with the large brass numbers indicating their address. He liked the contrast of the shiny 6, 1, and 9 against the dark wooden door. Their house was on the corner.

Monty looked at his hands. He was holding the remote

control to his favorite toy car. He looked back at the house and saw his mother in the kitchen. She stopped to look out the window. The house now resembled a book. His right hand hit the toggle on the remote control switch. He looked up at his mother waving from the window. The next instant she was gone as the book exploded and the shockwave from the blast knocked him down.

Mama Crossbones stood next to him in his dream, laughing and wheezing. She bent down and grabbed him by his shirt collar and helped him stand up. She continued to laugh. Then she abruptly stopped. "Here, let me introduce you to your brother." Monty turned his head and saw the boy standing beside him. It was himself. Then the boy was engulfed in a dark demonic shadow. His body burst into flames. Mama Crossbones was roaring with laughter. "Congratulations, you've been promoted." He felt dizzy. Everything started to spin. He could still hear Mama Crossbones' horrid wheezing laughter as her rant continued. "Your career is sizzling now! You are one hot commodity! You've been burning the candle at both ends. Whoops, you are the candle, hee hee!" The spinning was intolerable. He wanted to throw up. Still, he could make out the old woman's rant. "Welcome to hell, manflesh!"

Monty awoke from his nightmare as beads of sweat ran down his face. He was sitting up against the stack of pillows. Realizing that the Bible was still in his hand, he threw it against the wall. It hit the door jamb and ricocheted into the bathroom. He got up and paced around the room. He was breathing hard. After few moments of pacing, he ran to the toilet and threw up.

He felt like a bad hangover, except he hadn't been drinking. He knelt, hugging the toilet as waves of nausea forced his body to heave uncontrollably. Monty could not remember the last time he ate anything or the last time he felt this miserable. The content being expelled from his stomach was brown with green blotches and had the consistency of pea soup.

Monty's head lay against the rim of the toilet. His body was weak from all the heaving and vomiting. The bathroom floor was a rose colored marble tile. His eyes gazed at the patterns and accents. Some accents were darker and bolder than others. Each tile had its own unique pattern. He tried to see if any two were the same. As far as he could tell, they were all different. Their patterns swirled differently, but they all were part of the same floor. His eyes followed two tiles ending at the sink. The last section of tile was obscured by the bible which landed at the sink's base.

He noticed the flimsy book cover was torn. It lay sprawled opened beneath the sink. The edges of the pages were red. You couldn't really tell looking at a single sheet, but when they stacked together the red was clearly visible. His eye was drawn to the top of the page. He could barely read the writing but thought it must be the guy who wrote the book. Some guy named Luke, and there seemed to be a reference to his birthday. "Luke 6:19, How do you like that? The guy has the same birthday as I do, June 19." He looked at the words. "And the people all tried to touch him, because power was coming from him and healing them all."

"Yeah, a little healing sounds good right about now. I feel like I've just been run over by a truck, again. Who the hell am I? Am I really alive in someone else's body? I have no idea who I am, and now, I have no idea who I was. I always felt sure of myself. I was better than all of them. I had the looks and I had the brains. Were those my feelings? Were they really my own? Now I feel like someone's toy puppet. I feel like a reverse Pinocchio. I was real; now I'm not. Perhaps I was never real."

Another wave of vomiting took control as his body tensed and expelled more of the foul-smelling pea soup. He glanced at the book under the sink again. He re-read the words. Then he wondered, *"Who is the 'him' to which the page refers?"* His eyelids became heavy. With drool hanging from his lips and his face pressed against the rim of the toilet, Monty fell asleep.

10

Giving Mama the Finger

The doorbell rang several times then stopped. The ringing began again. They knew he was in there, so they just kept ringing. Monty's eyes slowly opened as the ringing continued. He slowly rose to his feet. He washed his face in the sink to bring himself around to full consciousness. "Just a minute," he hollered. After drying his face, he ran to open the door.

Wino chauffeur and wino butler stood at the door. "Are you ready to go?"

Monty wiped his eyes. "Go, where?"

"Mama's taking you to meet the Council," said wino butler.

"You're kidding! What time is it? You guys just dropped me off a few hours ago."

The winos looked at each other and laughed. Wino chauffeur said, "We dropped you off yesterday, almost 24 hours ago." They looked at each other, and laughed again. "Say, did you go to a party without us?"

Monty looked at them as though they were crazy. "Yeah, I had a party with the toilet bowl. It wasn't much fun. You boys have to wait until I get ready. Hopefully, the old bag left me some clothes. She's thought of almost everything else."

The two winos sat down and turned on the television. Wino butler picked up Monty's blade to examine it. Monty found clothes in the closet and went into the bathroom. While in the shower he heard the winos yelling at each other, but couldn't make out what they were saying. One of them sounded upset.

A few moments later Monty emerged from the shower. He put on the clothes. They fit fairly well, but were not nearly as nice as the clothes he picked out for himself in his past life.

Stepping out of the bathroom, he saw wino butler holding his blood soaked shirt around his hand. "He cut off his finger," said wino chauffeur holding up the severed finger for Monty to see.

"What?" Monty asked in disbelief. "What do you mean, he cut it off, by mistake? What the hell were you doing?"

Wino butler glanced at the blade resting on the coffee table. "I was admiring your blade. Wanted to see how sharp it was. I just put it against my finger, then I sneezed. It cut through my finger as though it was nothing."

"Great!" Monty buttoned his shirt. "Why don't you take him to the emergency room? I'll just take a cab to the old witch's place."

"No need. Mama Crossbones can take care of him. And she ain't no witch, doesn't like to be called one," Wino chauffeur warned.

Monty snickered. "Well, she's no beauty queen. What the hell else is she?"

"She's a high priestess, one of 666 holy ones that bear the mark. She is a powerful soul trapper, very powerful," Wino chauffeur explained.

Monty looked at wino butler who was clutching his hand. "Well then, let's go."

Monty and his two wino friends arrived at Mama Crossbones' place. Wino chauffeur explained what happened.

She motioned wino butler to come to her. "Where is the finger?"

Wino chauffeur took the finger out of his shirt pocket and handed it to her.

She examined the finger and looked at his hand. Then she took a small knife and cut herself on the arm. Surprisingly, no blood came from the wound. She squeezed the area around the cut. Thick black jelly oozed from the open wound. She scooped it up with the severed edge of the finger. Then she scooped up more of the black jelly with her finger, rubbed it on finger stump on wino butler's hand and fastened the finger with a cloth. She finished the job by using a candle to drip hot wax all around the finger and hand, to hold everything together.

Monty watch in amazement as her wound sealed itself almost instantaneously. "How did your wound heal itself like that?"

"Mama Crossbones cannot be hurt, manflesh. The evil one has rewarded his faithful servant with much power. You may yet attain such power as your deeds grow more hideous and to his liking." She looked at the two winos and instructed them. "Now, you will take Monty to the Council meeting where I will present him. I will meet you there."

Monty was a bit confused. "Where are we going and how will you get there?"

"They know where to take you. As for me, I do not need the aid of a vehicle to get from one place to another. Now go." As she said this, she turned and walked toward the wall with the poorly drawn Roman arch. There were strange symbols on the floor directly in front of that section of wall. She paused, uttered something under her breath, then walked through the wall. In an instant, she was gone.

Wino chauffeur looked at Monty. "Like I said, she's very powerful. Let's go."

11

The Investigation

Detective Lopez sat in a chair near Carl Petterson's bed. "I'm sorry to burden you with questions, Mr. Petterson, but do you think you can answer a few?" Carl nodded "Sure, why not. It only hurts when I breathe."

"Mr. Petterson, can you tell me exactly what happened?"

Carl gazed directly in front of him and thought for a moment. "As I was helping Paul get up from under the desk, he stabbed me. I remember my legs turned to rubber, then I hit the floor. Paul stood there with the knife in his hand. I lost consciousness."

"Was there anything else, Mr. Petterson? Anything at all?"

Carl thought for a moment. "I remember the water from the sprinkler hitting my face. I remember wondering why the body kept burning. I thought it might be a chemical fire. If so, whoever set fire to the body used a highly flammable chemical. Then, as I was laying there, I heard Paul mumble. 'My name is Monty,' but he seemed unsure. That's the last thing I remember."

Detective Lopez sat back in the guest chair and took notes. "Nurse Mitchell mentioned she thought Paul might be schizophrenic. Has Paul ever exhibited any prior behavior leading you to believe he might be schizophrenic?"

"No, he was a low-key guy, had a dry sense of humor and always seemed harmless. He was the last person I'd ever expect to want to kill me." Carl shifted a bit to get comfortable. "I've been doing this job for a long time, Detective Lopez. That night was the strangest one of my entire career. There was something strange about that corpse, the way it exhibited such extreme rigor mortis. Paul planned to use the corpse as an exhibit for his morning anatomy class."

The detective tapped his notebook with his pen. "You and your partner picked up the corpse earlier that night. Was there anything odd about the body when you first arrived at the scene?"

Carl explained how they found the body. "The guy had been hit by a truck. The body was badly beat up. His father arrived at the scene and stood there looking at it for awhile. It was his son. As I understand it, the son, Monty McPride, tried to kill Blake McPride, the father. The police set up a sting operation. Monty tried to flee when all of a sudden he was eating truck grill."

Detective Lopez raised his eyebrow "Wasn't that the name Paul said?"

"Yes, Detective. Maybe Paul is schizoid and took on the dead man's name, assuming a different personality."

Lopez agreed. "It makes the most sense of anything I've heard so far."

Carl's mind wandered to Blake McPride at the accident scene. "Did someone contact the father and tell him what happened to the body?"

Lopez nodded. "Yes, I got a chance to speak with him briefly. He will have the remains taken to a funeral home where they will arrange a proper cremation. This Monty was a real piece of work. He tried to take over his father's company and tried to kill him off."

Carl sat back in his bed. "For Paul's sake, I hope it is schizophrenia, and not…" Carl paused.

Detective Lopez was curious. "And not what, Mr. Petterson?"

Carl reluctantly brought himself to complete his sentence. "…and not possession."

12

The Council Meeting

The Mercedes with Monty and the two winos pulled into the parking deck of one of the tallest buildings in downtown Raleigh. They took the elevator to the top floor. The doors opened. Monty was surprised to see a row of men and women standing on either side of the room, all dressed in their finest, all looking at him. They formed a human corridor. He recognized a few local politicians, several famous actors and actresses and other television personalities. He did not expect such a grand reception; it looked like a who's who of famous and influential people, at least 100 on each side.

As Monty slowly stepped out of the elevator, everyone started to clap. They all smiled at him as he walked through the applauding gauntlet. Many of the people stuck out their hands to shake his. Some simply patted him on the back. Monty smiled and gained more momentum. His disbelief was replaced by a familiar and joyful sense of being the center of attention and importance. It was a feeling he remembered from his past life. It felt great. *"Now, this is more like it."*

Mama Crossbones waited for him at the end of the human corridor. She pointed to the head table. Waiters and waitresses escorted them to their seats. The long head table was situated at the front of the room, midway along the window wall overlooking the city. The large room had floor to ceiling windows on three sides. The view of the city was breathtaking. The sky was clear, the moon was full, and the city lights sprawled below them.

Waiters poured champagne into glasses. Once everyone was seated, Mama Crossbones tapped her glass until the room was quiet. She looked around at the audience and greeted them. "Welcome to all our regional members of the Council and to those watching via satellite from across the world. As you know, we've had a rising star whose career was cut short. Some of you may have seen it on the local news. But we are persistent, especially when it comes to someone with as much potential as our special guest. To his credit, he is one of the few recruits able to plan and carry out the execution of his own mother, or I should say surrogate mother, at just six years of age. He is my designee. And so, we gather tonight to embark on a new day of evil's reign. I present to you Monty McPride."

At this, everyone in the room broke into spontaneous applause. They arose from their chairs and gave Monty a standing ovation. As the applause continued, Monty stood and bowed in front of the entire assembly. He smiled, took a deep breath and proudly enjoyed the moment. Minutes later, he sat down and the applause subsided. Mama Crossbones continued. "Monty will slay Juan Arias who has been favored by our enemy. Then he will be assigned to a parish where he will unleash a torrent of corruption to bring down as many Catholic priests as he can. He will move from one parish to another, his agenda will remain the same. We have chosen the parish of St. Ignatius as his first target because of its large congregation. There, he will use his talents to corrupt and manipulate clergy and followers of the man Jesus into public humiliation. The result will be another scandal resulting in. disenchanted believers who will lose faith. Many will join our cause. Our strategy continues to work brilliantly, so we will continue to spread our veil of evil over the entire world."

The room broke into applause again as people nodded to acknowledge what Mama Crossbones was saying. She held up her hand in a gesture of hush so she could continue. "As members of the Council, you all are privileged to know first-hand how the power of darkness works, and in many cases, where it will work next. You all know it for what it is. The lust of evil runs through you. Its rewards have been lavished on all those gathered here tonight. Now that he has been presented to you and many truths revealed to him in his rebirth, let us hear from our special guest. Once again, I present our chosen one, my designee, Monty McPride.

The room once again exploded into applause and all eyes turned to Monty. He was again at ease and comfortable at being the center of attention. Mama Crossbones sat down. Monty looked intently at the crowd. "Wow, this has been the craziest 48 hours of my life…" He laughed a little "…and death." The crowd chuckled at his remark. "Much has been revealed to me and for that I am grateful." He looked over to Mama Crossbones and smiled. "I am grateful for this second chance, and I promise all of you I will not waste it by running in front of a large moving truck." The crowd chuckled again. After a short pause, he continued. "This celebration, meeting all of you tonight, learning how the unborn are recruited and how their souls are hijacked for the purposes of serving evil, has left me breathless. I feel more myself than I ever did in my past life, and I promise to partake of the pleasures of the work that lies ahead." Monty removed the Black Lamia from its holder and held it up. "This has been entrusted to me. It is with great joy I will use it for the important work before me."

After another few moments of applause and cheering, Monty returned the blade into its sheath. He waved to the guests and sat down. Mama Crossbones was clearly impressed. She looked at him like a proud mother would look at her child. "I knew you were special. You have exceeded my expectations with your passionate speech. You will go far and become very powerful. I think this will happen in a short period of time. The master will be very pleased."

The band began to play, and food was served. Monty was served some of the finest wine he had ever tasted. The appetizers were remarkable. It was as though he discovered a new set of taste buds. He had never enjoyed such a fine steak and all the trimmings. Everything was cooked to perfection.

During their meal, three guests came to the head table. All had business to conduct.

The first was Mr. Fredericks. He placed a small brown envelope on the table. "Here is your new identity." Monty looked at Mama Crossbones. She nodded for him to open it. He removed the passport to verify the picture. It was him. There was a new driver's license. His new name would be Charles Dubois. He also had a new social security card. Mr. Fredericks continued. "Here is your bankcard and account information. Your account balance is $1 million dollars."

Monty turned to Mama Crossbones with a look of surprise. "Is he serious?" She simply nodded.

Mr. Fredericks continued. "You can draw upon it any time." Fredericks congratulated Monty, shook his hand, and returned to his table.

Next, came Mr. Adolfo. He placed a small box in front of Monty. "It has all the available options. I think you'll enjoy it." Monty opened the top of the small box and pulled out a set of car keys. "It's black, just like the one you came in. If you need anything, just bring the vehicle around to the showroom, and we'll take care of it." He shook Monty's hand and returned to his table. Monty again looked at Mama Crossbones.

She squinted at him. "What were you expecting, frankincense and myrrh?"

Monty looked at her with a blank expression.

Her squint turned into a chuckle, then into a knee smacking guffaw. Monty's face remained blank. He didn't get her little joke. She composed herself and flapped her hand in a dismissive waive. "Never mind. I'll explain it to you some other time."

A third guest came up to the head table. Dr. Sinclair shook Monty's hand. "You come see me. We'll improve that face, make it so you're no longer recognized as Paul Herodias." The doctor glanced and smiled at Mama Crossbones, then back to Monty. "You know, bringing someone back is rare, you're lucky to receive such an honor."

Monty smiled. "Yes, I'm beginning to see that. I'm certainly glad to be here, even in this Paul suit." The doctor chuckled. "It's not too bad. With a little work, you'll be happy in your new skin; just call me when you're ready." He gave Monty his business card and returned to his table.

"I didn't realize what a big deal this is," Monty said to the old woman.

"The doctor is right. You have been given a great honor."

Monty held up his glass. The old woman did the same. They clinked wine glasses.

Mama Crossbones reached into her sleeve and produced a small black book. She placed it on the table then slid it across to Monty. He reached for it. As he did so, she maintained her pressure upon it and did not release it. He looked up at her. "You will need this as you travel the world." She looked intently into his eyes. "Guard it carefully. It contains important information." She released her pressure and he placed it in his pocket. "You are now officially a member of the Council."

He nodded. "I will be careful, thank you."

She took a sip of wine. "After the Council meeting you will meet me at my place. We have some unfinished business."

"Agreed." He surveyed the room and took it all in. It was surreal being in this place with all of these famous and influential people.

Finishing everything on his plate, Monty took a deep breath as he smiled and looked over at Mama Crossbones. "Extraordinary! That was by far the finest meal I have ever tasted. The steak was out of this world."

The old woman squinted as she smiled back at him. "That was not steak you were eating, manflesh."

13

The Little Chat

Pastor Bob sat in his office preparing his homily for the 5:30 Mass. He heard a knock on the door, looked up and said, "Come in, Oliver."

Oliver proceeded to take a seat. "You wanted to see me?"

Pastor Bob put his pen down. "I know you are preparing for your karate competition and, as you know, I encourage and fully support your sports pursuits. I want to talk to you about a couple of things." Bob's mild mannered tone was a stark contrast to Oliver's high octane, testosterone voice and mannerisms.

"Yeah, what's up, Bob?" Oliver did not understand why Pastor Bob could not get it through his thick head it was Wing Chun, not Karate. They are two completely different things. "And, it's not karate, for the hundredth time. It's wing chun, Bob. They are very different styles. It's what Bruce Lee practiced. Karate is what Chuck Norris practiced. You probably know those two guys from movies, right?"

Pastor Bob looked at Oliver as though he had just spoken Mandarin Chinese. "No, I never watched that stuff."

Oliver had to overcome his urge to smack Pastor Bob, the man leading the parish in spite of the fact he had no personality. He was known as the toast pastor. Oliver looked away, and focused on the picture of St. Joseph hanging on the side wall. He thought about Jesus as a kid. *"Were there moments when Joseph or Mary just wanted to pull him by the ear and tell him to behave?*

What about that time when Jesus was at the temple? His parents worried about him because they didn't know where he was. Jesus told them they should have known he was at his father's house. Did Joseph react like a typical father and say, 'Come here, mister. The next time you decide to do something like this, you let us know ahead of time. We were worried sick looking for you.' Do you think he might have pulled Jesus by the ear on occasion? After all, Jesus was fully human and fully God. He did exhibit human emotions. His experience in the Garden of Gethsemane was one of those times, when he feared what he knew was yet to come. He could have had his moments as a kid." Oliver took a deep breath and turned back to the Bob.

Bob looked at Oliver as a principal of a school would look at a child who misbehaved. "Oliver, I've been talking and you have not been listening to a word I've said. What is so fascinating about that portrait of St. Joseph?"

"Sorry, Bob. I'm on my training regimen, working out three times a week."

Pastor Bob nodded. Oliver recognized Bob's characteristically, concerned look. "Is anything bothering you? I've noticed you have been acting a little…" He paused to search for the right word, "short with some of our parishioners, in particular Dr. Sinclair who joined our building expansion team. He is a very wealthy new member. I'd hate for him to get the wrong idea, especially from our pastoral staff."

Oliver shifted uncomfortably in his chair. Pastor Bob had no idea what Oliver saw and felt when in the company of Dr. Sinclair. His demon face was big and grotesque. Oliver struggled to keep his mouth shut whenever in his company.

Because of his ability to see a demon face superimposed on a normal face, Oliver kept to himself for the most part. He attended few church functions other than presiding at Mass. Oliver developed the reputation of being a somewhat reclusive priest. Folks loved his homilies, and they liked him, but he was usually missing from parish celebrations and other events not directly related to Mass.

Oliver waved his hand. "Sinclair just gives me the creeps, that's all." He chuckled, trying to make light of it, hoping Pastor Bob would not pursue the matter any further. No luck.

Bob continued. "I get the impression several of our parishioners make you uncomfortable. I think it's more than heebie-jeebies from what I have observed. You will find any excuse to leave whenever certain people are around. It became obvious to me when I introduced you to Mr. Fredericks and Dr. Sinclair. Your reaction was the same, borderline rude. What is it about them that make you uncomfortable?"

Oliver wanted to finish this conversation, not get dragged further into it. "Perhaps you're right, Bob. It's more than the heebie-jeebies. Some people strike me as not being quite what they appear to be. Maybe, I'm just imagining things. I don't mean to be judgmental or rude. I will try not to let it affect how I act toward them. Thanks for pointing it out. I promise to work on it."

Pastor Bob's gaze was full of concern. "Oliver, the pastor at the church where you last served warned me you were prone to some strange behavior, well meaning, but strange. He told me several parishioners claimed you helped liberate their souls, or something like that. He was forced to send you to another parish when one of their top donors threatened to press charges, claiming you touched his wife inappropriately."

Oliver quickly clarified, "I tried to trace the sign of the cross on her forehead. She was an elderly woman, close to eighty years old. There was nothing inappropriate about it. I was just trying to bless her."

Pastor Bob pressed on. "At the church prior to that one, you had a similar thing happen. I must make sure it doesn't repeat in this parish. The last thing we need is a scandal or lawsuit or both." Pastor Bob had been putting off this conversation with Oliver, but after his recent reaction to some of the parishioners, he had to address it. He studied Oliver closely as he continued. "I mention this to you because if you think that you can benefit from some counseling, I would be happy to arrange it. We are under constant public scrutiny. I must be honest. You are beginning to worry me."

Oliver took a deep breath. There was an awkward silence for a moment. "Would it be best if I left the parish?"

Pastor Bob thought about the offer. "No, that won't be necessary. You may have a reputation of being a bit antisocial, but that is not something that would warrant your dismissal. What I need is your assurance you won't do anything to jeopardize the parish's reputation, causing us negative publicity and humiliation."

Oliver knew a conversation like this was bound to happen. He didn't expect it so soon. There seemed to be more people engulfed with darkness than ever before. Oliver knew he wasn't crazy or imagining things. He had to walk a fine line, helping in ways that would not bring attention to the parish or to the crazy priest who could see demons.

14

Getting Ahead

Monty pulled up to Mama Crossbones' place in his recently gifted Mercedes. He walked up to the house and the door opened as he was about to knock. It was the beautiful hollow. She smiled. He lowered his hand, returned her smile, and entered the house.

Mama Crossbones was sipping her glass of brandy and enjoying a fine Cuban cigar. "Come. Let us discuss important matters at hand." She waved her scrawny hand. "Sit." She pointed to the adjacent chair. "Tomorrow, you will kill Juan Arias." She took a sip of brandy. "This one is personal. I want him to pay for meddling in your affairs and mine. He will be a trophy kill." She handed him an address. "This is where he lives. I could have sent another, but I want you to do it. What sweet revenge. After you kill him, you can kill that idiot father of yours. Blake McPride must also pay. But before you kill him, let him know who it is that is doing the killing. It will be very amusing. You will enjoy it tremendously. After you have your fun, you will go to Dr. Sinclair. He will perform cosmetic surgery on your face so you can be free to be you and not mistaken for Paul Herodias. No doubt, the police will be searching for you. Do you have any questions?"

Monty sat taking in her instructions and nodded to signal he had no questions.

"Good." She puffed on her cigar. "This brings me to your assignment. You will join St. Ignatius Church as a parishioner.

You will give a generous donation to win over the pastor. You will have a great deal of fun in this role. Your goal is to facilitate corruption within the St. Ignatius parish. It is a huge parish, and we can convert more to our cause as they lose faith in the man Jesus by bringing shame and ruin to this church. Dr Sinclair and Mr. Fredericks are also working toward its demise."

She poured a glass of brandy for him and offered him a cigar.

Monty sat back and enjoyed the brandy and the Cuban cigar. "Nice." He puffed and then examined his cigar. "You sure have fine taste, Mama C."

She gave him a snarly smile. "Mama knows best. You remember that, my little manflesh."

He smiled as he continued to gently puff and blow smoke rings. "You bet!"

Mama Crossbones put down her brandy and turned to Monty. "There are pleasures and rewards waiting that you can't possibly imagine. Now, the next bit of business is one that we postponed yesterday. It is time for you to indulge me." The beautiful hollow approached Monty. She now appeared as Hernando.

Monty smiled. "Ah, I see you didn't forget my preference, Mama C. I am very much looking forward to this night." He glanced at the old woman then back to Hernando. Monty stood up, took Hernando's hand, then turned to Mama Crossbones and gave her a wink. He and Hernando proceeded into the adjacent room. They closed the door behind them. The old woman took a deep breath and sat back in her chair.

A moment later, the door opened, and Monty approached the old woman. "I need a Brandy for my Hernando." She poured another glass and handed it to him. He took it and put it down on the table next to the chair as his eyes were fixed on the wall next to her. "I see you have guns with silencers." He pointed to a section of wall behind her which held the weapons. "That is the weapon I would like to use for my business with Juan Arias and my father. This sword is great," he said holding up the Black Lamia, looking at its sharp edge. "But I think it would be neater if I just shot them. I don't want to risk getting caught. Which of those guns would you recommend?"

She turned and pointed to the 44 caliber magnum. "I would use this little gem. The more damage the better." She retrieved the weapon and turned to hand it to him. That's when Mama Crossbones saw a glimmer and felt the cold sting on her neck as Monty took her head off with the Black Lamia. He made one clean slice. It was effortless. There was a swooshing sound as the blade cut through the air and then through the old witch's neck. The expression on her face was temporarily frozen in utter disbelief.

The head fell, crashing onto the table, spilling the brandy, before hitting the floor, and rolling a few feet. Amazingly, the old woman's head started ranting and raving. "What have you done, you fool! What have you done? I will make you pay for this!" As she said this, her headless body lunged at Monty. He fell against one of the walls, managing to kick away the old woman's powerful body. It got up and began flaying its arms wildly, trying to get a hold of him. Then it turned as if by remote control and charged him again. Monty held the Black Lamia straight up. As the body lunged at him, he brought the blade straight down, performing a perfect bilaterally symmetrical cut down the center. The headless body fell in two pieces onto the floor. Each section continued to twitch and move aimlessly. Monty stepped out the way.

The next scream he heard was Hernando as he came running out of the bedroom at top speed, a twisted look on his face, screaming and charging straight for Monty. In a split second, Monty reached for the gun and shot Hernando in the chest. He slowed but kept coming. Monty fired two additional rounds. The charging hollow fell backward.

"You'll never get away with it, manflesh!" said the severed head.

Monty approached it slowly. He examined the head for a moment then picked it up by the hair. It continued to speak. "Why, manflesh? I gave you everything. You even made that fancy speech at the Council meeting."

He held it up, so the head was at eye level with him. "I meant every word I said. I'm glad for this second chance. I promise not to waste it." He became angry and shook the head violently. "Learning that you hijack unborn souls, how you hijacked my soul, has left me wondering if I have ever been me. I feel more myself right now than I ever did in my past life, and I have lots of work ahead for me. Yes, that is what I said, and it's what I mean. I may see you in hell, but before that time comes, I want to know what I am capable of doing without some old witch pulling my strings. I spent my whole life in the dark. It is ironic; it took dying to wake me up."

"You have signed your own death sentence, manflesh! Your death is the only thing left that you will enjoy. I will make sure to greet you personally when you get to the pit, which will be soon enough." She sneered. "Yes, I will enjoy welcoming you to hell!"

Monty reached for anything he could use to stuff the talking head's mouth. He took the head into the bedroom and stuffed a pillow case in its mouth. "There, that's better," he said as he looked at the witch's contorted face. "I knew if I shot you, it probably would have done no good. After seeing how your arm healed from that cut earlier, I figured my only option was to take off your ugly head and burn it." He approached the fireplace amazed the thing was still alive without its body. Monty wondered how long it could survive on its own. As he was about to toss the head into the fire, he paused. There was something he had to do first.

15

Sacramental Emergency

Oliver sat in his office after presiding over the 11:00 a.m. Mass. He heard a commotion coming from Betty's desk. She was the volunteer receptionist.

"I'm sorry Sir, but you can't just walk in there. Let me see if a priest is avail…"

Oliver's office door crashed open. Not sure of what was happening, he was taken aback. A looming demon stood in the doorway. It was different from anything he had ever seen. There seemed to be multiple creatures occupying the same space. There was a stench emanating from it. Oliver wondered if hell had been unleashed on the earth.

The demon entered the office slamming the door shut. The room was filled with an eerie silence. Oliver wondered what the monster wanted with him. The silence was broken by the demonic figure. "Tell the old lady everything is all right and that you know me. Tell her now or I promise you everything will cease to be all right. Please don't test me on this. It would not be wise."

Oliver took a moment to consider the request. Then he shouted out, "It's OK Betty, I know this gentleman. Sorry he frightened you. He's a friend."

Oliver heard Betty comment, "What in the world?" She went back to her desk.

"Who, what are you and what do you want?" Oliver stared at the dark figure.

The demon's face changed several times, each time revealing a different presence. Every once in a while there would be a flicker of a human face. "I need to be baptized." The man's face was visible as he spoke. I need you to do it right away."

Oliver fell back into his chair. "Why do you want to be baptized?"

"My name is Monty. It's a long story. The bottom line is I may be out of time. I'm told all hell will be after me in a very short time and I don't like the prospect of downward mobility. There is more to it than that: I can't begin to know what to do next until I'm sure I'm free of some nasty baggage."

"That's an understatement." Oliver thought. *"Nasty doesn't even come close to describing your baggage."*

"What makes you think baptism is the answer?" Oliver wondered why someone so completely enveloped in evil could honestly want to receive the sacrament of baptism. Could this be a ploy for some greater evil? If someone possessed by so much evil sincerely wants to be baptized, it was taking a great deal of courage for this man to come here. By the looks of it, he was almost completely engulfed in whatever evil possessed him.

"I think it may be my only option to save myself from this." Monty pulled Mama Crossbones' head out of a basket and held it up by the hair. The rag was still in its mouth, and her eyes still solid black.

Oliver jumped out of his seat. "What are you doing with that?" He noticed the head trying to spit out the rag, and saw the eyes blink several times.

I don't have time to play twenty questions, priest." Monty pulled out a gun and pointed it at Oliver. "I need to be baptized, and I need you to do it now, damn it! Now, get on with it!"

Oliver thought for a moment, not quite sure what to do. This was all crazy: Baptism at gunpoint while using a severed head as justification.

"Look priest, if you dion't get on with it, I'll kill you right here and go to the next church and get someone else to do it."

Oliver held up his hand. "OK, I'll do as you ask. It seems I have no choice in the matter. However, forcing me to perform the sacrament of Baptism at gunpoint will make the baptism invalid. If you shoot me and go to another church, they will tell you the same thing. If you really want me to baptize you, there are a few things we need to discuss. You have to lower the gun and that severed head."

There was a long moment of silence as Monty considered his options. He lowered the gun slowly and put the head back into the basket. He was resigned to the fact that he could not afford to mess this up. He intuitively knew that as soon as the head of Mama Crossbones was tossed into a fire, there would be hell to pay. He never gave much thought to the meaning of that expression until now.

Oliver signaled to Monty to have a seat. "Now, so we can get on with it, why don't you tell me how all this unfolded? I need to know a few things about you. Why are you carrying around a severed head, which appears to be alive?"

Monty sat down and placed the gun on his lap. "I'll give you the condensed version because time is of the essence. If the body from which this head came off is discovered, I'm a dead man. People and things will be hunting for me, and I'm not talking about the police. What I am about to tell you is all true. I am not crazy. You must believe me."

Oliver gave Monty a slight nod, signaling him to continue.

"My real name is Monty McPride. When my mother was pregnant, she and my father were accosted by an old woman who claimed to be selling souvenirs. She forced my father into buying a bracelet for my mother. My father inadvertently invited this soul hijacker into their world. They would never know what really happened that day. She cast a spell on the fetus growing in my mother's womb. That would be me.

"I was, am, evil. It has always been my nature. I've done reprehensible things. The worst was killing my mother when I was six years old. Later in life, I tried to kill my father by hiding his medicine, forcing him to have a stroke leaving him in a comatose state. I attempted to take over his business. I have always thought myself to be a superior person and master of my own destiny. I've never felt an ounce of remorse or experienced doubt about anything that I have done. My life was great until I was foiled by the police as I was about to put a bullet in my father's head. I tried to escape by running and got hit by a truck. My life came to an abrupt end. A few hours later at the hospital's morgue, I awoke in this body."

"Do you remember anything between the time you were hit by the truck and the time you woke up?"

"No, nothing, but memories of my previous life soon came back full and vivid. I escaped from the hospital by killing the guy who was trying to help me get up from the floor. During my escape, two of the witch's henchmen came to my aid. They escorted me to the house of the old woman who managed to bring me back to life in this body." Monty gestured by pointing at himself. "This body belonged to a Paul H. Herodias who had been performing some kind of exam on my corpse. When I came before the witch, she placed her hand on my head and killed the original owner. She informed me of how she had done me a great service by guiding me in the ways of evil, even before I was born. She calls herself Mama Crossbones. That's her head in the basket.

She and others are involved in the systematic hijacking of the souls of the soon-to-be-born for the purposes of perpetuating evil. She claimed that since my parents were wealthy and did not believe in the man Jesus, I was an ideal candidate. It seems that she and this Council of 666 have high hopes and great plans for me. Recently, I was the guest of honor at a gathering of many of the who's who, all of them functioning as part of this elaborate recruitment effort for the perpetuation of evil.

"What has made you change your mind? By your own admission, you have never felt remorse for anything. Evil has been your nature."

He pointed to the basket. "This thing claims to be my real mother. She has taken great pride in hijacking my soul. There are others like her. They are located at popular destinations all over the world. They prey on unsuspecting pregnant women who don't belong to the man Jesus. Even if my days are numbered and I go straight to hell, I want to know that my free will is really my own. I want to know what it feels like to be me. I want to know what it feels like to be un-hijacked, if even for a brief moment."

Monty paused and looked at the basket. "She is very powerful. I saw how a wound instantly healed from a cut on her arm. That's why I cut her head off. It seemed like the only thing that could work. As you saw, it is still alive. I plan to throw it into the fire as soon as I have some protection. That's why I came here, to be baptized, to find the man Jesus to see if he can help me."

"This is certainly not your typical confession," Oliver thought. "Why do you think being baptized will protect you?"

"The witch said those who belong to the man Jesus cannot be hijacked. That's why the demons target wealthy mothers-to-be. They figure since their money takes such good care of them, many would never turn to the man Jesus."

Oliver was struck by the odd way in which Monty referred to Jesus. "Why do you call him 'the man Jesus?'"

"It's how the witch refers to Him. I had not given Him much thought until I was brought back. I know nothing about Jesus, except that He might be able to help me."

Oliver leaned forward in his seat. "Jesus was fully man, and fully God. I know that might sound confusing, and it might be difficult for you to understand now, but you can refer to Him simply as 'Jesus'." Oliver reached for the phone and pressed zero. "Betty, would you be so kind and bring me a pitcher of holy water? You can get it from the baptismal font."

Oliver turned to Monty. "Now, I must ask you a couple of questions. How you answer will determine whether or not I can help you." Oliver noticed how all the demon faces were peering at him and how the man engulfed in them seemed nervous. He could detect a slight shaking in Monty's body, which seemed to be getting worse.

Monty felt uncomfortable and nauseated as he anticipated Oliver's questions. On one hand, he wanted to seek help. On the other, he had to fight the urge to kill the priest.

Oliver looked at the man with the demonic faces flashing across his countenance. "Do you repent for your sins and do you accept Jesus Christ as your one and only Lord and savior?"

Monty's trembling increased. He seemed to be thinking. He looked at the basket containing the severed head. "Repent? I don't think I know how."

Oliver asked again with different words. "Are you sorry for things you have done that hurt others?"

Monty thought for a moment. "You mean, do I feel bad about the things I did?" *"Kill the priest."*

"Yes." Oliver noticed the superimposed demon faces combine into a single hideous demon face. The eyes were piercing and full of hate. It was wearing a frown. Monty's trembling worsened. He got up and paced around the room, gun trembling in his hand.

After a moment, Oliver asked again. "Do you regret, feel bad, and feel sad about what you did? Are you sorry for what you did?"

Monty stopped pacing and turned to face Oliver. "I am not sure what those feelings are. I've felt angry and upset when I couldn't get my way. Then I would do what I had to do to get it. It always felt great to get what I wanted." *"Kill the priest."*

Just then Betty walked in with the pitcher of holy water. "Where do you want it?"

Oliver tapped on an area of his desk, next to his jar of jellybeans. "Right here will be fine."

Betty set the pitcher on the desk and looked at Monty. Then she pointed to the basket. "What's in the basket, Fr. Oliver?"

"It's an antique, Betty."

"Oh, I love antiques." She reached for the lid.

Oliver roared as he stood up, "That will be all Betty! Thank you!"

Betty froze. "You don't have to yell."

"You would not like this particular antique." Oliver's voice was low and calm.

Betty looked at Oliver's strange guest who seemed to have a case of the shakes. She turned to the priest with an inquisitive look.

Oliver noticed her curiosity. "Thanks Betty. I'll call you if I need anything else. Now if you will excuse us. I have important matters to discuss with this gentleman."

Betty simply nodded as if to say, "I hope you know what you're doing." She left the room and closed the door behind her.

Monty stood in the corner while Betty was in the room. When she left, he pointed to the pitcher of holy water. "What's that?"

"It's holy water. It's used for sacraments and blessings."

"I'm not sure why, but it makes me nervous. Get rid of it, priest." *"Get rid of the priest."*

Oliver observed Monty's trembling had ceased except for the hand gripping the gun. "You're the one who asked to be baptized, or have you changed your mind? In which case, why don't you take your severed head and get out of here? I can't help someone who doesn't really want to be helped. More importantly, Jesus cannot enter your life without your invitation. I can't do it for you. I can guide you, but you must make this decision of your own free will."

Monty turned to Oliver. "That's what she said," pointing at the basket. His voice quivered. "You must specifically invite Him in, whereas evil could sneak in without an invitation." *"Kill him."*

Oliver nodded. "You didn't think evil would release its grip easily did you? You must fight this, speak the words and feel them in your heart in order to make it happen. I'll ask you again. Do you renounce Satan and repent for your sins and accept Jesus Christ as your one and only Lord and savior?"

Monty's shivering returned. There was no answer. *"Kill the dammed priest!"* He pointed the gun at Oliver, hesitated as a sneered came across the demon's face, then he fired a shot.

Oliver had barely enough time to duck as the bullet zipped past his left temple.

He lowered the gun and approached Oliver to see if he was still alive.

As Monty got within a foot of Oliver, he found himself on the floor with the priest on top of him. The gun was now in the priest's hand. Monty's arm was burning with pain as the sneaky priest continued to pin it and his face to the floor.

Monty moaned in agony. Slowly, Oliver released his grip, stood up, and pointed the gun at Monty. "Get out and take your friend with you."

The man on the floor started to tremble. "No please, you have to help me." He sat up rubbing his arm.

After a moment of silence Oliver sat down behind his desk again. "How did you feel after killing your mother?"

Monty's trembling increased. "I didn't want…" He paused, stood up and paced again. "I dreamt of her last night. I saw her die again. She told me about my name. My father insisted on Monty. She wanted to name me Luke or Mark, after my grandfathers. Then she said to seek them out, they would help me. But, they're dead. Then I saw my birthday everywhere I looked. I saw myself on fire, and the witch was laughing."

"What is your birth date?"

Monty stared into space. "June 19."

Oliver flipped the pages of his bible. "Sit down, Monty." He stopped when he found the page. "Have you ever read the bible?"

"I did pick one up recently, and I threw it against the wall, but reading it, no."

"Monty! You must listen carefully. The bible is the Word of God. Reading it is one way of letting God into your life." Oliver motioned to Monty to sit down. He saw that Monty became stiff and sat down reluctantly. His demon face was contorting with anger.

Monty started to get up. "I don't want to listen to…"

"SIT DOWN!" Oliver boomed.

Monty fell back into his seat.

Oliver began to read. "This is a reading of the holy Gospel according to Mark 6:19 'So Herodias nursed a grudge against John and wanted to kill him. But she was not able to'."

"Why is Paul's name in there?" Monty was now sweating as well as trembling.

"What do you mean?" asked Oliver. He saw that Monty seemed to have difficulty speaking. His body was tight, and his lips were pursed. "Come on. This isn't going to be easy. You have to fight hard. That thing that has hijacked your soul will not give up without a fight. What do you mean, Paul's name?"

"The name," Monty blurted out. "It's the same as Paul's last name. The guy who owned this body, his name was Paul Herodias, just like the name in what you read. You said he had a grudge against John."

Oliver carefully observed Monty. "Do you think that is a coincidence? What about a grudge against John and wanting to kill him?"

Monty broke into loud laughter and a stutter. Oliver was startled at how loud and intense it was. "Is…n't J,J,John, J,J,J,Juan in S,S,S,paaaanish? I haaaate those spic ba,ba,ba,bastards." He pointed at the basket as he continued to laugh. "Sh,Sh,She waaanttss mme to kill J,J,Juan Arrrias. That waaas m,my fir,fir,first asssssignment afterrrr m,m,my reeeebirrrrrth." He was bent over. His laughter was gut wrenching. He continued his laughing fit as he gasped for air. After a moment of more intense laughter, he attempted to speak again. "bbbuuttt ssh, shh, shh" Monty got on one knee and opened the basket. He picked up the head by the hair. The hideous face contorted. He pointed to it as he continued to laugh. "B,B,B,B,uttt shheee wassss nnotttt aaaaablllle to." His laughter was out of control, his chest tightened up, he was laughing so hard now that he couldn't breathe.

Oliver reacted quickly, splashing holy water on Monty's face. The priest was instantly thrown backward and slammed against the wall.

Monty stopped laughing and dropped the head back into the basket.

Fortunately, Oliver was in exceptional physical condition, the result of his intense training for the wing chun competition. He got up slowly and sat back down. The demon's eyes were now slivers of hate. He could feel their intensity. Monty was quiet and still shivering.

After a moment of silence, Oliver flipped the bible pages once again. He stopped and looked at Monty. "This is a reading of the holy Gospel according to Luke 6:19 'and the people all tried to touch him, because power was coming from him and healing them all.'"

"Who? Who are they referring to?" Monty's voice was low and tired.

"Jesus Christ," replied Oliver. "So your mother asked you to turn to Mark and Luke for help? She must have loved you very much. She still does."

Monty's shivering became out of control trembling. A voice came from inside the basket. It was laughing hysterically. Monty jumped, knocking into the basket, tipping it over. The flap opened. The old witch's head rolled out, coming to rest against a bookshelf, looking directly at Monty. Its voice was hideous as it shouted. "You fool. Your time is up. I will see you in hell!" Her laughter erupted. The door to Oliver's office flew open as the wino pair stormed into the room.

Oliver immediately bolted out of his chair and jumped in front of the two before either of them could reach Monty.

"KILL THEM BOTH!" The severed head screamed.

They each withdrew guns. Oliver knocked wino butler to

the floor with a wing chun blow to the face. He reached wino chauffeur's arm with a kick, just as he was firing a round at Monty's head. The bullet missed its target by a couple of inches.

Oliver moved quickly thanks to his sparring training. He knocked wino chauffeur against the wall with a forearm strike to the throat. Wino chauffeur came at Oliver. As he charged, Oliver delivered a groin strike that took wino chauffeur out. It was an illegal move in competition, but this was not a competition.

After picking up both weapons, Oliver threw them in his waste basket. He grabbed the pitcher of holy water and rushed over to Monty who was lying on the floor face up. As Oliver knelt next to him, he found it harder and harder to move. It felt as though he were sinking in quicksand, the same way he felt when he was a child afraid of his Uncle Ned. He clutched the pitcher and bent over Monty's body. "Do you repent for your sins and accept Jesus Christ as your one and only Lord and savior?"

Monty's faced stirred, but all Oliver heard was moaning. Meanwhile, Oliver continued to feel as though he was sinking into quicksand. He fought to keep from sinking further. All he could do was pray. "Lord, please grant me the strength to follow your will. Fill me with your Holy Spirit. In Jesus' name I pray."

Oliver's feeling of sinking vanished. He slapped Monty across the face. "You've got to fight. You must want to be saved. You have to do it. Fight! Respond! Say, 'I do,' if you want to be saved. I cannot save you. Only Jesus is your savior. But you must ask for His help. You must say it." Monty was gasping violently. His breathing stopped.

Oliver tried to shake him, but the force crushing Monty was too strong. It was literally squeezing the life out of him. The witch's head was now shrieking with laughter. Oliver got up, stuffed the rag back into its mouth, threw it into the basket, and slammed the lid shut. He knelt next to Monty and said a blessing. "Dear Father, forgive this poor soul for his transgressions. Have mercy on him. In Jesus name I pray, Amen." He sprinkled holy water over Monty's body as he said this.

Oliver reached behind Monty's neck. Monty's face was turning blue. "This is your last chance. Do you repent of your sins and do you accept Jesus Christ as your one and only Lord and savior? Do you reject all evil?" Oliver asked as he sprinkled more holy water in the sign of the cross across Monty's body. "Damn it man, answer me!" Oliver yelled. After a moment of no movement a slight gurgling sound came from Monty's throat. His head nodded up and down ever so slightly as he struggled to utter "I do. I do. I do." Oliver poured the holy water over Monty's head and traced the sign of the cross on his forehead. "I claim you for our Lord Jesus Christ. I baptize you in the name of the Father and of the Son, and of the Holy Spirit, Amen."

The instant Oliver uttered those words there was an explosion of light so strong he covered his eyes. It was a soft explosion, no noise. The demons squeezing the life out of Monty instantly burst into ashes. Oliver felt the impact of the explosion traveling through him. It did no damage, but he was able to sense its intensity. He watched as the ashes floated to the floor and fizzled into red sparks. Then, they were gone.

Betty came rushing into the room "Is everything all right? I heard a commotion." She saw the two winos on the floor. "I tried to stop those two men from barging into your office."

"Call the police, Betty! Hurry! Those men are dangerous."

She ran back to her desk and dialed 911.

Monty stirred slowly and tried to open his eyes. He rubbed them and a moment later, he was finally able to open his eyes, like a blind man who could now see for the very first time. He looked at Oliver, who gently helped him sit up. He could see the man's face clearly for the first time. There were no demonic images superimposed on it. "How do you feel?"

Monty's gaze met Oliver's. "Sad, I feel very sad."

This was not the response Oliver expected. "Why are you sad? You have just been saved."

"I'm sad because of the anguish I have caused others." Tears rolled out of Monty's eyes. "I have never felt remorse for anything. Now, I am feeling it all at once." His tears ran freely, as he sobbed.

Through his weeping Monty asked, "How can I possibly be saved? Isn't it too late? That's what I was told." He looked at Oliver. "When is it too late to ask for forgiveness? I died. Doesn't that make it too late?"

Oliver shook his head. "If you are in the here and now, it is never too late to turn to Jesus."

"But, everything I've done…" Monty wept heavily for a few moments. "I killed my very own mother. I don't see how that can be forgiven."

Oliver put his hand on Monty's shoulder. "Just because you have been forgiven, does not mean you will not be held accountable for all you have done. To some degree or another, we are all flawed. We all have things for which we must account. I cannot say what the cost of redemption will be for any of us, but I know when our time comes, pay we must, you, I, everyone. Be glad. At least you will have the opportunity for that." Oliver paused and looked at the bible on his desk. "Is salvation on the horizon for all of us? I don't know, but I can't think of anything more worthwhile. Whatever the toll may be, it's between you and Jesus now. You must keep Him in your heart always. You have just met Him, you have a lot of catching up to do. Seek to know Him and to understand what His will is for you. You must spend time with Him. Reading the Bible will bring you closer. There is nothing more powerful than the Word of God."

Oliver stood up with bible in hand. He turned the pages until he found what he was looking for and placed a bookmark there. He handed it to Monty. "Please, take it. It's yours." Monty slowly got up from the floor and sat in the chair. He opened the Bible and stared into the bookmarked page and read the following text:

> *Blessed are the poor in spirit, for theirs is the kingdom of heaven.*
>
> *Blessed are those who mourn, for they will be comforted.*
>
> *Blessed are the meek, for they will inherit the earth.*
>
> *Blessed are those who hunger and thirst for righteousness, for they will be filled.*
>
> *Blessed are the merciful, for they will be shown mercy.*
>
> *Blessed are the pure in heart, for they will see God.*
>
> *Blessed are the peacemakers, for they will be called children of God.*
>
> *Blessed are those who are persecuted because of righteousness, for theirs is the kingdom of heaven.*
>
> *Blessed are you when people insult you, persecute you and falsely say all kinds of evil against you because of me.*

Rejoice and be glad, because great is your reward in heaven, for in the same way they persecuted the prophets who were before you.

Monty closed the bible slowly. He clenched it tightly. He brought the book up to his forehead, bent forward and slid out of his chair onto both knees. He wept as he prostrated himself.

Oliver approached the winos, now beginning to stir.

Wino butler wiped his mouth and sat up. "Curse you! You have no idea what trouble you're in." Then he turned to wino chauffeur. "These bodies are dispensable. We must get her out of here."

Both winos sprang up. Each now brandished knives. Wino chauffeur lunged at Oliver as wino butler lunged at Monty whose back was turned to them. Oliver moved quickly to avoid being slashed to death. Wino butler stabbed Monty in the left shoulder and reached for the basket. Monty was able to withdraw the Black Lamia with his right hand, slicing wino butler's reaching hand completely off.

Betty came back into the room. "What's going on...?" Wino chauffeur turned and grabbed her. He put his knife against her neck. "Now, hand over the basket and our guns or the old bag gets it." The police siren was approaching. "Do it now!" wino chauffeur yelled.

Oliver fetched the guns out of the trash can and handed them over. Wino butler picked up the basket and his severed hand. They made their way to the exit with Betty in tow. As they reached the door, wino chauffeur said to Oliver, "Follow us, and I will put a hole in her head. They both backed out of the building, leaving Betty at the entrance while still pointing his gun at her from outside.

"Get down, Betty!" cried Oliver. Betty immediately ducked as two bullets came through the glass door just over her head. As much as he wanted to pursue the assailants, Oliver thought it best to stay put and tend to Betty, Monty, and questions from the police.

The Mercedes screeched out of the church parking lot.

Moments later the police pulled up, and so did Pastor Bob.

16

The Interrogation

Monty woke up. His shoulder was numb. He couldn't remember what happened after he was stabbed in the back of his shoulder. He glanced across the unfamiliar room. Dr. Carlson was looking over some charts. "Where am I?"

Dr. Carlson approached the side of the bed. "You're at Raleigh Central," he replied. "Glad you turned up, Paul. We were all worried about you and the police have been looking for you. Fortunately, your wound is not serious. I think you should be ready to go home, or wherever the police decide to take you in a few hours. I just want Dr. Bradley to see you before you're released. Are you up to answering a few questions?"

Monty nodded.

Dr. Carlson turned to the middle aged man sitting in the chair. "He's all yours." Then, he left the room. It was not someone Monty recognized. The man had a mustache, an intense five o'clock shadow, and wore a trench coat. He sat quietly and looked Monty over.

A moment after the doctor left the room, the man broke the silence. "I'm Detective Lopez. What is your name?"

Monty looked at the detective and thought to respond carefully. "My name is Paul Herodias."

Can you tell me what happened?

Monty hesitated. "I don't remember."

"Paul, did you set fire to the body in the morgue?"

"No, I didn't set fire to anyone."

Lopez nodded as he scribbled on his notepad. "Can you tell

me what happened?"

Monty shrugged his shoulders. "I don't remember."

Detective Lopez got up from his chair and approached the bed. "Mr. Herodias, you were examining a corpse a couple of nights ago. The corpse was set ablaze. You stabbed one of the hospital staff while they helped you get up from the floor. Does any of that ring a bell?"

Monty had a faint recollection of a fire, but that memory was foggy. It seemed like a dream. "No Detective, I'm sorry. I don't remember anything."

Detective Lopez remained calm, although he was frustrated with the answers he was getting. "Do you recall stabbing your co-worker?"

Monty thought long and hard about how he would respond. He remembered the Bible passage he read recently. Blessed are those who hunger for righteousness. He wanted righteousness. That implied truthfulness in spite of the consequences it might bring. "Yes, I remember. I was not myself. I am sorry. I did not mean to kill him."

Do you remember threatening to kill Nurse Mitchell, then locking her in your vehicle?"

Monty took a deep breath. "I'm sorry about that as well, Detective. Like I said, I was not myself."

"What vehicle do you drive Mr. Herodias?

"I drive a blue minivan."

"Why would a fairly young single man choose to drive a minivan?"

"Is it a crime to drive a minivan, Detective?"

"No, I was just curious, that's all. If I was single, in my mid-thirties, I would be driving around in something a bit more exciting."

"Well, I'm a practical person."

"I see. Tell me, Mr. Herodias, where have you been the past three days? Why did you not take the BMW convertible? You threatened to kill Nurse Mitchell unless she handed over her keys. I think your words were; 'I wouldn't be caught dead driving a minivan', so Nurse Mitchell reported."

Monty was silent for a moment. "It doesn't sound like something I would do, but I guess I was confused and disoriented."

"What were you doing visiting the priest, Mr. Herodias?

Suddenly, Monty sat up "Where's the black…" He stopped short.

"Where's what, Mr. Herodias? Did you lose something?"

Monty relaxed back into the bed, hoping the police had not confiscated the Black Lamia. There was not much he could do at this point. He looked around the room but no luck. "Just want to make sure I've not lost my 'Black' bible."

Lopez looked at Monty curiously. "So, you are a religious man, Mr. Herodias?"

Monty shrugged. "I don't know."

"Where did you get the antique mask to which the priest referred? Why were those men after it? You know, the ones who tried to kill you?"

Monty tried to organize his thoughts. He looked into space for another moment then turned to the detective. "I know you must think I'm trying to hide something from you, Detective, but I assure you I'm not. I can't say where that thing came from."

"You can't or you won't, Mr. Herodias? I can't protect you from those goons if you are not honest with me. Those men tried to kill you!"

"It doesn't matter, Detective. I'm going to jail anyway, am I not?"

"I don't know Mr. Herodias. That is a very real possibility."

There was a long silence. "Very well, Mr. Herodias" The detective handed his business card to Monty. "If you remember anything, please call me."

Detective Lopez began to head toward the door. As he reached it, he turned. "One last question, Mr. Herodias; do you know anyone named Monty? It was the name of the dead man that you were examining when all this started."

Monty did not respond.

"Mr. Herodias, I asked you a question."

"I'm sorry, Detective, but my shoulder is killing me." He turned on his side.

"Have you ever been treated for schizophrenia, Mr. Herodias?"

Monty remained on his side. "No, I don't recall ever being diagnosed or treated for that."

Detective Lopez opened the door. "Very well, Mr. Herodias, I'll be in touch." He left the room and wrote on his pad.

A few moments later, two men entered the room. One had a sling over one arm. They approached the bed.

"Paul? What the hell happened to you?" asked the one with the sling.

Monty did not recognize them. They came closer. The one without a sling said. "Hey Paul, it's Carl and Jake. Don't you recognize us? Geez, you almost killed Carl. Why did you stab him like that?"

Monty stared at both of them for a moment. He looked at Carl's sling. "Did I do that?" Monty pointed at Carl's sling.

Carl nodded. "Yeah, and it hurt like the devil."

He put his hand to his forehead, feeling remorse for stabbing this man he didn't even know. He was not used to all this remorse. It was overwhelming. He looked at Carl. Monty could not hold back the tears beginning to pool in his eyes. Finally, he said, "Carl, I'm sorry. I didn't mean to do that. I thought I had killed you."

Carl and Jake glanced at each other. Just then, Nurse Ann Mitchell walked into the room. "So, you're back, Paul, how nice." She huffed over to the foot of the bed.

Carl looked at Nurse Mitchell. "He can't remember anything, Ann."

"Oh well, let me refresh his memory!" She yelled as she clenched the bed and leaned in. "You threatened to give me a…what was that now? 'Give your keys or I'll give you a mega chin tuck.' Do you remember now, Paul? You made me get into your stinking van while you made your getaway." She stood there, hands on her wide hips.

Monty feared this large, angry woman. "I'm terribly sorry I did that, really I am. I was not myself." Monty thought about what he had just said and knew the opposite was true. He did that because he had been himself, his old self, a person he wanted never to be again. He found himself apologizing more in these five minutes than he had in all of his previous existence.

"Carl, Ann, I'm sorr…"

"Don't you call me Ann; it's Nurse Mitchell to you, jackass!" She banged on the bed frame with her meaty hand.

Monty sat up straight. "I'm sorry for hurting you both. Can you forgive me? I'm sorry."

Carl and Jake looked at each other. Jake felt sorry for Paul.

Carl wondered if it really might be schizophrenia.

Nurse Mitchell rolled her eyes. "Yes, how convenient. I have a good mind to slip you some arsenic and then not remember doing it. I don't buy it, Paul! I don't buy your little act, not for one minute. If you ever come near me again, I'll be prepared. I won't tell you how. It will just be my little surprise. I hope your damned arm falls off!" With that, she stormed out of the room.

Monty turned to Carl and Jake. "Is there anyone else I should know about that I hurt recently?"

Jake stepped closer. "You've been missing for a few days, Paul. Who knows what kind of trouble you might have gotten into? Hell if I know."

Carl looked at Monty. "Don't worry Paul, I'm not pressing charges or blaming you for anything. For your sake, I hope you didn't get into trouble while you were missing. How much do you remember?"

"Not much." Monty let out a sigh. "There's very little I know about Paul Herodias."

Carl's eyebrows shot up. "What do you mean? You know what you do here, where you were born, and all of that, don't you?"

Monty glanced at Jake, then back to Carl. "I know that my name is Paul Herodias. I drive a blue minivan. I'm single, and I'd better stay away from Nurse Mitchell."

Jake covered his mouth. "You're kidding, aren't you? That's all?

Carl leaned forward. "How about teaching, and your stamp collecting?"

Monty didn't know what they were talking about. His look of dismay was sincere.

Jake walked to the foot of the bed, scratching his head. "Holy smoke, Paul, what are you going to do?"

"I don't know. Just take it one day at a time. Maybe my memory will eventually return." Monty knew, deep down, the original owner of this body was gone for good. That probably meant there was little chance of Paul's memory surfacing.

Carl gently touched Monty's shoulder with his good arm. "Well, I'll pray for you, Paul."

At once a smile came to Monty's face. "Thank you, Carl." He never thought he would be happy having someone pray for him. It never crossed his mind before today. It felt good. There was hope in it. He also felt grateful. It felt good in an odd kind of way. *What were those winos planning to do with the head? Could the damned thing be alive after all this time?*

Dr. Carlson came back into the room. "Sorry gents, I have to cut this visit short. Paul has one more visitor, then I need Dr. Bradley to check him out."

Carl turned to Monty. "You let me know if you need anything, OK, Paul?"

Monty nodded. "Thanks, Carl."

Jake waved his hand. "Yeah, take care of yourself, Paul."

Carl and Jake left the room with Dr. Carlson.

A moment later, Oliver entered. He approached the bed. "How are you feeling?"

Monty pointed to his shoulder. "Other than a numb shoulder, I feel all right, all things considered."

"I waited around because I wanted to let you know if you want to talk, you can always reach me. It has been an unusual day for both of us, to say the least." Oliver placed the bible on the bed next to Monty. "You have a lot of catching up to do. My contact information is on a piece of paper in the front of the Bible." Oliver glanced at the door. "The doctor asked me to make it quick. So, I'd better get going." He placed his hand on Monty's right arm. "Take care of yourself." Oliver waved and headed for the door.

"Wait!"

Oliver stopped and turned to face Monty.

"I haven't thanked you for saving my life." He paused and added, "and perhaps my soul. Thank you."

"You're welcome. But if you want to thank the one who really saved you, thank Jesus. I was simply the intermediary." Oliver wondered how Monty would get on with his life. If what he said was true, Monty inhabited a body and assumed a life of which he had no previous knowledge. "What will you do now?"

"I don't know." Monty glanced at the bible on the bed. He picked it up. "I guess I'll start by reading this."

Oliver smiled and gave him a nod. "That's a great place to start. When you're better, we need to talk. I have a few questions of my own." Oliver walked to the door. "Oh, and I stored your sword in my office for safe keeping. Pick it up whenever you are up to it. I didn't think bringing it here would be a good idea." He gave a slight wave and left the room.

Dr. Bradley entered the room shortly after Oliver left. He approached Monty's bedside. "Well, Paul, it seems you've suffered some trauma to your shoulder, and I understand you seem to be having some memory issues. I'm going to conduct a few tests. Is that all right with you?"

Monty nodded, and Dr. Bradley began his examination.

17

Patching Things Up

Wino butler and wino chauffeur rushed into Mama Crossbones' house with the basket containing her severed head. They rushed over to the perfectly sliced torso. It had stopped quivering and flailing. Wino chauffeur took the head out of the basket and removed the rag from its mouth. He set it gently on the chair.

"What do you want us to do?"

"Call Dr. Sinclair." She gave them the numbers. They dialed. "Now, put the phone next to my ear. The phone rang twice, and a female voice answered. Mama Crossbones cut her off. "Put me through to Sinclair. It's Mama, and this is an emergency.

Dr. Sinclair came on the line. "What's happened?"

"We've been betrayed by manflesh. My body is in pieces. You must come over right now. I need to be made whole."

"I'll be right over."

The head looked at the winos. "Put the two halves of my body side by side on the bed and place my head just above the neck. Dr. Sinclair will be here soon."

The two winos got busy with the grizzly business of placing the two body halves on the bed. They placed the head at the top and waited for Dr. Sinclair.

18

Awkward New Life

Dr. Bradley reviewed his findings with Dr. Carlson. "I'm afraid Paul is suffering from complete amnesia. He may regain his memory in time. It's hard to tell in these types of cases. It may come back quickly or very slowly. The best thing to do is send him home and put him on a leave of absence. Perhaps being at home for a few days will start triggering his memories. Being in familiar surroundings is the best therapy right now."

Dr. Carlson informed Monty that he was being released. Since no one had pressed charges, including Nurse Mitchell, he was free to go home. He would be on a leave of absence until his memory returned.

After Dr. Carlson left the room, Monty got dressed. He was careful not to bump his bandaged shoulder. He took out his wallet to check his license for a home address. As instructed by Dr. Carlson, Monty proceeded to the check-out desk adjacent to the customer information desk. Standing at the desk signing a patient release form, he did a double take when he saw Blake McPride standing at the customer assistance counter.

Monty froze. His senses went on high alert. His thoughts shifted into overdrive. *"There's my father, who I tried to murder. Here I am, and he has no idea that it's me inside this body. I'm a complete stranger to him and will probably need to remain so for the rest of my life. How I wish I could tell him what really happened on that damned cruise. How I wish I could tell him all I did and how sorry I am. I don't think I've told him that I loved him. I don't think I've ever told anyone that I loved them, not even my own mother. What a miserable human being. How could I have been so completely cut off from my own conscience? Now, I'm in a prison of sorts, my true self in the flesh of another."*

Blake stepped up to the counter. "I'm here to sign for the body of my deceased son, Monty McPride. He was taken to the morgue a few nights ago, and I understand there was a fire. I was instructed to wait until the police could investigate what happened. I was notified earlier today that I could claim the remains."

"Just a moment, sir." The woman searched through her papers. She glanced at her computer screen, then at Monty. She recognized Paul and waved to him, signaling him to come over.

Monty was shocked into full attention as he looked behind him, trying to identify the person with whom the lady was trying to communicate. The woman then pointed at Monty and signaled again with a wave. "Come here, Paul."

Monty was speechless. He slowly approached the counter, and froze momentarily, not knowing how to act. "Paul, can you escort this gentleman down to the morgue? What happened to your arm?"

Monty smiled nervously. "Oh, it's nothing, just a minor accident."

The woman turned to Blake. "Sir, what is your name?"

"My name is Blake McPride. The remains are those of my son, Monty McPride."

She wrote on the paper attached to her clipboard. "OK, Paul here will show you where you need to go." She turned to Monty. "Thanks, Paul and take care of that arm."

"Oh uh, sure, you're welcome." Monty stood there trying to think of what to say. He avoided making eye contact with Blake. Crazy as it might seem, he was afraid Blake might recognize him just by looking him in the eye.

"Come this way," Monty instructed as he walked toward the elevator. From his escape, he remembered where the morgue was located. He walked ahead of Blake, stopping at the elevator. Monty's mind continued to race.

The elevator arrived. Monty pressed the button for the lower floor B1. "I'm sorry for your loss."

"Thank you. He was my only son." Blake sighed as the elevator doors closed. "I'm afraid I was not a very good father."

Monty felt like telling Blake everything right then and there. It might be worth going to the loony bin if he could get it off his chest. He wanted to tell his father that he was a good father, and that he loved him but didn't know it until recently. He wanted to tell him he was sorry for not breaking the witch's spell on his own. He was sorry he never listened to the crazy Jesus lovers who had crossed his path so many times. *How many opportunities did I have to discover Christ? Countless, each one was dismissed with disdain and contempt. My blindness was complete. But I could have broken the spell, and made a different life for myself just by listening and making a few choices differently. That's all it would have taken to avoid all the pain and suffering, just a few right choices - just one choice, to follow Christ, would have changed the course of my life. Even as a child, could I have come to Christ on my own somehow? But no one guided me there. I know I must have had opportunities, but I can't remember. How could I have discovered Christ on my own? Why didn't you and mother have faith? How could I discover something I didn't know I needed to discover?"* The regret in Monty's heart burned like acid.

Finally, the doors of the elevator opened, and they proceeded down the hall to the morgue.

Monty stopped to look at Blake McPride. He risked discovery, however, Blake showed no sign that he recognized the inhabitant of Paul's body. "I'm sure your son loved you very much."

"He tried to kill me. He wanted to take over my company. I would not necessarily call that love."

Monty was silent a moment. "I'm sorry to hear that. Perhaps he was not completely himself."

"Do you have children, Mr...?" Blake looked at Monty, waiting for a reply.

Monty paused for a moment. He knew he was single, but had he fathered any children? He guessed not. "Mon...I mean my name is Paul, Paul Herodias. No, I don't have any children, sir."

"Well, when you do, you will understand." Blake thought of his encounter with Monty. "After all the heinous things my son did, and mind you, there are probably lots of things I don't know, after all of that, I must admit I still loved my son."

They proceeded into the morgue. Monty looked at the labels on the shiny metal doors and spotted the one with his name on it. "OK, there it is. I'll leave you alone now." He turned to leave.

"Open it, please."

Monty froze. "Are you sure? Perhaps it would best if you didn't."

"Open it, please. I was told of the fire, but I want to see the remains before folks from the funeral home arrive. They will transport what is left to complete the cremation." He looked at his watch. "They should be here shortly. Please open it."

Monty felt chills run up and down his spine as he clutched the door latch and pulled. It clicked open and the table slowly rolled out revealing the charred remains of Monty's body.

Blake gasped and brought his hand to his mouth. "Dear God!"

Monty looked upon his dead self in shock and amazement. *"What has happened to me? Why am I here? Why am I here and not burning in the pit of hell? How many people have looked upon their dead remains through the eyes of someone else? There must be a point, some purpose, to all this. How ironic, the evil that blinded me, has, inadvertently, given me another chance to see."* He was glad he sought out a priest when he did.

Blake lowered his head. "Thank you. You can close it now."

Monty slid the table back into the container and closed the door. It clicked shut. He turned to Blake. "Mr. McPride, if there is anything I can do, please let me know. I realize that we've just met, but in a way, I feel I know you, perhaps because you remind me of my own father. I realize this must be very painful for you."

Blake returned Monty's gaze. "Thank you. Thank you very much. You're very kind. I think I will be all right. Life goes on. I will go on. It's what I must do."

Two men from the cremation center entered the morgue. "We're here for the remains of Monty McPride."

Monty gestured them to come in and pointed to the metal door with his name on it. He turned to Blake and extended his hand. Blake took it. As they shook hands, Monty said, "Mr.

McPride, it has been my pleasure to meet you today. I must confess I have not been a very good son to my father. You have inspired me to try being a better person."

"Perhaps there is still time to make amends to your father if he is still living," Blake replied.

"Fortunately, he is still living. That would be a true miracle. Nothing would make me happier."

Monty left the morgue wishing he could have hugged his father.

~~~

Monty parked the minivan in the driveway of the small brick ranch. He double checked the numbers to make sure it was the address on his license. After a moment, he got out of the vehicle and approached the front door.

The door of the adjacent house opened. An elderly man stepped out. He was wearing a tee shirt, light blue shorts and shoes with black socks that came almost up to his knees. A dog shot out of the house and ran to Paul. It started to jump and run around in circles. "Paul, where the heck have you been? I called the hospital, and they didn't know where you were. The police came by looking for you. Fred and I have been worried to death." Suddenly the dog stopped running around in circles. It made a whimpering sound and ran back into the house.

Monty looked at the old man. "Is your dog all right?"

"My dog? Fred is your dog, Paul. What's the matter with you? Don't you recognize your own dog?"

"I've had a rough few days. *A dog? I've never had a pet. My parents knew better. I probably would have killed it.* I had an accident and the doctor says I have severe amnesia. That's why I haven't been home. I don't remember much. I don't even remember your name." Monty watched the man's expression turn to one of concern.

"When you didn't come home, I had Fred stay with me."

"Please refresh my memory. What is your name?"

"Bill, Bill Freely, we've been neighbors for five years. Gee, Paul, this is not good. Have you spoken with Barb or Joe or your folks?"
~~~

Monty thought for a moment. "Bill, would you mind coming in and helping me try to remember things? The doctor said being in familiar surroundings was the best therapy."

"Why sure, Paul. Let me get Fred. I'll meet you inside."

Monty opened the door and entered the house. It was neatly kept. It had standard finishes and simple furniture. On one wall were pictures of Paul with various people. On the adjacent wall he saw several pictures of Paul and Fred.

Monty took a quick tour through the small house. The bedroom was neat. He looked in the closets and drawers. *"No women's clothing. That's good. Hopefully, Paul did not have a girlfriend. That would be one less person worrying about his condition."*

Bill entered the house carrying Fred, Paul's long haired dachshund. He put Fred down, and the dog immediately ran into his kennel in a corner of the kitchen.

"Fred seems spooked, like he doesn't recognize you, Paul."

"Yeah, I know. He must sense my amnesia."

"You can't fool a dog. They can sense things we can't. It's like you are a stranger to him. Normally, he would be all over you, especially after not seeing you for a few days."

"Thanks for taking care of him, Bill. Can you tell me who these people are in the pictures?"

Bill looked at Monty. He was amazed that Paul could not recognize members of his own family. "You really don't recognize any of these people?"

Monty shook his head, "I'm afraid not."

Bill approached one of the photographs. He started telling Monty about the people in his life, in Paul's life. "It's going to be a long night, Paul."

"That's OK, Bill, I'll order pizza if it's all right with you." Monty entered the kitchen looking around for anything indicating whom to call for pizza. He grabbed one of the magnets off the refrigerator.

"I like pepperoni on mine, Paul."

19

Humpty Dumpty Together Again

Dr. Sinclair arrived at Mama Crossbones' place. He let himself in, proceeded to the bedroom, and stopped short when he saw the two torso halves and the head. "Oh my!"

"Let's get on with it, Sinclair. I need to be made whole."

"Who did this?"

"It was him, the one I thought was the chosen one, the one I brought back. He has betrayed us, but not to worry. I gave him back his life and I can take it away just as easily."

Dr. Sinclair looked worried about something other than Mama Crossbones' condition. "This has never happened before. You presented him to us at the Council meeting, and he has seen us. He's a threat and must be eliminated."

"Yes, that will be easy enough once I am whole again. And you, Sinclair, must notify the others. You must contact Fredericks. Under no circumstances should manflesh have access to the money or the apartment. If he shows up at the bank, bring him to me."

"If he did this to you, who knows what else he might try to do." Sinclair removed several long rolls of gauze tape from his travel case.

"You need not worry. I will see to it that my little mistake is eradicated."

Dr. Sinclair carefully wrapped both halves of the torso together. No organs were visible. The exposed innards were a mass of thick congealed jelly. Nothing spilled out of the body when it was cut in half. "I won't pretend to understand your biology or how you are still alive. If this was something I could market, we'd make a fortune."

"My powers are my rewards for several lifetimes of dedication to the master. Fortunately, manflesh did not throw me into the fire when he had the chance. There was no one around I could have inhabited. Fool that he is, now he will pay. He should have finished me when he had the chance. He won't get another." Her face contorted, and her eyes became slits. "I will hunt him down like a dog, and he will die a slow and painful death. We must also recover the Black Lamia. It is no ordinary blade."

Sinclair continued bandaging her body parts together. "What do you mean?"

"It has a power all its own. It executes the will of the one who wields it. Space and time are irrelevant. That's why manflesh was able to use it against me. It carried out his will in an instant. I had no time to react. He is cunning; I will admit that, but he will be dead before too long. I promise you that."

"I hope you're right. I hate to think of that lunatic running around with such a weapon." Dr. Sinclair completed his task of joining both halves of the torso. Shortly thereafter, the hands on the torso reached for the head.

"Lift me into a sitting position," she instructed.

The doctor slowly sat the body up as it continued to hold the head just above the neck. When it reached a fully upright sitting position, the hands placed the head on the neck.

"In a few hours I will be whole." Her eyes returned to normal. No longer were they completely black. "Your job is done here, Doctor. Go and inform the others. When we catch him, let's make sure it is a clean kill. Then we will celebrate with a special meal in his name."

20

Home Sweet Home

Monty sat alone in Paul's house, now his house. Bill spent the better part of the evening going over Paul's family history, at least what he knew of it. Monty discovered much about the man who originally occupied his host body.

Paul was an avid stamp collector. He had an older brother living in Colorado with his family and a younger sister who lived in Washington DC with her family. His folks also lived in Colorado. His retired father had worked for the Internal Revenue Service for twenty five years. His mother was a retired school teacher.

Paul was not in a relationship with anyone. He seemed to like his privacy. His house was simply furnished and lacking in décor. He was a penny pincher. After examining the record files neatly kept in his home office, he found Paul had put away a good bit of money over the years. His current bank balance was $235,000. He also owned mutual funds, worth $143,000. His house was paid off, and he seemed to live a plain vanilla life, his only passions being his stamps and his dog. There were pictures of him and Fred in several rooms of the house and on the refrigerator.

Judging from the DVD collection, Paul was a fan of vampire movies. His laptop password Monty quickly guessed correctly as "FRED."

Paul was the forensic pathologist at Raleigh Central. He also taught advanced anatomy class to interns at the hospital.

Monty sat on his sofa to read the bible Oliver had given him. Fred lay on the floor in the kitchen looking at Monty.

"Come here, boy!"

Fred didn't respond. After repeating it several times, Fred reluctantly and cautiously approached Monty. He was whimpering the whole time he approached the strange man in his master's body. Monty reached out to pet the dog lightly on the head. "I know you know, Fred. You know I'm not really Paul. I'm somebody else, some stranger who has just showed up looking and smelling like your master. "I'm sorry, Fred. I'm afraid all of this is new to me too, little buddy. No, you're not crazy."

Fred withdrew to the kitchen and into in his kennel. Monty didn't press the dog to stay. "Hopefully, he'll feel comfortable around me in due time." Monty went back to reading the bible. Within twenty-minutes, he was asleep and dreamt of his mother.

Monty sat at the kitchen table having his freshly baked chocolate chip cookies with his cold milk. She turned and smiled at him. After he finished his cookie, she said "Come outside sweetheart. I have a surprise for you." He followed her with great anticipation. "Look!." She pointed to his new red bicycle.

"Wow, mom!" He shouted. "It's just what I wanted." He ran to get on the bike and began to pedal around the driveway.

"Be careful, dear." She was concerned for his safety. He continued to pedal it around.

"Look, mom, I can ride it just great! Wait'til dad sees this!" He pedaled faster.

"Be careful Monty! Stop, before you…" She ran over to him. He had taken a tumble and was lying on the driveway crying. She leaned over and stroked his head. "You'll live," she said with a smile. "Now get up." Monty continued crying. She repeated, this time a bit more sternly, "You'll live. Now get up!"

He continued to cry while holding his knee, which had a nasty scrape on it. She grabbed him by the arm and yanked him. "You'll live, I said. Now, get up!" She screamed. He momentarily stopped crying, looked at her disfigured face and gasped. It scared him so much that he jumped straight up in the air.

Monty looked at the clock. It was 3:00 am. Everything was quiet until he heard a car pull up in front of his house. He peeked out through the blinds. It was the familiar black Mercedes. Wino butler and wino chauffeur had found him.

"Definitely not a social visit," he thought.

Monty scrambled to gather his belongings and stuffed everything into his computer bag, then went into the kitchen and grabbed Fred. He ran out the back door and climbed over the low fence into Bill's backyard. He put Fred down, patted him on the head several times and made his way toward the front far end of Bill's house. As he peeked around the corner at the Mercedes, he saw the doors open and the two winos get out. They were not alone. The smaller figure getting out of the back seat was an elderly woman.

"It can't be." He continued to look *"It is that old witch! But how?"*

Monty got a chill in his spine realizing they wouldn't stop until he was dead. He watched as the winos approached his minivan. Wino butler examined the license plate. He looked at the old woman and nodded.

She proceeded to the front door, opening it as though it was not locked. The three entered the house. Monty ran quietly to the driver side of the Mercedes. *"Yes!"* Wino chauffeur left the keys in the car. Monty climbed in, started the car and sped away.

Wino chauffeur came running out of the house. Monty could see him in the rear view mirror. Mama Crossbones came out immediately after him and slapped him on the head. Monty didn't bother to look back again. He just kept going.

Mama Crossbones waited until wino butler came out of the house. She backed away from it and stood on the far side of the sidewalk. The winos did the same. She turned toward the house and lifted her arms. She stood that way a moment, murmuring words at the house. Both winos covered their eyes as the house and the minivan were instantly engulfed in flames.

As the fire lit the night, she turned and walked down the street with both winos following her. They walked until they came upon an unlocked car in a neighbors' driveway. All three got in and sped away.

21

Managing Risk

Oliver's morning workout consisted of a series of wing chun techniques followed by power training exercises. He typically began his workout at 6:00 am. He would visit the wing chun school and take part in sparring exercises two days a week.

On this particular morning, he reviewed a few of his favorite techniques focusing on leg exercises. He worked out for an hour, took a shower and had a light breakfast. Daily Mass was at 9:00 am, and it was his turn today.

At 8:00 am, Pastor Bob asked Oliver to join him in his office. Oliver grabbed a handful of jelly beans from the jar on his desk and headed for the toast pastor's office. He was fully aware of the unavoidable interrogation coming, after the events of the previous day.

"Oliver, we didn't get a chance to talk yesterday about everything that happened. I had a funeral as you know, then I had to head back out to Chester Hill nursing home for a special Mass. After that, I attended a meeting with the Bishop. As you might have guessed, word of what happened at our parish reached the Bishop before I did.

"Betty said the fellow who came in with the basket was a friend of yours. How do you know him?"

Oliver shook his head. "Actually, I had just met him. I told Betty that so she would get back to her desk and stop worrying."

"Why exactly did he come here to see you?"

"He didn't come here to see me. He was looking for a priest to baptize him. He wouldn't take no for an answer."

"What do you mean, he wouldn't take no? We have ways in which we conduct the sacraments, you know that." Pastor Bob was not pleased. He liked everything to be done just so and done his way. He would have made a good Pharisee.

"Yeah, Bob, but he had a gun and threatened to shoot me if I didn't comply." Oliver wondered what Bob would have done had Paul barged into his office instead. The toast pastor had a tendency to be condescending and rigid. Once he made up his mind about something it wouldn't matter if Jesus himself came down to talk sense into him. He would not change it. In Bob's mind inflexibility and being rigid minded were part of being a good leader. He wanted the parish and congregation to know that he was numero uno.

Pastor Bob sat back in his chair. "So, these other two men just came in and tried to kill the both of you over some antique mask?"

"That's right, Bob. They took the basket and made their getaway."

"Did you get a chance to see this mask?"

Oliver nodded. "Yes."

"And? Was there anything special about it, Oliver? What did it look like?"

Oliver sat back, popped a few jelly beans into his mouth and thought. *"Beside the fact that it was really an evil severed head, which continued to speak without any help from a nearby ventriloquist, it was perfectly normal."* He popped a few more jelly beans. "No, it was just an old Mardi Gras mask of an old woman."

Pastor Bob reached down and placed the Black Lamia on his desk. "What do you know about this?"

Oliver tried not to reveal his surprise at seeing the blade. "Where did you get that, Bob?"

"Betty found it in your office." The toast pastor had that irritating "gotcha" smirk on his face.

"What is Betty doing going through my things?" Oliver was miffed, and didn't try to hide it.

"I asked her to look around for anything that might help shed some light on the strange attack that almost got you and her killed. I'm sure you understand."

"No, I don't, Bob. You had no right."

Pastor Bob continued to wear his annoying smirk. "Oh? I beg your pardon. I am the pastor. It's all my business. Betty said she saw this man, Paul, with it when he arrived. She saw it on him when he stormed into the reception area insisting to see you."

"He wanted to see a priest. He was not looking for me in particular, Bob, if that's what you mean. And that sword belongs to the man who came in here with it." Oliver picked the sword up off Pastor Bob's desk.

Pastor Bob sat back observing the handsome priest with more muscles and hair than he. "Oliver, remember when we talked the other day? You asked me if you should seek a transfer to another parish. I'd like for us to move towards that. I just don't think I'm getting the whole truth from you. I can't afford to have this parish riddled with scandal. I received a call from Dr. Sinclair late yesterday. I don't know how he got wind of it so fast, but he did. Need I remind you that he is a new and very wealthy parishioner? And then, there's the Bishop. He wanted to know what is going on here."

Oliver took a deep breath. "OK, the truth of the matter, Bob, is that the man, who came in here and threatened to kill me unless I baptized him, had a severed head in the basket. It was still alive and talking. The winos that came in here were possessed by demons. Their demonic entities tried to squeeze the life out of him but, fortunately, he gave himself to the Lord just in time and I immediately baptized him. The demonized winos attacked us and were willing to sacrifice the two wino bodies, which they referred to as 'expendable.' Betty then appeared at the door. They grabbed her, threatening to kill her unless we gave them the head. This sword belongs to the man I baptized. It is what he used to sever the head from the body of a powerful witch. He was planning on throwing the head into the fire."

Bob sat back in his chair and folded his hands as a smile forced its way onto his face. He chuckled. "I'm going to miss your sense of humor, Oliver."

"Has Pastor Bob helped himself to my jellybeans? Certainly one must be taking up too much space in that thick head." Oliver got up from the chair. "I'd better get going. I have

morning Mass today."

Pastor Bob waved a motion for him to sit back down. "Don't worry about Mass duties, Oliver. I'm having Fr. Ken preside at morning Mass today. He and I will manage the weekend Masses. You are on pastoral leave as of now, until we can find you a new parish."

"What?" Oliver was shocked at how fast he managed to get himself kicked out of yet another parish. Perhaps this was not the way God wanted him to serve. *"Why give me the ability to see evil so clearly, if I can't do something about it?"* One minute he was the presider; the next, he was on pastoral leave.

"Bob, I understand why you feel you must do this. I think I'll just retire to my room if you don't mind. I need to reflect and pray about all of this."

"Of course, Oliver, and please let me know if there is anything I can do. If you want to talk to a professional counselor about anything, I can arrange that." Pastor Bob seemed very pleased with the outcome of the meeting.

Oliver smiled and did his best not to let Pastor Bob get to him. "Very well, thanks for the offer." Oliver left the office. It would be the last time he would see Pastor Bob. Life would never be the same from this moment on.

As Oliver entered his room at the rectory, his cell phone rang. He answered without checking the caller.

"Fr. Oliver, please, I need to talk with you. I don't have anyone else I can turn to. Can we meet? It's Monty, or Paul, if you prefer."

"You had better not come to the church office. I'll meet you at the coffee shop on Hargett, Cup-a-Hoot. Do you know where it is?"

"I'll find it. When can you get there?"

"I'll meet you there in forty-five minutes."

"OK, thanks, see you then."

22

I'm Going to Enjoy Killing Him

Mama Crossbones sat in her favorite chair sipping her brandy and smoking a rather large Cuban cigar. Mr. Fredericks, the banker, and one of the local Council members sat in guest chairs. After taking a few puffs, she turned to the two men and waited for their report.

Fredericks shifted nervously in his chair. "I expect we should be able to catch up with him today. The Mercedes was spotted in a public parking garage in downtown Raleigh. When he tries to drive off again, if he is that stupid, we will be waiting. He won't get far. We have people looking out for him. His picture was circulated to the Council members."

She sat back and relaxed in her big chair as she examined her cigar. "I'm going to enjoy killing him." She took a puff. "And that damned priest." She took another puff. "I should have left manflesh rot in hell, when he was killed the first time. Now, he has sought the man Jesus, and thinks he can somehow redeem himself." She laughed, coughed, and hacked up something. She coughed again and spat on the floor. Her laughter roared. A moment later, she continued. "He thinks the man Jesus will have him, after everything he's done? Ha ha ha, he lost that chance when he died the first time, the fool.

His house is burned to the ground; he has no vehicle, no one he can turn to for help, except the meddling priest." She stopped and turned to Fredericks. "Send someone to the church

and have the priest followed. He is liable to try to help manflesh.
When you locate them, make sure you retrieve my Black Lamia.
What a fool I was to entrust it to him. I was so sure he was the one.
Now get out of here, Fredericks, and let me know when they turn
up."

23

A Priest and a Dead Man Walk Into a Bar

Oliver entered Cup-a-Hoot and glanced around. He noticed the familiar face looking at him from the corner table near the back.

Monty stood up and reached out to shake Oliver's hand. "Thanks for coming."

Oliver sat down across from him. "How's the shoulder?"

"It's sore, but not too bad. The pain medicine helps." Monty leaned forward as he took a quick look around the coffee shop. "Listen, Oliver, I'm in big trouble, and there is no one else I can think of calling. Last night I woke up in the middle of the night. Within minutes, a car pulled up to my house. It was those two winos and the head, only the head was reattached to the body. The old witch was with them. I snuck out the back door, put Paul's dog in the neighbor's backyard, and took off in the witch's car while they were all in the house looking for me. They were there to kill me."

Monty pointed to the large television screen on the side wall of the coffee shop. Oliver turned to look. The news reporter was standing in front of a house that had burned to the ground. Fire engines had blocked off the street. The sound was off so he couldn't hear the report.

"That's my house – what's left of it, anyway. I don't know any of Paul's family, and I don't have any friends. I grabbed the essentials and left last night. I must have known I would not be returning. I didn't know they had set fire to it until this morning."

Oliver looked at the house on the television. It was in ruins.

Monty continued "I wish I had tossed that damned head into the fire when I had the chance. I was just too afraid to do it. I thought as soon as she was in the fire all hell would know what I had done and come looking for me. I've seen her demon friends. Those two guys that came into your office were not just winos. They were possessed by demons. In her house, she called them out of the host bodies so I could see their true forms. She introduced them to me as my brothers.

"I've been an evil man all of my past life. Never did I think hell was real. Never did I think my actions were propelling me closer and closer to it. Even though I was under the spell of that witch before I was born, I could have broken free any time. I chose to ignore all the invitations to goodness. I don't think you could have found a more self-centered, hateful individual. Then, in an instant, I was dead. Had the old witch not brought me back, I would be in the farthest corner of the pit of hell, alongside the world's most despicable characters. That was my fate. But for some reason, through the hand of evil itself, unbeknown to what they were really doing, I was given a second chance."

Oliver leaned forward in his chair. "And so you came searching for Jesus after you came to believe there is a hell?"

"Yes, although I'm sure I've exceeded the statute of limitations on being forgiven, destined to be damned forever. I've died already. My previous life was full of self-gratification. I would not think twice to hurt or kill for it. I received tremendous pleasure from the suffering of others. The witch claimed to have liberated me, but she did not liberate me. She imprisoned me. I was seduced enough by the pleasure of it, not to realize that I was enslaved by evil. Ironically, after you baptized me, I feel more my true self in this stranger's body than I ever did in my own.

"After hearing her brag about how she knew what was best, how much she hated Jesus Dand his followers, I knew my only hope was to find Jesus. I needed to find him somehow, so I decided to start by finding a priest. If I could find Jesus, then maybe I could burn the head and perhaps survive the onslaught of hell. That's when I came to your office."

"How did you come by our church and my office?"

"Shortly after I was brought back to life in this body, I was the honored guest at what they call the Council of 666 meeting. I was introduced as some kind of agent-of-evil. My job: to proliferate more chaos in the world. There were powerful people at the gathering. Many of them are people that you would recognize as political leaders, doctors, lawyers, you name it. It was a who's who of the evil elite. I was given a new car, a luxurious apartment, and a bank account with a million dollars in it. My second assignment was to become a member of St. Ignatius parish and help create scandal and embarrassment for the church. My previous life of self-indulgent evil was on-the-job training for this life of organized and highly leveraged evil. The Council's purpose is to bring down followers of Jesus and convert the masses to the ways of evil. The campaign has been in full swing across the world. They have made a great deal of progress."

Oliver nodded "Yes, we just had another mass shooting at a high school not too long ago and a scandal with a priest in our Diocese. There is more hatefulness and perversion, like a swell in the evil tide. I can see it. People are killing each other at an alarming rate. Meanwhile, God is politically incorrect. It seems aggressive secularism is one of evil's best weapons. People are choosing the wrong side, thinking they aren't on any side."

"So, what was your first assignment, Monty?"

"My first assignment was to kill Juan Arias. He is a parishioner at your church. He is the fellow who helped the police catch me in my former life.

"I realized God was trying to speak to me as you read Mark 6:19. It frightened me to my core, but at the same time gave me more hope than I ever had before. When you read Luke 6:19 it reinforced my hope and gave me clear instructions how to proceed. I knew I must follow Christ. Saying yes to Jesus in your office was the hardest thing I have ever done in this life or my past life. I literally could not speak. I felt as though I was being crushed to death. I wanted to say 'I do,' more than anything. I knew that my eternal soul was hanging by a thread. I had never felt so desperate or lost. I may be headed straight for hell after all, but I am grateful to you for this opportunity to be out of evil's grasp. I am sorry that those winos caused trouble at your church. I hope it didn't cause too much trouble for you. Is the lady all right?"

"Betty is fine. She was a little shaken up. However, I have been placed on a pastoral leave of absence as of this morning."

"Can I get you gentleman anything?" came the voice from a young waitress. Both men looked up.

"Oh, yes. What would you like, Oliver? I'm buying. It's the least I can do."

Oliver smiled at the waitress. "I'll have a cup of your black coffee no sugar and a Turkish coffee."

She turned to Monty. "And for you?"

"I'll have a cup of your Cappuccino."

She smiled "Thanks, I'll be back in a moment with your coffees."

Monty turned to Oliver. "What does that mean? Did you get fired because of me? Can you get fired from being a priest?"

Oliver chuckled. "Politely fired, I guess that would best describe it. They will find another parish for me to serve. I'll probably be fired again. It's a pattern with me." Oliver thought about past parishes where he served and eventually was asked to leave. "You know those demons you mentioned that were in the two wino attackers?"

Monty nodded in anticipation.

"I can see them in whomever they choose to possess. I have seen them everywhere in all kinds of people possessed by evil. I saw it in you when you came to my office. You had quite the gorilla on your back. You had several demons engulfing you. I have been able to see them clearly since I was five years old. You are the second person with whom I've shared this. My church doesn't know. I manage to get myself into trouble at every parish. It happens when I help someone possessed by evil get rid of their demon, thus, my current leave of absence. If it hadn't been you, it would have been someone else, just a matter of time."

It occurred to Monty this was the first time he ever expressed a genuine interest in someone's life other than his own. "I'm sorry to have cost you your job. Where will they send you? Do you get to select the place?"

"No, it's not up to me. They send me wherever they feel I am needed. With every reassignment, parish options become fewer. The church will not tolerate scandal, especially, with the media ready to make it their feature story."

The waitress came back with their coffees. "Here you go gentlemen. Will there be anything else?" She asked in her perky voice.

"No, thank you," they replied simultaneously.

She smiled and walked back to the counter.

Monty recalled what Mama Crossbones had said about fallen clergy. "The witch said that causing religious leaders to fall was one of their strategies." He reached for his rich aromatic coffee. "They figure every time clergy is caught in scandal, multitudes leave the church. They take that as a victory because evil provides disgruntled Christians with a secular and rational alternative. Many question their faith as a result of religious scandal. It creates an opening to allow evil into the hearts of those whose frustration and anger at their religious leaders leads them to search for a new faith or simply abandon it."

Oliver contemplated his coffee. "Unfortunately, she is right. There has been an exodus of the faithful, I'm afraid. It has been fueled, in large part, by child abuse scandals. It's very sad. No man is immune to the power of evil, not even clergy. The flesh is extremely weak. Evil knows what can easily corrupt someone. Many underestimate evil and find themselves stuck in its quicksand unable to get out."

"So, what are you going to do? Will you continue to be a priest?"

Their conversation was interrupted by a woman's voice. "Well, hello, handsome!"

They both looked up to see Regina approaching their table.

"I'd know that head anywhere." She looked at Oliver and then at Monty.

Oliver smiled and stood up to greet her. "Hi, Regina, it's nice to see you."

"I see you are enjoying your Turkish coffee fix."

"Would you like to join us for a cup? By the way, this is a friend, Paul."

Monty shot up from his chair. "It's nice to meet you, Regina." He shook her hand. He noticed her firm grip. Oliver had noticed it, as well.

"Sure" I have a little time before work. She grabbed a chair from the adjacent table.

"I'll get your coffee. What would you like?" Monty asked as she sat down.

"I'll take a large cinnamon cappuccino, thanks."

"I'll be right back." Monty made his way to the service counter.

Regina grinned as she remembered their last meeting. "So, how have you been? Have you come to your senses, and decided to quit being a priest?"

Oliver laughed as he thought of their conversation a few days earlier "You are something else. As a matter of fact, my situation has changed a bit since we last met."

Regina's curiosity was sparked. She leaned in and looked intently at Oliver. "I hope it's good news!"

Oliver smiled "I don't know if it's good or bad, but I have been put on pastoral leave. I'm to be relocated to another parish."

Her smiled faded. "That is not good news. What's the matter with your boss? Where are they sending you?"

"I don't know yet. I was informed this morning."

Regina never thought she would be disappointed hearing that a priest was being transferred. She couldn't remember the last time she stepped into a church. But this was no ordinary priest. "How long will you be around?"

"I'm not sure. I think the sooner they find a new home for me, the happier the pastor will be."

"You boys had a falling out or something?" She was curious why any pastor would ask such a fine priest to leave. It was like asking your star quarterback to play for the other team. Only in this case it would be the best looking quarterback. *"Who cares how good he can throw the ball."*

"I wouldn't call it a falling out. It's rather complicated. Let's just say I can serve the Lord better in other ways, in another place."

She glanced at the order counter with a keen look in her eye. "Is your friend part of the problem or part of the solution?"

Oliver sat in amazement as he looked at this hairdresser, whom he realized also had razor sharp instincts. "Wow, maybe you should have continued to be a reporter. You have great intuition and instincts."

She smiled. "I know. That's why I'm such a good catch."

"To answer your question: both. He is part of the problem and part of the solution, but I can't really get into it." Monty was approaching with her coffee.

"Here you go, Regina, one large cinnamon cappuccino." He placed her coffee on the table.

"Thanks" She had a curious look in her eyes. She examined Monty as he sat down.

He noticed her scrutiny and smiled at her. He looked at Oliver and then back at Regina. "What? Did I miss something?"

"I don't know what you two have going on, but if there is anything I can do to help, let me know, OK?" She looked back at Oliver.

There was an awkward silence for a moment as they each looked at one another.

"Paul knows my secret." Oliver sipped his coffee and continued. "The two people who know I can see demons are sitting at the same table. I find that unusual. First, is the fact that you both know, and second, the fact that you are both here."

"What's going on?" Regina's tone became serious. She looked at each of them.

Oliver took another sip of his liquid sand, Turkish coffee. "The short of it is, my friend here is in real trouble. He has made some very serious enemies. They are trying to kill him. They burned down his house last night."

Monty shifted uncomfortably in his chair. "I'm afraid there's more, now."

Oliver and Regina both looked at Monty. Oliver seemed more surprised than Regina by Monty's statement.

Monty continued. "I'm afraid you might have to pay a very high price if you help me, and I don't mean being put on Pastoral leave. They are after me. They burned down my house, and they will probably come after you because of your intervention. They know where you live, Oliver, and if your pastor is trying to avoid a scandal, what happened yesterday might only be a prelude to what will happen next at your church."

Oliver's phone rang. He glanced at the caller ID and decided to take the call. "Excuse me." He got up and walked toward the front of the coffee shop.

Regina studied Monty. "So, how long have you and Oliver

been friends?"

"I met him yesterday."

Regina settled back into reporter mode. "Why are these people trying to kill you?"

"I betrayed them. They wanted me to do awful things and I backed out. The other reason is I can identify many of them. I am a threat to them as long as I'm alive." Monty refrained from including the bizarre parts of his story.

"How did you meet Oliver?"

"I went to his church and asked him to baptize me." He looked intently at her as he recalled Mama Crossbones severed head and her awful laughter. "Thankfully, he was able to do it. It's the reason I'm alive." He paused and held her gaze. "In more ways than one, I am a new person. Evil had a very powerful hold on me. I did not comprehend the power of that hold until recently."

Oliver returned to his seat. He took a gulp of his black coffee. Regina looked at him inquisitively. "Everything OK?"

"Yeah, I need to meet with one of our big donors who requested a private meeting with me. I guess he got the jitters after hearing what happened and is threatening to leave the parish, unless he hears from me that I'm not involved in any craziness."

She seemed irritated by this request. "Do parishioners usually threaten to get their way if they donate big bucks to the parish?"

"I wouldn't necessarily say they get their way, but Dr. Sinclair is relatively new to the parish. I think the pastor wants me to reassure him. I guess this is the kind of thing he was trying to avoid. I can't say I blame Pastor Bob for wanting to relocate me. People are skittish and fickle. Those with money are ..."

Monty cut him off. "You can't meet with him. It's a trap. He is one of them. Dr. Sinclair, if it is the same man I met at the Council meeting. He is one of them. I was to make an appointment with him for facial plastic surgery to alter my appearance." Monty was nervous about the possibility of this meeting actually taking place.

Oliver knew Dr. Sinclair was host to evil. He should have guessed he was part of this. Fredericks was probably involved, as well. "Do you know Mr. Fredericks?"

Monty nodded. "Yes, I think he is the banker. He is part of

the Council. He was also there. They set me up with a million dollar bank account and a new Mercedes which I obviously cannot use since I want to remain among the living. These folks are powerful."

Regina drank her coffee and glanced at Monty then at Oliver. "Crap! You boys are into some nasty business."

Oliver thought for a moment. "Are you sure about this, Paul?"

"Yes, they must figure if they can get to you, they can get to me. After all, you fought off those two goons and you are a member of the clergy. You are an easy target. As a bonus, the scandal potential is enormous."

"Hey, I have an idea!" Regina chimed in. "Why don't you arrange a meeting with this Dr. Sinclair in private, perhaps at his office? Then, you can do what you did to the woman at the salon and drive the demon out of him. After he is free from the demon, you can recruit the Doctor to the side of the good guys."

Oliver gave it some thought. "I'm afraid that may not work, and it would be too risky to try."

"Why? You were able to free the woman at my salon. Why not the Doctor?"

"You are assuming the Doctor wants to be free of evil or that he has some subconscious desire to be free of it, but that may not necessarily be the case." Oliver paused to gather his thoughts. "Some people are quite happy with their demons. They don't see evil as something keeping them from a relationship with God. They see it as a tool that has helped them get where they are. They are quite comfortable living in evil. The woman who walked into your salon was not. I don't know how I knew that. Perhaps, I just sensed it. I suspect people on this Council of 666 have embraced evil of their own free will. If there is no desire to repent, not even on a subconscious level, my actions would be ineffective. God does not override anyone's free will, even though you and I might see the benefit to that person." Oliver took the last swig of his Turkish coffee and then reached for a swallow of his black coffee.

Monty nodded in agreement. "I can tell you with certainty that underestimating any of them would be a mistake. You might go missing and turn up on someone's plate."

Regina wrinkled her nose. "That's disgusting. You're not

serious?"

"At the Council banquet, when I commented on the delicious steak, Mama Crossbones corrected me and said it was not steak, no need to explain any further. The meat had a different aroma. I never smelled or tasted anything like it before, and I hope I never again."

Regina put her hand over her mouth. "Oh my goodness that is sick! And, this Dr. Sinclair was there?"

"Yes," Monty replied, "As I explained to Oliver, there were many famous and notable people in attendance. They were all part of the Council, and this was a safe meeting where I was presented as one of them, one with great potential. I don't think it's safe for you to go back to the church, Oliver." He paused and lowered his head. "I'm sorry I dragged you into this mess."

They all sat quietly for a moment as each thought about the gravity of the situation.

Monty broke the silence. "It's as though they are casting a dragnet. They have the resources to find me, us. It's just a matter of time. With all of these high powered wealthy individuals involved, I wouldn't be surprised if they have people in every law enforcement agency. I wish I could see them as you can, Oliver."

"Perhaps this is the reason I've been given this ability," Oliver replied. "It occurs to me that what is happening here is much greater than the sum of its parts."

"What do you mean?" Regina looked at her watch. "Go on, I want to hear this. I have a few minutes before I need to get going."

Oliver glanced toward the front of the store. No one appeared to be eavesdropping. "Because what Paul has shared with me about his past, the fact that evil has given him a second chance at life, my ability to see demonic possession in the flesh, the fact that he found me when he could have found any other priest in the city, I must believe God's will is placed in our hands. We are part of something greater that is taking place." He reached into his pocket and pulled out a rosary and showed them the cross. "Think about it. Evil does not give you a second chance. Evil only consumes. The fact that Paul has been given a second chance can only be due to God willing it to happen. That witch, or whatever she is, was used by God for a higher purpose, and that was to keep you alive. I believe there is work ahead of you and ahead of me, that is part of His greater plan. I won't pretend to know what it is, but coming together like this, under these circumstances is no accident."

Regina looked at her watch again. "It sounds pretty far-fetched to me, Oliver."

"God is far-fetched," Oliver replied as he glanced at her. "Sending His son to be tortured and hung on a cross; for a bunch of sinners? Oliver paused and looked at Monty. "Did you happen to read your bible? In particular, have you read about the apostle named Paul?"

Monty shook his head. "No, I've been too busy dodging demons and possessed people."

You might want to read about Paul, and while you're at it check out St. Michael. The parallels are interesting." He handed the Black Lamia over to Monty. "St Michael uses one similar to this, only his is much bigger. And, Paul was an ardent persecutor of those who followed Christ until he had a change of heart, a second chance. Pretty far-fetched stuff," he said smiling at Regina.

Regina looked on as Monty took the sword and put it under his jacket. "I take it that little item also has to do with why they're after you?"

Oliver looked at Regina somewhat worried. "Hey, I don't want to get you involved in any of this. Perhaps we should part company. The less you know the better. You've probably heard more than you wanted to, or should."

She laughed heartily. "Are you kidding? What I wouldn't do for a little adventure! No, you can count me in. I meant what I said. If I can help, just let me know how. It sounds like you've got some major creeps on your tail and I can't stand creeps." She took a quick sip of her coffee and continued. "Oh, and by the way, I recommend you boys disengage any tracking function on your cell phones. It sounds like you have the mafia after you, but you might as well make it more difficult, just in case."

Oliver reached for his cell phone and checked the settings.

"This is worse than the mafia," Monty added. "At least the Mafia is human."

Regina looked at Monty. "Aren't you going to check your phone, Paul?"

Monty felt his pockets. "I don't think I have one."

She was mildly amused by that statement. "Why? Aren't you sure whether you own a phone or not?"

"I must have lost it." He did not want to have to explain to Regina that his recent arrival into a stranger's body left him unsure of quite a few things.

Oliver smiled and turned to Regina. "Are you serious about helping us?" he asked, hoping she would not be scared off by his question.

"If I can, I will. It depends what you want me to do." She set her coffee cup down. "As long as it's not too racy."

Oliver smiled. "I was hoping you might really mean it. There is something you can do!"

24

A Visit to the Doctor

"She must be a product of the Dr. Sinclair's handiwork." She appeared to be in her twenties. Her hair was silky auburn, as though she had used some kind of magic shampoo. Her face was made up meticulously, with just the right amount of blush on her cheeks. Her eyebrows were flawless. Her skin resembled porcelain, and she articulated every syllable when she spoke. "How may I help you, sir?"

Oliver noticed her expression. It was neither pleasant nor unpleasant. She was expressionless. "Perhaps she is afraid to express a smile. It might release a temporary crease on areas of her face." He leaned on the edge of the white granite counter. "I was hoping to see Dr. Sinclair. He requested a meeting with me, and I happened to be in the area." Oliver smiled, revealing normal smile lines on his face.

She did not return the smile. "What is your name?" She asked with minimal movement of her lips.

"My name is Oliver. I'm a priest at St. Ignatius where Dr. Sinclair is a parishioner," he replied, again with a smile.

Again, no smile. "Just a moment, I will check." Oliver wondered how such a person could articulate words so well while barely moving their lips. He also wondered if she ever smiled, period. She turned, dialed the phone and spoke in a low voice. When finished, she turned back to address Oliver. Her eyebrows went up slightly and the edges of her mouth moved slightly upward, then halted as if on command. They had reached their acceptable smile limit. Her cheeks hinted at a smile.

"What are you doing?" she asked in her articulate minimalist way.

Oliver took the pen out of his nose and put it back in his pocket. "I just wanted to see if you would smile." He was amazed at her level of smile control. "I thought I saw the beginnings of one, but it disappeared before it could blossom."

Her eyebrow rose slightly. "Yes, well, that was very amusing. Dr. Sinclair will be out in a few minutes. Please have a seat."

Then Oliver stopped dead in his tracks. He was on his way to go sit in the waiting area. That's when she winked, still no smile, but a perfect wink, almost mechanical. He was about to make a comment after he closed his mouth, but her phone rang. *"Maybe she's really a robot and that wink was a malfunction of some sort."* There were no magazines or newspapers, so he sat and looked around at all the artwork. Each canvas was approximately three feet square with colors and rich dark lines creating overlapping geometries. Stylistically, it appeared to be the work of the same artist. The signature at the bottom right hand corner of each canvas confirmed it, 'Sigmund Sinclair'. No doubt it was the same Dr. Sinclair.

As Oliver looked at the signature on the painting directly across from him, the painting and the entire panel on which it hung started to swivel open. A man with a demonic face emerged, dressed in a white lab coat. The beastly Dr. Sinclair emerged from behind the wall panel, a decoratively concealed door.

Taken by surprise as the doctor demon stepped out and extended a hand, Oliver did his best to remain calm as he shook the doctor's hand.

"Hello, Fr. Oliver. I am surprised to see you here. Come, let's go to my office where we can chat." He held the panel door open and gestured Oliver to enter.

Oliver followed his host down a corridor into a large corner office furnished with comfortable, luxurious furniture. The doctor's office was decorated with smaller copies of the original art, about eighteen inches square, and hung in the same regular intervals as the art in the waiting area.

A large mahogany desk resided on one side and a plush leather sofa and a set of chairs on the other. He motioned to Oliver to sit in one of the chairs. The doctor took a seat in the other.

"Can I get you anything to drink, Father?" His voice was pleasant. The nostrils of the demon's face flared as its lips parted revealing jagged teeth and dark brown gums with yellow blemishes.

Oliver guessed the expression was supposed to be a smile. "No, thank you, doctor. I'm fine."

The doctor took his seat. "What brings you to my humble office, Fr. Oliver?"

"Pastor Bob said you wanted to meet with me. I happened to be in the area, so I took a chance and dropped by. I hope I am not inconveniencing you in any way."

"No, not at all, Fr. Oliver. As it happens, I am between appointments. Your timing is perfect."

"Good, I'm glad. Pastor Bob said you had something on your mind that you needed to discuss." Oliver pretended to have no idea why the good doctor would want to meet with him.

Dr. Sinclair sat back and smiled. "Yes, that is correct. I was a bit concerned about some things I heard took place at the church recently involving the police and gunfire. As you know, I recently joined your parish. I became concerned about a possible backlash, which would reflect badly on the church and its members. So you see, I was just curious about the situation. Can you tell me what exactly happened?"

Oliver gestured with his hands. "I think it was just a big misunderstanding. A gentleman came in and asked to be baptized. Then two men broke into my office and robbed us. After a brief struggle, they took the receptionist hostage and ran off. Fortunately, they left her behind and nobody was seriously hurt."

Dr. Sinclair put one hand on his chest in a dramatic gesture of concern. "Oh, my! Yes, you were fortunate indeed. What were the thieves after? You said they robbed you. What did they take?" Dr. Sinclair's eyes squinted as he waited for Oliver to respond.

If what Monty said was true, Dr. Sinclair probably knew exactly what was taken. Oliver played dumb and revealed a viable version, one that a normal person might believe. "They stole, what I think was, some kind of animatronics. The fellow who came to my office kept it in a basket. It was an amazing piece of craftsmanship. It was a Mardi Gras head with a full range of facial expression and a recorder which played sounds, so it would appear to be talking. I guess it must have been a prototype or something. They made off with it."

The doctor nodded continuously as Oliver spoke. "What happened to the fellow who came to you seeking to be baptized? Do you know where he is now?" Dr. Sinclair's voice was soft and caring. Oliver found it interesting that a demonic face could be speaking so softly and with such care. It was a bit un-nerving.

Oliver shook his head. "No, I don't know where he is."

The doctor leaned forward, and his voice got even softer, as though he were sharing a secret with his best pal. "Can you find out where he is? Has he been in contact with you since coming to the church?"

"Why do you ask, Doctor? Do you know this man?" Oliver faked complete surprise.

Dr. Sinclair sat back in his chair. "Well, Father Oliver, I am a little embarrassed by this but, yes, I know him, but not well. I met him once a few nights ago. But more importantly, the owner of that 'animatronics' is a dear friend. As I understand it, the man has something else which belongs to this friend. They would like to retrieve it, and asked me to find out anything I can about the man's whereabouts. I'm sure you understand. If something was taken from you, you would want it back."

Oliver nodded in agreement. "Yes, of course." He paused, and added "I'm sorry that I can't help you."

"That's too bad, Father Oliver. I thought he might have contacted you after all that had happened."

There was a momentary silence. The doctor stood up and signaled to Oliver to follow him to the other side of his office. He walked over to the large mahogany desk and sat down. "Please, take a seat here. I want to show you something." Dr. Sinclair pointed to a chair on the other side of his large desk. He pressed a button and a large screen came down from the ceiling.

The doctor closed the blinds by pressing another button. As the room became dark, several images of nude women appeared on the screen. "Fr. Oliver, I thought you might want to see the kind of work I do. These are some of my clients. I perform plastic surgery of which I am quite proud." He continued to show more women, each in a slightly more suggestive pose. "I don't suppose you get to see these kinds of images too often, being that you are a priest. Or, maybe I am wrong about that, hey Father? But this is just for your information, of course, and it permits me to brag about my work a bit." Dr. Sinclair came to a stop on an image of a beautiful woman fully nude, in a highly suggestive pose. "This is the client I was telling you about. The one who would like to have her property returned. She has asked me to inform you that should you be instrumental in returning her property, she would be most appreciative. She emphasized this to me, and I think it is safe to say she would deliver whatever method of appreciation you request. She is quite beautiful, isn't she, Father?

"Why, yes," Oliver replied. "She is very attractive."

The room became bright once again as the blinds opened. Oliver noticed the demon's grizzly expression. There was some white foam-like residue at the corners of its ugly mouth. It had a broad smile. Then it licked its lips and peered at Oliver as if knowing its seductive weapon was sure to bring down the pathetic priest.

Oliver did his best not to stare at Dr. Sinclair. He thought his demon vision would be found out. "This has been very enlightening, Doctor. That is quite an incentive package."

"Yes, Father Oliver. Please understand, I'm simply the messenger. I will treat this in the strictest confidence. You can be sure of that. You are free to accept the lovely lady's offer without fear of retribution or judgment from me. Pastor Bob need not know of our conversation."

"I appreciate the very fine offer, Dr. Sinclair, and wish you luck finding whatever it is your client is seeking. But, I cannot help you."

Dr. Sinclair's left hand tapped nervously on his desk as he listened to Oliver. "Are you sure you don't know where he is, Father?" The Doctor's voice was noticeably less soft and caring.

Oliver looked at his watch as he stood up. "My goodness, look at the time." He glanced at Dr. Sinclair. "No, I'm sorry Dr. Sinclair, I cannot help you. Thanks for your time and for showing me your very interesting work." Oliver turned to leave the office. As he did so, he was shoved violently backward into his seat by the

old woman who now stood before him.
    "Sit down, priest!"

25

Temporary Shelter

Monty exited the taxi and walked several blocks west. He would need to walk another half mile to reach Regina's apartment. He did not want to risk being followed, so he took a convoluted path to get to his destination. He knew better than to attempt to use the stolen Mercedes. It would stay in the public parking garage until someone discovered it. Oliver had warned him that Mama Crossbones' recruits would be waiting for him there. After leaving the coffee shop, Monty headed to the mall. He made the four mile hike on foot. There, he purchased a cell phone. He dialed Regina's number and let her know his number then he dialed Oliver's number and left a message with his new number. After purchasing his phone, Monty took a cab to a location near Regina's apartment. That was the favor Oliver had asked of her. It was either really nice or really stupid of her to agree. He wasn't sure which, but he was glad to have a place to go while he could figure out what to do.

Monty entered the subdivision and found Regina's house. Upon arriving at the front door, he double checked the number before unlocking it. She had given him a spare key and told him he could hide out there temporarily. Oliver would join them later after his meeting with Dr. Sinclair, then they would figure out what to do next.

26

Ambushed

Oliver sat in the chair dumbfounded.

The ghastly decapitated head he confronted in his office was now joined to its body. The demon witch seemed no worse for having lost her head. She peered at him, then pointed with her bony finger. "I want to know where manflesh is hiding, priest. I know that you know. He is alone, and I suspect he has reached out to you for help, now that he has been baptized into your miserable religion. You are a fool if you think you can help him. He is mine. I will exercise my revenge and collect what he has stolen."

She approached Oliver and stopped directly in front of him. "Tell me where he is priest, and I will let you live. Refuse and I will kill you."

Oliver turned to Dr. Sinclair "Is she a friend of yours, Doctor?"

Dr. Sinclair stood up and approached the front side of his desk. "Fr. Oliver, meet Mama Crossbones. She is one of my benefactors, a colleague if you will."

Oliver smiled at Mama Crossbones. "Yes, we've met." He paused. "What I mean is, I met her head. I'm not sure how Humpty Dumpty got put back together, but I liked her better before."

Doctor Sinclair stepped forward and slapped Oliver across the face. "Show some respect, foolish priest. You are speaking of one of our most sacred ambassadors of evil. She is one of the 666 soul reapers present on earth. They take their place throughout the world serving the master. Monty McPride was recruited for a great mission. You have ruined his prospects and caused a major inconvenience to the Council. It would be wise to comply. The alternative is not a pleasant one for you." Dr. Sinclair used his best bedside manner voice.

"A dead priest in your office? I don't think that would be good for business, Doc. I did come here at the request of Pastor Bob. He will know where I was."

"No one will ever find your body," Mama Crossbones smirked. "There would be nothing left of it for anyone to find." She looked Oliver over up and down. "Your flesh might be a bit tougher than most, but our chefs have ways of tenderizing meat. Unfortunately, you would still be alive while they do it. It makes for a more flavorful meat that way."

There was a long pause as Oliver waited to see what came next. He mentally prepared himself for an attack.

"I'm afraid she's right, Fr. Oliver. The situation is quite serious." Dr. Sinclair spoke in a conciliatory tone. He sounded like someone giving heartfelt advice to a dear misguided friend who was in need of counseling and perhaps, a hug.

Mama Crossbones' face came within inches of Oliver's face. The stench of her breath almost caused him to heave. "You have 24 hours to bring me manflesh, that traitor who came to you for help. If you do not comply, I will kill you. If you dare to divulge any of what you have seen or heard here, I will kill you and your pastor."

Dr. Sinclair, the good cop in these negotiations, provided more heartfelt advice. "It would be best for all if you did as she said, Fr. Oliver. There is nothing you can do. We will find him sooner or later, with or without your help. However, if you cooperate, you can go back to being a priest at a new parish and not make things worse for Pastor Bob and St. Ignatius. Do as Mama Crossbones asks and no one will be harmed."

Oliver turned to Doctor Sinclair. "What will you do with him?"

"That's none of your business, priest," sneered Mama Crossbones. "You should have stayed out of it. He would not have escaped without your help."

At that moment, a tall slender man entered the room. He

was dressed in a black leather outfit and held a gun. Dr. Sinclair politely waved in the direction of the man in black. "This is my personal assistant, Mr. Smith. You will take him to our beloved Monty. He will bring him back to us, and you will be free to worship your little god at another church. Then he looked at Mr. Smith "Stay with him. If he tries anything, kill him."

Mama Crossbones turned to Oliver and raised her bony finger, "You have exactly one hour, priest, and the clock starts now."

"You said I had twenty four hours."

Mama Crossbones laughed and coughed for a moment. She stopped abruptly. "I changed my mind, priest. I'm tired of wasting time. We will get him with or without your help. I'm tempted to kill you right here. I was in the mood for sushi, but priest tenderloin sounds pretty good right about now."

Dr Sinclair smiled at Oliver. "I suggest you go and find your friend before Mama Crossbones changes her mind. Mr. Smith will make sure you stay on task." He motioned with his hand. "Now, go."

27

Rocky Future

Oliver and the black clad demon left Dr. Sinclair's office. Demon Smith walked behind Oliver, gun in hand, but concealed under his jacket. Once clear, Oliver stopped and looked at Mr. Smith. "I'll see if I can reach him, and have him meet us somewhere, I really don't know where he is right now. So, I think that would he our best bet."

Mr. Smith did not respond. His snake-like demon head faded to a human blank poker face for a few seconds, then back.

Oliver reached for his phone and dialed the number Monty had left when he purchased his phone.

After a moment, Monty answered the call. Oliver jumped right in, "It's Oliver, I don't have time to explain. Meet me at the Cary mall. It's very important. Come alone." As soon as Oliver said "mall," Mr. Smith shook his head from side to side signaling it was not an acceptable rendezvous point. Oliver corrected himself. "Make that the Raleigh Mall." Mr. Smith again shook his head, signaling that this, too, was an unacceptable choice.

"Hold on." Oliver held the phone and looked at Mr. Smith.

"Rock quarry on Westgate," Smith said while maintaining his poker face.

Oliver turned to speak into his cell phone. "Meet me at the rock quarry on Westgate Road. How fast can you get there?"

"I can be there in…" Monty paused for a moment. "Tell him forty five minutes."

After Oliver ended the call, he looked at Mr. Smith.

Mama Crossbones' henchman was a man of few words. He looked at Oliver. "Your car."

They reached Oliver's car, a four wheel drive SUV. Both men got it in. Oliver realized this was going to be a one way trip. Meeting at a rock quarry? How convenient. He didn't need to be a rocket scientist to know what Smith planned to do, which was kill them both and dump the bodies in the quarry.

Forty minutes later, Oliver and Mr. Smith pulled into the gravel parking area in front of the rock quarry. An office trailer and a couple of large storage sheds were on the property. A little further back, behind the office trailer, the gravel road snaked its way through the quarry.

Oliver stopped the car in front of the office trailer. It was set back 100 yards past the entrance. The quarry was closed since it was after business hours. Both men sat in the parked car. Neither spoke. Mr. Smith kept his gun pointed at Oliver as he glanced around the area. After a few moments, Mr. Smith turned to Oliver. "He'd better show, priest. You've got thirteen minutes."

Cars drove by, but none pulled into the rock quarry parking lot. Both men continued to sit in the car. Smith looked at his watch. "You've got five minutes, priest."

Finally, a car turned off the road and pulled onto the gravel parking area. It slowed and parked in front of one of the storage barns, located 20 yards to the left of the office trailer.

Mr. Smith waved his gun. "Get out, priest."

Oliver opened his door and stepped out of the car. Smith came up behind him and held the barrel of the gun against his head. The door to the other car opened. But no one got out.

"Get out or the priest gets it. He has less than a minute." Smith extended his arm and cocked the trigger.

"OK, OK," came the sound from the parked vehicle. "I'm coming out. Don't shoot." Both hands were raised in the air as the occupant of the vehicle began to emerge.

A faint hissing sound came from the other side, then it quickly zipped by them. Smith turned, just in time to feel the sting of Black Lamia as he watched his hand drop to the gravel driveway still clutching the gun. The slice was so clean and precise it was not immediately evident what happened. Smith was about to say something when his hand simply slid off at the wrist.

Oliver didn't hesitate. He struck Smith with a blow to the throat knocking him backwards. Smith staggered and was temporarily unable to breath. He grasped at his neck with his right hand and the stub of his left wrist.

Oliver removed the gun from the severed hand and used it to knock Mr. Smith unconscious.

Monty approached from the second storage shed. "Are you OK?"

Oliver turned to him. "Yeah, thanks."

A woman emerged from the other vehicle and came running. "Are you all right?"

Oliver turned to her. "Thanks, Regina." Then he got busy tying a tourniquet around Mr. Smith's wrist. He used a piece of leather which he cut from Smith's jacket. Then he checked Mr. Smith's pocket and removed his phone. Oliver propped Smith up against the office trailer door, put the severed hand in his lap, and dialed 911 using Mr. Smith's phone. When the operator answered he said, "I'm at the rock quarry on Westgate. My left hand has been severed. I tied a tourniquet around my wrist. Please send an ambulance. I think I'm going to faint." Then he ended the call.

Oliver turned to Regina and Monty. "There's a coffee house three miles up the road. Do you know the one I'm talking about? It has the giant coffee cup sculpture at the entrance.

Regina nodded. "That's where I split up with my ex-husband. He was double timing me."

Oliver looked at her. "Maybe we shouldn't go there."

She smiled. "No, that's fine. They have good coffee. Besides, if he shows up I'll just have to borrow that blade, and it's not his wrist I'll be cutting off."

Mr. Smith's phone rang. They all looked at each other. Oliver spoke. "We'll regroup there. We need to get out of here."

They jumped into their corresponding vehicles and left the quarry.

~~~

Ten minutes later, seated in a quiet corner of the coffee shop, Oliver turned to Monty. "How did you manage that bit of
~~~

James Bonding?"

Monty took a sip of his coffee. "When you kept changing meeting locations I wondered what was up. Then I heard someone tell you to meet at the rock quarry, which you then repeated to me. I figured our visit to the quarry would not be for a geology lesson. I asked Regina to drop me off so that I could hide. She was to come back later and park by the other storage shed to draw your attention. I wasn't sure what to expect, but I had to try something, so I hid in the first storage shed. With your attention on the other vehicle, I figured I would have at least one chance to make a move.

"How did you manage such a precise throw of the blade? If you had missed, it might not have turned out well for me." Oliver looked at Regina.

She nodded. "I was wondering the same thing."

"The blade seems to know my intent and facilitates it. I felt it the first time I used it on the old witch, then again when I was in your office and used it on one of the winos. I knew your friend with the gun would have heard me coming if I tried to get close. So, I took the chance that my theory about the blade was correct. As soon as it left my hand, I knew it would meet its target exactly one inch along the wrist. I don't know how it knows, but it has been dead on every time."

"No wonder they want it back. That is no ordinary blade." Oliver shook his head and pondered all that was happening. "We have to leave town. We cannot afford to fall into their hands again." He nodded at Regina. "Thus far, you are not on their radar. If we continue to be in your company, however, you will eventually become a target."

Regina hated the thought of Oliver leaving town. "Where will you go? What about your church?"

"I'm thinking of the church. My presence will only bring more danger to the parish. I'm not sure where we will go, perhaps Mexico. How about it, Paul?" He looked at Monty.

"Is there anything I can do?" Regina asked.

Oliver smiled. "There is one more thing you can do to help."

"What do you have in mind?"

Oliver pointed at Monty "I recommend Paul make you a co-signer on his bank account. We can call you in the event we need to do a more complex transaction than simply using the credit card. I think it would be best to disappear for awhile.

Regina looked surprised. "How do you know I won't take off with the money?"

"Somehow, you just don't strike me as the dishonorable female gold digger type. As a matter of fact, your willingness to help two virtual strangers who run the risk of getting you into trouble, leads me to believe you are a trustworthy and kind person." He paused and smiled. "I think it was a blessing to have met you. You're not bad on the eyes, either."

Regina blushed.

"Well what do you say? Would you be willing to help us manage the money? I don't think it would place you in danger. Paul and I need someone we can trust."

Regina glanced at Paul. "I would be glad to help. But, if it's Paul's money, he must have the final say."

Monty seemed pre-occupied. He hesitated for a moment, then said "Oh yeah, that's fine, whatever you think." He rubbed his forehead.

Oliver noticed the bags under Monty's eyes. "Are you OK?"

"I have a headache, feel like I could sleep for a week."

Oliver looked at his watch. "It's been a long day. We can take care of business tomorrow then head out of town. Regina, can you meet Paul at Cup-a-Hoot at noon and take care of signing the proper forms?"

She nodded. "I can do that. It shouldn't take long."

"In the meantime, Paul and I will stay at a motel. We'll grab some fast food on the way." Oliver took a deep breath and let it out slowly. "I need to call Pastor Bob. I will have to tell him I've had a family emergency and I'll be out of town for a while. The less he knows, the safer he'll be."

Regina looked at Monty. "That sounds like a plan. See you at noon." She glanced at Oliver and gave him a smile as she got up to leave the table. "Stay safe, boys."

28

Cover Story

Oliver and Monty checked into a motel after stopping for some fast food. Once they were settled, Oliver called Pastor Bob.

"Hi Bob. It's Oliver."

Pastor Bob wondered why Oliver did not arrive at the rectory after visiting Dr. Sinclair. He did not yet suspect foul play and was eager to hear how it went with the good doctor. "Oliver, where have you been? Did you meet with Dr. Sinclair?"

"Yes, I sure did. I met with him a few hours ago." Oliver was careful to keep his normal tone so that he would not arouse Pastor Bob's suspicion.

"Well, how did it go? What did he say?" asked Bob.

Oliver could hear the concern in Pastor Bob's voice, hoping he not made matters worse. "The doctor has quite an office. He showed me some of his work. It was not what I expected. I spent an hour or so and then it was time to leave. That's about all I can say." Oliver carefully left out information that might be hazardous to Pastor Bob's health.

"Did you put him at ease about what happened the other day? He seemed nervous about being associated with any kind of scandal."

"Bob, he did not look nervous to me. By the time I left his office, I guess you can say that he felt perfectly in control."

"Good, I am happy to hear that, Oliver. I'm glad you responded to his request to meet."

"Yes, well, Bob, not to change the subject, but something has come up. I have to deal with a family emergency and I'm not at liberty to get into details. Suffice it to say I have to take a short leave of absence to sort this out. I will be leaving in the morning."

Pastor Bob was alarmed at this unexpected news. "Is there anything I can do?"

"Thanks, Bob. No, unfortunately, it's something that's been brewing for a long time. I just was not aware of it. I hope it's not too much inconvenience for the parish if I'm away for awhile."

Pastor Bob was happy to have Oliver away from St. Ignatius while he found a suitable parish for him. "We'll manage. Take care of your family business. How long do you think you will be gone?"

"I honestly don't know. I'm hoping it sorts itself out before too long. Oh, and the next time you see Dr. Sinclair, please tell him I understand his situation more clearly after our talk and thank him for his time."

"I sure will, Oliver. Keep me posted, and if there is anything I can do, please let me know."

Oliver knew that further communication with Pastor Bob would endanger the parish. He would continue to serve God, but wasn't quite sure what that meant at this point. While having demon vision would seem to be useful, thus far it had managed to get him kicked out of every parish he ever served, and most recently, almost killed.

That night Oliver sat in his motel room pondering what the future might hold. He had no clue. He knelt down and prayed. "Here I am Lord. Guide your servant and fill me with the Holy Spirit so I may have the wisdom and strength to do your will."

29

Bank Business

Next morning Monty and Oliver sat in the motel dining room enjoying their free continental breakfast. Monty ate a bagel with cream cheese. Oliver had cereal and a muffin.

Oliver finished the last of his muffin, wiped his mouth and looked up at Monty. "I think we should head to Mexico."

"Why Mexico?"

"It's warm. There are great beaches. Besides, there's a monastery in a little town just north of Durango where we might be able to stay for a while. Fr. Antonio is a good friend. He runs the monastery, and I think he would allow us to stay a while. We can't stay here trying to dodge these people until we're caught and killed. We might take out a few of their chiefs so their taste for hunting us turns sour. Unfortunately, I don't think they'll stop coming after us until we are dead. There's no telling how extensive the Council 666's influence is in the states. We need to get off the US grid. After you and Regina are done with the banking business, you and I will hit the road. The sooner we leave town, the better."

Monty finished his bagel and orange juice. He began writing a few items on a napkin. "I think we should pick up a few things before you drop me off to meet Regina. That way we can head out right after we're done at the bank. And here, hang on to this." Monty handed the Black Lamia to Oliver. "I don't want to risk being spotted with it while I'm at the bank."

Oliver took the weapon. "Good idea."

Monty reached into his pocket. "Oh, and I almost forgot to show you this."

Oliver looked at the little black book in Monty's hand. "What that?"

"I think it's my contact list of the 666 nasties. The witch entrusted it to me at the Council meeting. Here take a look."

Oliver flipped through the pages. "I suspect this might be more valuable than the blade. They definitely don't want it to be in your hands, now that you're a defector." He returned it to Monty. "You'd better keep that safe."

After breakfast they headed out to pick up the items on Monty's list, before heading to downtown Raleigh. Oliver dropped Monty off at the coffee shop. They would rendezvous back there at 2:00 pm. That would give Monty and Regina plenty of time to visit the bank. In the meantime, Oliver would visit the rectory and get a few of his personal belongings, including his jar of jellybeans. Pastor Bob would be at his weekly lunch meeting with the Bishop, so Oliver was grateful he would not bump into him.

<center>~~~</center>

Regina walked into Cup-a-Hoot at exactly noon. She joined Monty at the counter and ordered a cup to go. "You ready to do this?" She got up from the stool with her coffee in hand.

"I guess so. I feel kind of funny impersonating myself."

"What do you mean?"

Monty got off the stool. "Oh, nothing, I guess this whole thing seems like a dream to me. Correction, nightmare," he replied as they exited the coffee shop.

A short walk later, they entered the lobby of Raleigh Trust Bank. It had been recently acquired by a larger bank. Signs were being changed in the interior of the bank first. The outdoor sign still read "Raleigh Trust Bank." The new interior signs read "Council 666 Bank."

Regina noticed that Monty seemed stiff and nervous after they entered the bank. "What's the matter?" She asked in a discreet low voice.

"I think I'm just a little nervous about the future, but I'm OK. Let's do this and get out of here."

They approached Mr. Prescott, one of the personal bankers. He looked at them over his bifocals. "Hello, how may I help you?" He was a rather large man in his fifties with multiple chins. His white shirt wanted to explode off his chest. Regina approached with caution. She imagined one of those buttons popping lose and taking out somebody's eye. His tie was loosened and yet the man still looked uncomfortable.

Monty took out Paul Herodias' bank card and prepared to hand it to Mr. Prescott. "I need to have a cashier's check for the full amount of my bank balance made out to Regina O'Neil. I realize this will close my account."

Regina tried not to show her surprise as he said this. She understood that she would be made a co-signer on the account. Now, all of a sudden the plans seemed to have changed. She glanced at Monty without letting Mr. Prescott see her surprise.

"Oh my, I see." Mr. Prescott took the bank card. "And, how much is in your account?" He typed away on this computer to access the account.

"Right around $250,000" replied Monty.

Mr. Prescott did not respond. He typed away and looked at the information on his screen. "Your account balance is $247,890.19." He looked over his bifocals at Monty then at Regina. "And, may I ask why you are withdrawing your entire balance, Mr. Herodias?"

Monty paused and looked at Regina then back at Mr. Prescott, "Yes, I'm purchasing a piece of real estate from her and I promised to pay cash. We settled on $250,000 as the sales price, and she will hold a note for the remaining balance. I need to close today."

"I see. Who is your closing attorney?"

Monty thought for a moment. He could not think of an attorney's name. He should have one at the tip of his tongue. There was an entire legal department at McPride Industries.

"Jameson and Vanderbilt." Regina impatiently looked at her watch.

Monty was relieved at Regina's quick thinking. He looked at Mr. Prescott and smiled. "I'll transfer some funds from one of my other accounts to replenish this account as soon as I can. This opportunity came up rather suddenly, and this was the only way I could close the deal." Monty paused then continued "As a matter of fact, rather than closing the entire account, why don't we leave $5,000 in it so that I don't have to re-open it again. That's if you will agree to carry the balance on the note," he said as he turned to Regina.

Regina paused for a moment and then reluctantly said "All right, we'll have to alter the total of my note on the closing documents."

Mr. Prescott handed Monty a piece of paper and a pen. "Please write down the recipient's name exactly as you want it to appear."

Monty slid the paper and pen over to Regina. "You fill it out. That way we can avoid me misspelling your name."

Mr. Prescott looked somewhat surprised. "I thought you said that Jameson and Vanderbilt were your closing attorneys. Typically we make the cashier's check out to them, and they put it into an escrow account."

"That won't be necessary in this case. It needs to be made out to me. I am paying attorney's fees and closing costs separately. Since there is no bank loan involved, they advised me to do it this way. They will hold the cashier's check until the title is transferred to Mr. Herodias."

"Very well." Mr. Prescott got up from his desk. "But I will need the bank manager's approval." He walked across the lobby to a corner office on the other side.

Monty and Regina looked at each other. "Thanks. I couldn't think of a lawyer's name. I'm sure glad you were able to come up with one."

"I gave him the name of the firm I use for my hair salon business. I do the wife's hair. If he checks, he will find that they are a real firm. I wasn't expecting this whole real estate transaction story. I thought you were going to add me as a co-signer. What happened?"

"I can't go into it now, but once we entered the bank, I thought it would be best if you deposited the money in another bank, any bank that is not associated with Council 666 Bank would be fine."

"Why is that?"

Monty looked around at the bank tellers. "Let's just say I

don't like their management style, and the way they do things."

They saw Mr. Prescott talking with a man dressed in a pinstripe suit that appeared to be the bank manager. He was nodding his head up and down, and he glanced over to where Monty and Regina sat.

Mr. Prescott made his way back. At three hundred and fifty pounds, he waddled over to the desk. "Mr. Herodias, will you come with me please?"

"Why, is there a problem?"

"No, sir, it's our policy. The bank manager has a couple of items he needs you to address before he can release the funds." Monty looked at Regina then he stood up and followed Mr. Prescott to the bank manager's office.

Once inside, Mr. Prescott introduced Monty to the bank manager. "Mr. Rowland, this is Mr. Herodias. He would like to withdraw the funds in his account minus $5000." Then Mr. Prescott left the office and closed the door behind him.

"Please sit down Mr. Herodias." Mr. Rowland took his seat behind his desk.

Monty reluctantly sat down. "Is there a problem with my account?"

"No, your account is fine. But I must ask, are you withdrawing these funds of your own free will? Is anyone coercing you to withdraw this money?"

Monty shrugged. "No, I want to buy her property, and this is the only way I can do it. She is not coercing me to do anything."

"Mr. Herodias, are you absolutely sure? Once you walk out of here with that woman and a certified check made out to her, there is nothing we can do should she decide to disappear with your money." Mr. Rowland got up from his chair and went over to the side of the office that faced the bank lobby. He signaled to Monty to get up and join him at the window.

Mr. Rowland pointed at Regina. "Is that the woman to whom you are going to make the check payable?"

Monty glanced out the office window, "Yes, that's her."

"She is on the phone, Mr. Herodias. Do you know with whom she is speaking?"

Monty turned to face Mr. Rowland. "How would I know that?"

Mr. Rowland walked back to his desk and sat down. "On your way to wherever it is that you are going, you could easily be accosted, and you would never see her or your money again. You understand that I have to point this out to you for your own protection, don't you, Mr. Herodias? Do you still want to continue with this transaction?"

Monty sat down and politely smiled. "Yes, I would like to continue with the transaction. I can understand why you are so cautious under the circumstances. It is a large transaction, and you are only doing your job. I do appreciate that, but I am not being hustled or set up, Mr. Rowland."

"Very well, Mr. Herodias, I will need to call the attorney to confirm the transaction and then I will be happy to release the funds."

Monty sat for a moment not sure what to do. This thing was about to blow up in his face. "I don't have their number."

Just then, there was a knock on Mr. Rowland's door. The door opened, and Regina let herself in. "Sorry to interrupt, gentlemen, but I do need to get going. Is there a problem Mr. Herodias?" She was polite but firm.

"I was just telling Mr. Herodias that I will be happy to release the funds as soon as I contact the attorney to confirm your transaction. Mr. Herodias does not seem to have the telephone number."

Regina approached Mr. Rowland's desk. "I'll be happy to give it to you."

Monty was amazed at the woman's ability to think on her feet.

Mr. Rowland dialed as she said the numbers. He put the call on speakerphone and sat back in his chair.

Two rings later there was an answer. "Jameson and Vanderbilt, how may I help you?"

"Hello, this is Mr. Rowland and Raleigh Trust Bank. May I speak with…" He paused and looked at Regina and asked "Who is handling the transaction?"

"Mr. Vanderbilt," she replied.

Mr. Rowland spoke into the speaker phone. "Mr. Vanderbilt, please."

"One moment, please."

A moment later a man came on the line. "Yes, this is Mr. Vanderbilt, how can I help you."

"This is Mr. Rowland at Raleigh Trust Bank. I'm here with a Ms Regina O'Neil and a Mr. Paul Herodias."

"Hi Will, it's Regina. Mr. Rowland needs to confirm a few things before he will allow Mr. Herodias to withdraw the funds and make a check payable to me."

"Yes, Mr. Rowland, Ms. O'Neill is a client of mine. I have worked with her since she started her business."

"Mr. Herodias is requesting to withdraw $247,000 in the form of a cashier's check made out to Ms. O'Neill," said Mr. Rowland. "Is this correct?"

"Is that the amount you both agreed upon?" asked the voice on speakerphone.

"Yes," replied Regina.

"Yes, that is right Mr. Rowland. Is there anything else?"

"No, I just wanted to confirm this large sum withdrawal."

"Certainly, Mr. Rowland, I agree," replied the attorney.

Mr. Rowland looked up at Regina and Monty. "OK, Thank you, Mr. Vanderbilt."

"You're welcome. Thank you." Click.

"Well folks, I won't keep you any longer. Please wait here and I will go make this out." Mr. Rowland opened the door and headed toward one of the tellers.

Monty simply looked at Regina in amazement.

She smiled and winked. "Never underestimate the power of a hairdresser."

A few moments later Mr. Rowland returned with cashier's check in hand. "Please make sure everything is correct on the check before you leave."

Monty looked it over and nodded. "Yes, this looks right, thank you."

Monty and Regina shook Mr. Rowland's hand and made their way out of the bank, attempting to stroll leisurely through the lobby.

Once outside Monty turned to Regina. "We should deposit this money now. Where do you bank?"

"I bank at Southern Central Credit Union. It's down the street, past the McPride Industries building before you get to the courthouse."

Monty pointed to the large clock in one of the office windows. "It's almost 1:15. We should have plenty of time to make the deposit and meet Oliver at 2:00." They headed South on Fayetteville Street in the direction of the credit union.

"So, have you and Oliver decided where you will go?"

"We're headed to Mexico."

Regina smiled. "Well, I'm a bit jealous. Sounds like you boys are going to have a little vacation."

"I don't know about that. I wish it was a vacation and I could lead a normal life." Monty was deep in thought as they walked past the McPride Industries building where, not too long ago, he sat in his father's office, scheming to take over the company, and after that, head to Hollywood and become a movie star. At the time, he was sure the studios would be fighting over the handsome new star. As he thought about his past life, he shook his head. *"How could I have been such a fool? I had it all; money, a fancy job I didn't deserve, and a father who was trying to make up for something not his fault. And, I milked it. Boy, did I milk it for all it was worth. My life has turned out to be a joke. Now I'm in another man's body. Although, I'm free of the evil engulfing my whole life, I can't help feeling disgusted by who I was. I hurt so many, not the least of whom was my poor mother."* Monty was torn from his reverie by a yank on his arm.

Regina had been talking to him.

"Earth to Paul." He finally looked up. "We're here. Are you all right? You were zoned out."

Monty looked up. "Sorry."

They entered the credit union and set up a new account on which both were authorized signers. The clerk recognized Regina from her frequent visits. Within fifteen minutes of entering the credit union they were on their way back to the coffee shop. As they headed north on Fayetteville Street, they passed the McPride Industries building once again. Monty stopped and thought for a moment.

Regina also stopped. "What's the matter?"

Monty glanced at the building's entrance, then back at Regina. "You go on ahead. I just need to run in here for a minute to see someone one last time. I'll catch up with you and Oliver in a few minutes."

Regina was not sure what Monty was up to, but she needed to get back to the salon. "Are you sure?"

"Yeah, I really want to see him before I go."

"Who?"

Monty paused and replied, "My father." He turned and walked into the lobby of McPride Industries.

Regina watched Monty enter the building, then headed for the coffee shop. Two minutes later she arrived at Cup a Hoot.

Oliver was already there. He spied her from their table in the back and stood up to greet her. "Where's Paul?"

She sat down. "He'll be here is a few minutes. He's at McPride Industries just down the street. He said he needed to see his father one last time before you both head to Mexico."

"How did it go at the bank?"

"Withdrawing the money was a bit tricky, but I called in a favor with one of my clients. He vouched for the story we told the banker about Paul wanting to buy my property. Making the deposit at my credit union was no problem."

Oliver stood up. "Can I get you a cup of coffee?"

"Sure, then you can tell me all about what you boys plan to do while you're in Mexico. I'm a little jealous not to be going."

30

Saying Goodbye

As Monty entered the lobby of McPride Industries, he was overcome by the familiar chatter and the people, all of whom he recognized. Yet, none recognized him. "They all must have heard of my untimely demise while trying to outrun the police. What I wouldn't give to have my old life back without the hatred and evil which kept me prisoner. If only I had found Jesus then. Better late than never, I guess." Then he laughed to himself. *"You can't get any later than being dead."*

As Monty made his way through the lobby, he noticed the Latino janitor mopping a corner of the lobby floor. Monty recognized the man, to whom, in his previous life, he had spoken to in a loud, condescending manner. *"I was a bigot. I hated this man for no reason."*

The janitor did not notice the stranger approaching. He was pre-occupied with doing his work. By the looks of it, he was engrossed in his mopping and didn't seem to mind doing it. He pushed the mop, but it was more than pushing. He wanted to do a good job, even in an inconsequential corner of the lobby. His world was making the floor clean.

The man looked up to see Monty standing there watching him. He gave him a polite smile and continued mopping.

Monty returned the smile. "Excuse me, sir."

The janitor stopped his mopping and looked at Monty. There was no animosity. His full attention was upon the stranger.

"Yes, sir?" The man had a strong Latino accent.

Monty was unsure what to say to the man. He had seen this person countless times in his previous existence, but not as a person. This man he had perceived as an inferior species, one to be despised and mistreated. The thought, now disgusted Monty. "Um, Oh, I just wanted to tell you that you are doing a good job here." Monty paused for a moment. "I've been in and out of this building many times. Occasionally, I see you mopping the floor. It's as though there is nothing more important to you than making sure each section is equally clean." Monty looked at the man's name badge. "Pedro? Is that correct?"

"Yes, sir. I like doing good job" Pedro smiled and patiently waited for the stranger's response.

Monty extended his hand to shake Pedro's hand. Pedro quickly extended his hand and shook Monty's. "It's nice to meet you, Pedro. My name is Paul."

Pedro nodded "Nice to meet you, Señor Paul, I am Pedro."

Monty stood there for a moment looking at the brown skinned Latino man who seemed perfectly happy mopping floors. He realized he had probably taken enough of Pedro's time. "Well, Pedro, keep up the nice work. The floors look beautiful."

Pedro smiled "Thank you, Señor Paul." He gave a little bow of the head and waited for Monty to turn to leave before he resumed his mopping.

Monty hesitated for a moment. Not quite sure of how to say something else that was on his mind. Pedro stood patiently wondering what else Señor Paul wanted. The coming and going in the lobby at McPride Industries continued as on any other day. No one seemed to notice the janitor and the other man standing at the corner of the lobby, facing each other in complete silence as the world continued to buzz around them.

Monty vividly recalled the last time he encountered Pedro. It was in his other life as acting CEO of McPride Industries. He ordered Pedro to clean the bathroom and treated him like scum. It was the way Monty typically behaved before his death. He took great pleasure in putting down a low life like Pedro. Monty's recollection of his hateful behavior gave rise to a lump in his throat. His eyes became red and watery. *How could I have been such a person? I'm embarrassed simply thinking about it. How much happier might my life had been if only..."*

Pedro noticed the change in the man's demeanor whom he had just met. "Are you OK, Señor Paul?"

Monty's eyes met Pedro's. "Pedro, I just wanted to say that I am very sorry for what that man said to you the other day when he ordered you to clean the bathroom. I was here, and I heard every miserable word he shouted at you. Can you forgive me, I mean, would you forgive that man, Pedro? Could you forgive him if he asked?

"Oh, Señor Paul, that man, Mr. Monty, died."

"Yes, I know Pedro, but can you forgive him? Would you forgive him, please?"

Pedro seemed a little puzzled at Monty's question and sensed a kind of desperate urgency in it. However, he smiled and gave a dismissive wave of the hand. "No problem, for me. I OK to forgive him, si'." Pedro lowered his head. "He not OK with God, I think. I hope he OK with God now."

Monty lowered his head and wiped his eyes. "Thank you, Pedro. It is probably too late for Mr. Monty, but thank you."

Pedro watched his strange new friend walk away. A moment later, he began mopping the floor where he had left off and Monty stepped into the elevator.

When the elevator doors opened again, Monty stepped onto the floor where the CEO's office was located. He proceeded to the reception area where several administrative assistants were busy at their workstations. He approached one of them in particular. She was a young black woman. The nameplate on her desk identified her as "Latisha Jones."

Monty slowed as he got near the woman's desk. He thought of his last encounter with this bright young woman whom he had labeled, in his previous life, as a no good nigger. He noticed himself trembling as he came nearer her desk. *"This is not a good idea."* He began to have second thoughts about coming this far.

"Hello, sir, how may I help you?" It was a familiar voice.

Monty stopped and forced a smile. His mind was again vividly replaying video of his contemptuous behavior toward another human being. In this case, he had taken pleasure in spitting into her coffee when she wasn't looking. It was his little game. He would ask her for a file or something to distract her. Then, while her attention was focused elsewhere, he would do his deed and place the coffee cup back where she had left it. It made him sick to think of how he enjoyed this outrageous perversion. *"God, I hate myself. What on earth was I thinking? How could I be so disgusting and cruel? I wasted a lifetime hurting people."*

She observed the stranger who seemed lost and repeated her greeting. "Sir, may I help you?"

Monty snapped out of his self-hating and stood in front of her workstation. His forehead was moist with perspiration. His eye twitched. He hoped it wasn't noticeable. His voice quivered. "Um, yes, Ms. Jones, I was here when a man knocked over your coffee cup by accident, which was really not an accident. You see, there was something gross in it and he did not want you to drink it."

Latisha's eyes widened and she got up from her workstation. "Was that you? Were you the man who called to warn me not to drink the coffee, and about that sadistic bigot, Monty?"

"No, but I was here when it happened. I just wanted to say I am very sorry it happened to you. That was a despicable thing to do."

"Well, thank you. That's very nice of you to say, but you don't need to be sorry. It was that sorry ass, Monty McPride, that should be sorry. But he was killed trying to escape from the police. So, I guess he got what he deserved."

Monty wiped his forehead with his hand. His throat was dry. His voice still wavered a bit. "Yes, I'm afraid he did. But, would you forgive him if he asked?"

Latisha snickered after thinking about it for a moment. She shook her head. "Why are you asking? Are you some kind of preacher? Or did you just find Jesus or something?"

Monty smiled at the thought of him being a preacher, a square peg in a round hole, indeed. "No, I'm not a preacher but, as a matter of fact, I did just recently find Jesus, or maybe He found me and knocked me on my ass to get me to listen. Either way, He's got my full attention."

"So, why are you asking me to forgive that creep? He's dead, and I think just about everyone in this building, including me, is glad." Her expression soured as she recalled her encounter with Monty McPride.

"You could say I knew him pretty well. I feel responsible. I should have done more to help him change his behavior. Your forgiving him would also, in a way, be forgiving me. And I could use a little forgiveness right about now." Monty knew he sounded a little crazy. He felt her gaze upon him. She was probably wondering whether or not he was loony.

Latisha thought for a moment. "If he asked, I guess I could forgive him. But he can't ask because he's dead. Besides, you shouldn't feel responsible for somebody else's actions. What he did was not your fault, no matter how well you knew him."

"Of course, you're right, Ms. Jones. I guess that's why I'm asking. He can't ask. He's dead, but I feel I should ask for him, although, it probably will make no difference at this point. Just the same, I feel I need to ask on his behalf. It's something I can't really explain." Monty paused for a moment. "Please Ms. Jones, would you forgive him for what he did to you?"

Latisha looked intently at the strange man asking for her forgiveness on behalf of a dead man. She was about to say something then hesitated. Monty did not say another word and hoped she would not call security and have him thrown out. She raised her left eyebrow and looked straight at him. "Sure, OK, if it's that important to you, I forgive him."

Monty was surprised after thinking he might be removed from the premises. "Really?"

"Yes, Mr....? What's your name?"

"Paul is my name. Paul Herodias."

Latisha's forehead wrinkled. "You mean like Herodias from the bible, the woman who had her daughter ask for the head of John the Baptist on a platter?" She smiled.

Monty did not understand. He had never heard of John the Baptist. "What's funny about that?"

"You asked forgiveness for someone whose head many people would like to have seen on a platter and your first name is Paul, the apostle who started out hating Christians and then turned out to be one of the most fervent disciples. I don't know if it's ironic or paradoxical, or perhaps a little bit of both. Either way it's an unusual last name." She paused to look at the clock hanging on the wall. "So, Mr. Herodias, now that we've gotten that out of the way, are you here to see someone?"

"Yes, I came to see. Mr. McPride. I was on my way to see

Peggy, and noticed you."

She pointed to her left. "I take it you know where Peggy's desk is located?"

Monty nodded and started walking in the direction of Peggy Simmons. "Thank you, Ms. Jones."

As Monty walked toward the CEO's office, he contemplated the fact that he might never see his father again. Heading to Mexico this afternoon and who knows where after that, the future loomed with uncertainty. Even if he had to do it as Paul Herodias, Monty wanted to see his father one last time. He recognized Peggy as he came to the section of the hall with her workstation set in its large alcove. *"Not too long ago she was my personal secretary as I wreaked havoc on the company. What an idiot I was."* He approached the desk. "Hello, Peggy."

She looked up from her computer screen at the stranger who called her by her first name. "Do I know you, sir?"

Monty reached the alcove and stood in front of her desk. He smiled. "No, I don't believe we have formally met."

"How do you know my name? She asked.

"Your nameplate." Monty pointed to her desktop, but there was no nameplate on her desk.

She turned and reached into the back of her credenza to examine the nameplate then looked up at him. "You mean this? You could read this from way over there?" She nodded in the direction from where he had come.

"I have pretty good eyesight."

"How can I help you, sir?"

"I came to check on Mr. McPride. I was at the hospital when he came for his son's body. I was the medical examiner on duty when the body arrived. We spoke briefly. I know it was difficult for him." Monty paused and looked in the direction of the CEO's office. "I'm heading out of town and thought I would check on him before I left. I don't have an appointment, but I was hoping I could say goodbye personally."

Peggy nodded. "I'll see if he is available. What is your name?"

"Paul Herodias."

"Have a seat Mr. Herodias and I'll check." Peggy dialed the CEO's extension.

Monty took a seat and looked around at the familiar surroundings. He noticed the art on the wall next to Peggy's desk. He had been in this building enough times, he should remember every detail. Yet, he didn't recall ever stopping to look at the art hanging throughout the building. This particular picture was an abstract. The interweaving lines of gold and purple seemed to dance on the canvas. The lines could be hair with other shapes and colors coming together in the form of a woman's face. He continued to analyze the painting. The more he looked, the more he could see a face emerging on the canvas. Monty's eyes were transfixed on the picture as he saw his mother's face appear in the painting. His eyes bulged. He blinked, then, it was just the lines and colors forming an abstract of a face.

"Mr. McPride will be with you in a moment, Mr. Herodias"

"OK, thanks." Monty's voice was low. He continued staring at the painting. He sat back and took a deep breath. His heart was pounding as the face in the painting brought on an adrenaline rush. *"How could this be? Now, I'm hallucinating."* He tried to gain his composure by looking around the alcove and down the hallway. He distracted himself from the painting by observing the courier approaching from the elevator. As he drew nearer, Monty's nervousness dissipated. The guy reminded him of Groucho Marx. He tried not to stare.

Just then the CEO's office door opened. Blake McPride approached Peggy's Desk. Monty began to rise from his chair, not sure of what he would say. His knees felt weak, and his throat was dry again. His hands started to sweat. He wiped them on his pants before standing up. Monty walked over to his father.

Blake recognized Paul from the hospital. "Hello, Mr. Herodias. What happened to your shoulder?"

"Hello, Mr. McPride. Just a minor accident." Monty shook his father's hand wishing that he could hug him instead.

The courier arrived at Peggy's desk. "I have a package for Mr. McPride."

She smiled "Thank you. Where do I need to …?"

The courier looked at the two men. "McPride?"

Blake looked up, a bit surprised at hearing his surname called out.

The top of the courier's package slid off revealing a gun.

Groucho took aim at Blake. His intent was clear. Monty's adrenaline kicked into high gear. Everything slowed to a crawl. Monty could see the fake bushy eyebrows and mustache beginning to detach from the madman's face. He might have noticed the gunman's disguise earlier but did not look too close. Underneath the disguise was a man with whom he dealt during his short stint as acting CEO of McPride Industries. It had to do with creating one of the most addictive drugs ever manufactured. The plan was foiled when Monty met an untimely death and his accomplice, Fred Wilkins, was arrested for a series of crimes as Monty's right hand man. The drug lords no longer had a connection into McPride Industries. No doubt, this was intended to be a revenge killing. Monty had not given much thought to the promises he made about a new wonder drug to be manufactured under the code name of BD109. Someone would pay for not delivering the goods. Blake McPride would do just fine.

Monty watched as the killer squeezed the trigger. Three muffled shots discharged in rapid succession. Monty moved the instant his brain registered what was happening. He stepped in front of Blake McPride, the man who, not too long ago, he tried to kill. He felt the first slug hit his left shoulder. The second slug tore into his chest. The third one ripped through his abdomen.

Peggy screamed.

Groucho ran to the exit stairway.

Monty stumbled backward and fell to one knee as he clenched his shoulder. Then he dropped to both knees as he placed his right hand over his chest. Finally, he collapsed onto the floor. He didn't feel any pain, only the energy being drained from his legs and his upper body.

"Call 911, Peggy!" Blake leaned over and looked into the dying man's eyes. "Mr. Herodias, thank you for saving my life. You protected me from that lunatic gunman. I don't know how to thank you. We've called for a medic. Please! You've got to hang on."

The dying man gasped for breath. His eyes were red. Tears ran down the sides of his face. A slow but steady numbness was taking over his body. He turned his head and looked up at Blake McPride. He spoke, but his words were inaudible. Blake moved closer and lifted the man's head to make him more comfortable.

Again, the dying man looked into Blake's eyes. He spoke. This time his voice was audible, but just barely.

"Father, I'm sorry."

Blake thought it was not unusual for someone who had been shot to go into shock and hallucinate. He remembered Paul Herodias said he reminded him of his own father. No doubt, he was hallucinating after being shot. Blake said nothing, simply held the bleeding man in his arms.

Again, Paul struggled to speak. Blake listened to the faint voice. "Father, I'm sorry for what I did to you. You were right. I was a fool." Blake applied pressure to the chest wound while holding the man's head up. "I'm sorry for being so cruel to you and for what I did to mother. I'm sorry I ran from the police at the nursing home and for trying to steal BD109."

Blake's eyes widened. "Monty?" He looked closely into the eyes of Paul Herodias. "How can this be?" Tears pooled in Blake's eyes. He wondered if *he* might be hallucinating.

Monty gasped and fought to maintain eye contact with his father. With his last bit of strength, he continued. "You and mother on the cruise - the old woman you met…" He coughed and gasped. "She's evil. I should have fought. I could have…" He coughed up blood. His eyes were losing their focus. He continued. "I blew up the kitchen killing mother. I was evil. I didn't know…" Tears ran freely from the face of both men. "Thank Oliver for me. Forgive me father…." Monty lay in a pool of blood. Blake continued holding the dying son he never knew. Blake could feel the life draining out the wounded body. With a last gasp, Monty clenched Blake's arm. With eyes opened wide, he looked into his father's eyes. It was an intensity that startled Blake. "Find Him. Find Jesus. Father I lov…." Monty closed his eyes and died a second time.

Blake McPride cried as he held the dead man in his arms. He had lost his son for the second time in less than two weeks, this time, the result of successful rescue rather than an attempted murder.

31

Groucho Delivers

Oliver sat in the coffee shop anxiously waiting for Monty to arrive. It was almost 2:45 pm and Regina had since returned to the hair salon to take care of her customers. With each passing moment, Oliver became more worried. Noticing a commotion in the street, he stepped out of the coffee shop and onto Fayetteville Street. Several people were pointing to the south end.

Oliver caught sight of a man walking rapidly, looking from side to side. He had a demonic face. The man was dressed in a brown uniform like that of the package delivery service. As he passed one of the city trash containers, he deposited a brown paper bag into it without breaking his stride.

Oliver approached a young man wearing a Wolfpack shirt who was talking with his friends. "What's going on?"

"Somebody's been shot at McPride Industries." He pointed in the direction of the building.

A sinking feeling came over Oliver. He started to walk toward McPride Industries hoping that Monty was not involved. His gut told him otherwise, but he dismissed it as pessimistic thinking. His walk quickened turning into a jog. He reached the McPride Building just as the police cars were arriving. He ran into the lobby and approached the lady behind the information counter.

"I'm a priest. Where is the shooting victim?"

The young woman pointed to the elevator. "Third floor,

CEO's office."

Oliver ran toward the elevator then decided to take the stairs. He ran up the three flights with an increased sense of dread, making it up to the third floor in no time. He approached the crowd surrounding the victim. "I'm a priest. Please let me through."

Oliver's worst fear could not be denied. His heart sank as he saw Paul Herodias' dead body lying in a pool of blood. Blake McPride was still holding the dead man in his arms. Oliver's mind raced, but he kept his cool. He knelt before the body and looked at Blake. "I'm Father Oliver." He felt for a pulse.

Blake's eyes met Oliver's. "He's dead."

Oliver bowed his head and made the sign of the cross on Monty's forehead. He placed his hand on the dead man's head and gave him his last rites.

Blake remained silent until the priest concluded praying. "You said your name is Oliver?"

Oliver nodded. "Yes"

"You knew him?" The paramedics and the police finally arrived at the building.

"Yes, I met him recently."

"Before he died, he asked me to thank Oliver for him. Are you that Oliver?"

"Yes, I am that Oliver. Did he say anything else?"

"He said he was sorry for everything he did. He said things that could only have been known to my son, Monty, who died recently." Blake took a deep breath and wiped his tears. "What do you know, Father Oliver? Was this man really my son? How is that possible?"

As the police and the paramedics approached, Oliver placed his hand on Blake McPride's arm. "You must not speak of this to anyone, not even the police. Doing so will place you in great danger and will get you killed." Oliver reached into Monty's pocket and withdrew the little black book. "This will certainly get you killed." He looked into Blake's bloodshot eyes. "We will probably never see each other again, but I assure you, what you suspect is true. And, if it's any consolation to you, Monty found Christ before dying a second time. I baptized him myself. Perhaps you should seek Christ yourself, Mr. McPride. I'm sure it would help you." Oliver removed his hand from Blake's arm. "It would also be wise to forget my name and forget the little black book. Now I must go."

Two paramedics rolled a gurney into the area. Carl and Jake looked at each other. They did not expect the victim to be their colleague. They hurried to his side.

"Is it really Paul?" asked Jake as Carl felt the body for a pulse.

"I'm afraid so," replied Carl.

Oliver stepped into the back of the crowd, made his way down the stairs. He exited the building and walked back toward the coffee shop. He could not stay in the area longer for fear someone from the Council might spot him. He walked up to the trash container where he saw the courier drop something. The brown bag was there. He carefully lifted it out of the container. It was rather heavy. He peeked inside the bag and saw a large caliber handgun, which he assumed was the murder weapon. He took the bag, made his way to his vehicle, got in and drove toward Mexico.

32

Just Two?

Oliver drove his unassuming vehicle toward the interstate. He pulled into a gas station, filled up, and called Regina to let her know what happened. She answered her phone on the first ring.

"I know. He's dead," she said as soon as she answered the phone. "It's all over the news. I'm watching it right now. Where are you?"

"I'm on my way to Mexico. Hanging around would be hazardous to my health."

"Well, I'm sorry to see you go."

"Thanks for all your help, Regina."

"You bet. I'm sorry Paul is dead. He was a little odd but seemed to be a good guy. Call me if you need anything. The money is safe in my account. I can wire it to you wherever you might be."

"OK. Thanks. Stay out of trouble. I'll talk to you as soon as I'm settled in Mexico."

"OK. Drive safe. Bye."

Regina's phone rang as soon as she hung up. She was a little confused. The call was coming from Paul's phone, but he was dead. "Hello?"

"Hello, Regina? This is Inspector Lopez calling. I found this phone on the body of the man who was killed this afternoon. It has only two numbers listed, yours and one for a man named Oliver. I was wondering if you might be able to come down to the station so I can ask you a few questions about the murdered man."

Upon hearing this, Regina knew it would only be a matter of time before Detective Lopez would suspect her in the killing, especially after he discovered that the man who was murdered withdrew a large sum of money and deposited it into her account shortly before he was shot. That also meant the people pursuing Oliver would learn about her involvement with Paul. She might wind up on the same hit-list as Oliver.

She managed to remain calm as she spoke. "I'm seeing it right now, Detective. It's on the news. Did you apprehend the killer?"

"No, I'm afraid not. I was hoping, with your cooperation, we could discover who would want to kill him." Detective Lopez spoke in a casual manner. His tone implied this was nothing more than a courtesy call.

"Very well Detective, I'd be happy to help in any way I can. I just recently met the man. When would you like me to come in?"

"How about this afternoon?"

"Very well, but I have two conditions."

"Oh, and what would they be?" he asked with great interest.

"First, you keep my name out of this. I want to remain completely anonymous. My gut tells me that if you reveal my name to anyone, including some members of the press and your department, I might turn up dead." Regina's tone was serious. She knew if what Oliver told her was correct, she could not trust anyone. Not even this detective. But she had to play along, at least for now.

"That sounds quite serious. Why would you think such a thing?"

"I wouldn't have believed it myself until I saw the news today. I'll explain when I see you."

"Very well. What's your second condition?"

"That we meet in a place other than your police department. I can meet you at the Tri City Mall in the food court at noon tomorrow."

"Why not now, Miss Regina?"

"I can't right now. And don't try to track my phone because

tracking is disengaged." Regina ended the call.

~~~

Oliver's phone rang. He pulled over to answer it. "Hello?"

"Hello, Oliver? This is Detective Lopez..."

Oliver sat in his car after his talk with Detective Lopez. His phone rang again. It was Regina.

"Did you get a call from Detective Lopez?"

"Sure did. Just got off the phone with him. I gave him a partial description of the killer."

"You saw the killer?"

"I'm pretty sure it was him. He was dressed in a brown uniform like a courier delivery man. I saw him deposit a paper bag into a city trash can. When I checked later, I found a gun in the bag. I told the detective that I removed the gun from the trash can and put it in my car for safe keeping. He wasn't too happy about that part. He told me I could be arrested for tampering with evidence. He doesn't know I'm a priest, headed for Mexico. I thought it best to limit our conversation. He's going to be quite upset when I don't show up at the police station with the evidence. You will be seeing him tomorrow. Do you think that's wise?"

"I don't think I have much choice. He's going to track me down eventually. I might just go stay with a friend in Maine until this whole thing blows over."

"I'm coming back. It's gotten too dangerous really fast. I never wanted you to be dragged into this."

"Don't, I'm a big girl. I can take care of myself. Besides, I've got friends in pretty high places. You'd be amazed the people you meet cutting hair."

"I don't doubt it. But I feel responsible for getting you involved. I'd hate anything to happen to you."

"Nothing's going to happen to me. I have a plan. I'm going to visit my lawyer first thing in the morning and have the money deposited into a foreign bank. Then, I'll meet with Detective Lopez, under the condition that my name and face be kept out of this."

"How do you know you can trust Detective Lopez?"

"I'm meeting him at the food court in the mall. That was my second condition for agreeing to meet."
~~~

Oliver didn't like it, but he reluctantly agreed. "OK, but call me after your meeting. If I have to come back to get you, I will."

"I'll call you. Drive safe. Bye."

33

New Lead

Mr. Fredericks examined the footage from the security cameras.

"That's Regina O'Neil. He wanted to buy her house, but she wanted cash," explained Mr. Rowland.

"I see. Well, this certainly is interesting. That will be all Mr. Rowland."

Mr. Harold Fredericks was the new Director of Finance for Council 666's east coast operations. Two weeks earlier, he had created a new identity for the man who was now deceased. He remembered the celebration banquet where Paul Herodias was officially introduced to the Council. *"He had great potential."* Fredericks had personally selected the Charles Dubois identity for the special recruit. The million dollar bank account remained untouched. *"What a fool, he threw it all away, corrupted by that priest."*

Fredericks hit speed dial. He sat back in his chair waiting for his call to be answered.

"What is it?" came the voice over the speaker.

"You might find this interesting. A woman was with the priest. This could prove helpful, not that we need help, but it's simply too convenient to pass up."

"Who is she?" asked the voice on the speaker.

"Regina O'Neill, I'm sure she is involved with the priest. They both were trying to help him. I spoke with Vanderbilt. He was trying to help her since she cuts his hair. It was the first time he had heard about a house deal. Vanderbilt didn't know she was helping your little manflesh."

"We could make them the prime suspects in the murder of Paul Herodias and send out an All Points to the other departments. We should have them by morning."

There was silence on the speaker phone, then the voice said, "I want that priest. I can almost taste it. She will lead us to him." There was a click, then a dial tone.

34

Mama's Calling

Regina awoke from her sleep and immediately tried to scream. She could not. The cold gnarly hand holding her mouth closed was pressing hard against her face. She was barely able to breathe. She tried to get up but was held down by another pair of hands. She struggled to no avail. All she could move were her eyes.

The horrid old woman standing over her looked like something out of a bad fairy tale. Her hideous face came right up to Regina's face. "Hello dear." The old witch sported a smile that revealed missing teeth. Her breath was so noxious it almost rendered Regina unconscious. "Mama Crossbones knows all about your treacherous little friends, you little slut." The old woman laughed and tightened her grip on Regina's face so hard it forced tears to roll down her cheeks. "You didn't think I knew about how you have the hots for that priest? Oh, did I squeeze your pretty face too hard? Well, I certainly don't want to do that. Now you and I are going to have a little chat. When I release you, you may scream. If you do, however, I will feel obliged to give you something else to scream about, so my friend will cut off both your legs. You'll still be able to scream. You'll just be a lot shorter. Got that?"

Regina attempted to nod, but the old woman's grip was too strong. Then the hand came off her face and she dared not move or say anything.

"Good, I can tell you and me are going to get along just

fine." The old witch smiled and motioned to Regina to sit up.

Regina sat up slowly, turned on her night lamp and looked around her bedroom. There were two other men in the room. One had been holding her by the legs. The other held a large sword. "What do you want from me? Who are you people?"

"We're the best of friends as long as you cooperate. I am just a feeble old woman looking for a little justice."

Regina could see the old witch clearly now. She had jet black hair, flaking skin, bad lipstick on paper thin lips, a large welt on the side of her jaw and long bony fingers with neatly painted and polished claws for fingernails. Regina thought it was strange the old woman seemed to have just gotten a manicure. All she was missing was a broom to complete her ensemble. "Justice? What are you talking about?"

The old woman pursed her lips "I want that damned priest! You're going to tell me where he is."

Regina pretended to be surprised. "I don't know where he is."

Mama Crossbones seemed happy by Regina's response. "Well, in that case maybe we can help you remember." The old witch gave a nod to wino butler who held a large blade and seemed delighted at the chance to use it. "Remove her left eye, perhaps she will remember then."

Wino butler approached the edge of the bed. Regina recoiled backward. He reached for her. 'Wait!" she yelled. "I don't know where he is right now; all I know is that he is on his way to Mexico."

"Mexico?"The old woman approached the bed. "He's on a little personal vacation, and he didn't take you with him? Tired of you already?" She laughed out loud at her own unfunny remark.

"It wasn't like that. I tried to help him, that's all." Regina felt powerless. She had always been able to handle anything life threw at her. This was out of her league, but she couldn't afford to lose her wits. She had to focus on escape and not think like a victim. She had to come up with a plan. "I can call him and have him come back."

The old witch looked intently at Regina. "By all means, you do that. Tell him you love him or whatever it is that horny priests want to hear. Just get him back here." Mama Crossbones looked over at wino butler, then back at Regina. "And if you tip him about us, it will be your very last and very painful phone call."

Regina got up from the bed and started to walk toward the bathroom. "OK, but first, I need to use the bathroom."

Regina felt her body being flung violently backward. She crashed onto the bed and slammed into the headboard before she knew what happened. She struggled to gain her composure as she looked into those wretched evil eyes. "Call the priest and don't play games with me."

Regina grabbed her phone off the night table. She thought the call would go to his voice mail.

He answered. "I'm here."

"I need you to come back." She paused. "Yeah, I'm home. I'm kind of lonely, and I know how badly you wanted me. I was playing hard to get. So, I'm giving you a second chance."

He spoke in a low voice. "You're in trouble. How many are there?"

Regina looked at her clock. "Why, it's only three o'clock. Did I wake you?" She did her best to not arouse suspicion from the witch.

"Tell them I am only an hour away. I'm actually closer than you think. Whatever you do don't underestimate the old woman and be ready to duck and roll under your bed. I'll..."

She cut him off. "So you're coming back? Great. I'll be ready and waiting. See you in an hour." Sensing that Mama Crossbones was getting suspicious, she couldn't afford to let the call continue.

"Don't end the call. Leave the line open."

Regina looked at Mama Crossbones as she pretended to end the call. "He'll be here in an hour."

The witch took a seat in Regina's reading chair. "Damned priest will do anything for a piece of flesh. He'll be here in less than an hour, I guarantee it. He's probably drooling at the mouth trying to keep the car on the road. Oh, yes, I knew he had the hots for you."

"May I please use the bathroom? I really have to go." Regina pleaded with the old woman.

Mama Crossbones looked at wino chauffeur. "Go move the car. I don't want that horny priest to know we are here. I want this to be our little surprise." Wino chauffeur nodded and headed out to the car. Then she looked at wino butler. "Go with her to the bathroom. Watch her. If she tries anything, kill her."

Regina slowly got up from the bed and headed toward the bathroom with her escort. She opened the bathroom door and stopped just inside. Wino butler was right behind her preventing her from closing the door. "Do you mind?" She tried again to close the door. She had one hand on the door knob. With the other, she reached into the pouch hanging on the bathroom side of the door.

Wino butler grinned and stood there. He smiled, revealing his rotten teeth. Mama Crossbones started to laugh and seemed to be enjoying the battle for the bathroom. "She said to watch you, so that's what I'm gonna do," he said, as he started to chuckle. He looked at Mama Crossbones who was now roaring with laughter. He let loose a couple of snorts and looked back at Regina as she hit him in the face with two doses of pepper spray and pushed him out of the bathroom. She quickly locked the door.

Wino butler screamed and put his hands to his face. He fell backward. The witch started to get up from the chair. That's when the lights went out. She shoved wino butler out of the way and darted to the bathroom door. The old woman opened the door with very little effort as Regina was climbing out the window. In a flash, Mama Crossbones darted across the bathroom to the window. As Regina landed on the lawn, the old woman reached outside and grabbed Regina's hair just as she was about to run. "No, you don't, you little whore."

Mama Crossbones once again felt the sting of the Black Lamia. This time it cut the upper part of her body, severing her neck and right shoulder from the rest of her body as she leaned out the window. Regina continued running. The witch's hand remained tightly gripped around her hair. The arm was attached to a shoulder and a head. The rest of the witch was frantically running around in the bathroom, bumping into walls.

Regina screamed as she continued to run, "Get it off me! Get it off me, please!" Oliver grabbed Regina's hair and cut it off just above where the witch's hand was gripping it.

The head, shoulder and arm continued to grab at them as they both stepped away. The head dragged itself using the arm to pull itself closer to them. Regina backed away from it again as

Oliver used the Black Lamia to sever the head from the shoulder.

The head stopped moving. The arm continued to grab at the grass and wandered aimlessly. From the head came the witch's voice. "You and your little whore will be mine. I promise you that. You cannot hide. You cannot run. We will find you."

Regina looked at Oliver. Her eyes wide in disbelief. "How can she still be alive?

"I don't know. She seems to be maintained by the power of evil. Come on. Let's get out of here before her two friends come after us." Oliver pointed down the street to where he had parked. He turned and picked up the head by its hair.

Wino chauffeur came around the side of the house with gun drawn. "Stop where you are."He stood a few feet behind them. "Now give me the head."

Oliver froze. With one hand on the Black Lamia's handle, he turned and tossed the head to wino chauffeur. Not expecting to be up close and personal with the witch's head, he fumbled to catch it. The hand holding the gun, immediately felt the sting of Oliver's blade. The hand and gun fell onto the grass as the Black Lamia sliced them clean off.

Regina looked on in amazement. Oliver grabbed the witch's head. She unleashed obscenities at them. He picked up the gun and handed it to Regina. "Take this. I don't want to leave it lying here." He stabbed the witch's arm with the Black Lamia and carried it like an arm kabob. "Let's go before the other one comes after us."

They ran to Oliver's car and looked back to make sure wino butler was not following. Oliver popped the trunk. The old witch was still rambling obscenities. He stuffed a greasy rag into her mouth, and ripped a piece of duct tape to keep her mouth shut. He put the head into one trash bag and the arm into another. He shut the trunk and tossed the bag with the arm onto the back seat.

Oliver dialed 911 and reported a break-in at Regina's address. He did not give his name. After he ended the call, they drove off.

Regina sat in the passenger seat and nervously turned to glance at the back seat to make sure the arm wasn't moving. She looked at Oliver. "What happened to Mexico?"

"I turned around after you told me you were going to meet with Detective Lopez. I figured if he had your number, maybe more of these nasties knew about you. I just had a bad feeling about this. This network of evil is unlike anything I have ever seen. I knew they would come for you. I hurried back and parked down the street from your house. They showed up just as I was about to get out of my car. After they entered your house, I went around to the back. When you called me, I hid in your shed so that they wouldn't hear me. I'm glad you left the phone line open because when I heard you were going to the bathroom, and then one of them screamed, I knew you were attempting an escape. I shut the main power from your electrical box on the wall in the shed."

He looked over at her. She looked tired and confused. "I'm sorry you were dragged into this." He reached into his pocket. "Here, wear this."

"What is it?"

"A baptismal cross on a string. We give them to folks after they are baptized to wear around their neck as a symbol that they belong to Christ. This one was blessed by Pope Benedict."

"Why are you giving me this?"

"I want you to wear it as a precaution."

"Why? I haven't been baptized."

"Just wear it for good luck then."

She held the little cross in her hand and examined it. She did not put it on.

Oliver gave her a "what are you waiting for?" look.

Regina rolled her eyes, put the cross around her neck, and sat quietly as Oliver drove. She looked out the window at the sleeping city. It was 3:30 am. It occurred to her just how tired she was. "Where are we going?" She tried to fight back a yawn but could not.

Oliver was tired, as well. "I'm not sure. I'm trying to think of a safe place until we can figure out what to do."

Let's go to the salon. "I need to get some sleep and so do you. There's nothing open this late. We might as well go there for now."

35

Closing In

Bonnie entered the hair salon at 9:30 am as she does on any other day. Since the salon's hours are 10:00 am to 6:00 pm, she and Regina typically get there in time to do a bit of housekeeping before the doors open.

Bonnie was surprised to find Regina on the small sofa in the staff lounge and a man sleeping on the floor. She approached Regina and gently nudged her. After the third nudge Regina popped up and screamed, "Get away from me, you witch!"

Bonnie stepped back and Oliver jumped to his feet clutching the handle of the Black Lamia.

A moment later Regina, rubbed her eyes. "Oh, Bonnie, it's you. I'm sorry. I thought you were someone else. I had a bad dream."

Oliver relaxed his grip and took a deep breath.

Bonnie looked at Oliver then back at Regina. "You look like crap. What the hell happened to you? Isn't this the guy who freaked out everyone the other day?"

Regina brushed the hair out of her face. "Bonnie, meet Oliver. Oliver, meet Bonnie."

Oliver gave Bonnie a smile. She ignored him. "What happened, Regina?"

"I was the victim of a home invasion last night. Oliver helped get me out."

Bonnie put her hand over her mouth in disbelief. "You're

kidding! Did you call the police? Did they catch the people?"

"Oliver called the police. We left and came here since it was so late."

Bonnie sat down next to Regina. "You should have come to my place if you needed a place to crash. You know that."

"Thanks Bonnie. I know."

Bonnie looked at Oliver. "Did they do anything to you?"

Regina shook her head. "No, I think it would have been very bad if we had not escaped."

"What did they want? Were they there to rob you?"

"I don't know, Bonnie. But I do need you to do me a favor."

"Sure, what is it?"

Regina looked down at her own nightgown. "I need you to get me something to wear. I don't want to go to the house just yet. Not until I'm sure it's safe." Regina got up, walked over to her small desk located in the tiny administrative office and pulled out her company credit card. She kept one in her purse and one here for staff to use on salon supplies. She walked back and handed the credit card to Bonnie. "I don't have my purse. You can use the company credit card. The mall should be open by now."

While Regina was giving Bonnie her dress and shoe size, Oliver stepped into the bathroom. When he had finished, he examined his reflection in the mirror. Then he bowed his head and prayed for guidance and wisdom.

As he stepped out of the bathroom, Regina stepped in and closed the door. He glanced at the clock. It was 9:45 am. Bonnie had gone to the mall. As Oliver was about to sit down, he heard a knock at the salon's front door. He peeked from behind the lounge door. Two men dressed in dark suits stood outside. Clearly they were not there for hair appointments. As Regina stepped out of the bathroom, he signaled her to keep quiet and pointed at the front doors.

She tiptoed over to where Oliver stood and peeked. She looked at Oliver and shrugged her shoulders. Then she heard the sound of keys unlocking the front door. It was Alice, one of the hairdressers.

Alice entered the salon with the two men. "No, she's not here yet. She and Bonnie are usually the first ones here. Do you want to make an appointment to see her?"

"It's bank related business. We're with Council 666 Bank, and it's regarding a recent transaction. It is important she come by the bank as soon as she can. The credit union deposit will be put on hold until she can clarify a few items."

Alice wrote down the information on a pad. "OK, I'll make sure I tell her as soon as she arrives." The two men turned and left.. Alice prepared her station for her 10:00 am appointment.

Oliver whispered, "Sounds like a trap. I would not recommend you visit that bank."

"What am I supposed to do? What if we can't get the money because they are holding it until I go down there?"

"Forget the money; your life is more important."

A moment later an elderly woman entered the salon. "Hello, Mrs. Jacobs," Alice said as she continued her set up. "I'll be with you in a moment." Alice stepped into the back of the salon and stopped short as she saw Regina and Oliver. "Oh, you are here! There were a couple of men from the bank looking for you. I didn't think you were here. They said that they need to see you about some transaction." Alice looked over at Oliver. "Hello."

Oliver smiled. "Hi."

Unlike Bonnie, Alice refrained from asking Regina to explain why she was in the back room in her nightgown, alone with this handsome guy. She filled in the blanks all on her own.

Bonnie returned a short while later with a pair of jeans, a blouse, socks, and a pair of cheap sneakers. "Here you go." I hope everything fits.

"Thanks." Regina took the clothes and hurried to the bathroom to change.

Oliver's phone rang. He did not answer the call. It was Pastor Bob. A minute later his phone beeped. It was a voice mail from the Pastor.

"Oliver, it's Bob. Call me as soon as you can. I hope you are all right. It's important that we talk. I have been hearing some ugly rumors about you and some woman. The Diocesan office contacted me asking if any of these rumors were true. Evidently, something's going on, and everyone wants answers. I contacted your brother in Maine. He knew nothing about a family crisis or your trip up to visit them. He assured me there must be some mistake. What's going on? Call me, please."

Oliver checked his other two messages. They were from his brother, Mike.

"Oliver, it's Mike. Call me. Pastor Bob said you were on your way up here due to some family crisis. What's up?"

"Oliver, it's Mike. Pastor Bob called again, and he's worried about you. He says you might be in some kind of trouble with some woman. Call me."

Regina came out of the bathroom in her new clothes while Oliver was listening to his phone messages. She checked her phone list then dialed Leonetta Locksmith to ask them to change the locks on her door. They helped her with the renovation of the house back when she purchased it two years earlier. Mr. Leonetta senior was the owner. He spoke with a thick Italian accent. "We take a care of it, Ms. Regina. You place will be a like a Fort Knox when you come a home. Justa stop by our shop for you keys."

Regina felt relief her locks would be changed. She also asked them for prices on installing a surveillance system. She was not going to sleep in her house until it was secure.

She then called her friend, Mandy. "Hey, it's Regina. I might need to stay with you for a few days until my place is secured. I had a break in last night. Do you mind?"

Mandy, a long time friend of Regina's, was used to having her visit. They had been friends since high school. "What? Are you alright? Why of course you can. What happened?"

Regina looked at Oliver. He was pointing to the clock. "I can't get into it right know, Mandy. I've got to run. I'll tell you about it when I see you this evening. Thanks for being there. Bye."

"What time did you tell Detective Lopez you would meet with him?"

"Noon, at the mall."

Oliver retrieved the phone number from his recent calls menu. Soon he had Detective Lopez on the line.

"Hello, Lopez here."

"Detective Lopez? Father Oliver here. The meeting with Miss Regina today. Plans have changed. We'll meet you at the farmers market, but you must come alone. Grits Heaven, you know the place?"

"Know it well. So, you will be there as well, I take it?"

"Yes, I have your evidence, the gun that killed Paul Herodias."

"I thought you were headed out of town."

"Like I said, plans have changed. Come alone or we will be no shows."

"I will be alone, I assure you."

Oliver ended the call and was about to tell Regina of the change in plans when her phone rang. It was Leonetta's Locksmith.

"Hello a Ms. Regina. It's a Gino."

"Hi Gino"

"Why you no tell me about the fire? I thought you wanted locks today. I no can do. Have to wait for..."

"What are you talking about Gino?" Regina's heart started to race.

"You place, it's burn down. I send Mario to measure for price for surveillance system just now, since you live so close to the shop, but he no can do noting until place is fix..."

"Are you sure you went to the right address?"

"Why, of course I know. We do work for you before."

Regina sat down. Her face turned pale as she clutched her cell phone. "I can't believe this." Tears ran down her face. Her voice quivered. "Are you telling me that my house burned down, Gino?"

"Why, you not know? Nobody tell you, Ms. Regina? Yes, I am so sorry."

Regina dropped her phone and put her head in her hands.

Oliver knelt in front of her. "Is there anything I can do?"

She looked up at him. Her face was red. Then she started to punch him repeatedly "This is all your fault. Damn you!" She continued to punch him. "I wish I'd never met you." After unloading her barrage of punches and slaps, she stopped and collapsed onto the chair.

Oliver sat quietly and waited for her to calm down.

Then her phone rang. She let it ring and finally grabbed it. She didn't bother to check who was calling. "What is it?" she asked, trying to mask how upset she was, but not doing a very good job.

"Regina, it's Mandy, a couple of guys just came by here asking for you. They said they were with Council 666 Bank. They didn't look like bankers to me. I'm not sure it's a good idea for you to spend the night here. Those guys might be hanging around waiting for you. Do you know why they're looking for you?"

"Yeah, but if I tell you, they will probably kill you. So, I best not. This is worse than I imagined. Thanks for letting me know. I'll call you when it's safe."

Regina looked at Oliver. She wished she could set back the clock. How different her life would be if he had sat in Bonnie's chair for his haircut.

36

Evidence

After departing the hair salon through the service entrance, Regina and Oliver made their way to his car and headed to the farmers market. It was just a matter of time before someone caught up with them. He needed to head out of town. He had taken a dangerous detour to save Regina and managed to protect her temporarily, but she must decide what she wants to do. It wasn't safe for her in the city. He knew that she knew it, but he didn't want to bring that up right now. She sat silently in the car as they drove to the farmer's market. He couldn't blame her for being angry. Without realizing it, he had dragged her into something which would never let her go until she was dead. It seemed this evil had zero tolerance for being discovered or threatened with exposure.

As they pulled into the farmers market, Oliver was on the lookout for any kind of police vehicle. There were no marked cars in sight. He hoped Detective Lopez would come alone. Finally Regina spoke. "Can you trust him?"

Oliver was relieved she actually said something. "I think so. I met the detective at the hospital not too long ago when he was there to interrogate Paul Herodias. I didn't see any demon faces on him."

Regina rolled her eyes. "Oh, that's right. I forgot. You have demon x-ray vision or some crazy crap like that. Isn't that convenient?"

He pulled into a parking spot in front of Grits Heaven. She got out of the car slamming the door so hard the glass in the passenger side mirror popped out. Remarkably, it landed on a patch of sand. "Whoops." She picked it up and handed him the mirror. "Sorry."

"That's all right. He took the mirror. Don't worry about it."

"I won't." She walked to the restaurant's entrance.

He put the mirror in the side pocket of the driver seat. Then he retrieved the brown paper bag with the gun from under his seat and locked the car.

They entered the restaurant. Oliver quickly scanned the room for demonic faces. He saw none. He did see the Latino man at the corner table who stood up and waved to them. He would have to trust Lopez was really alone.

They approached the table. Oliver remembered the detective from their meeting at the hospital. He wore the same light colored trench coat. He looked like a Mexican Columbo. Lopez stood up and extended his hand.

"Hello, Miss O'Neill." He then greeted Oliver. "Hello, Father Oliver. It is good to see you again. Thank you both for coming."

Oliver scanned the room one more time as he took his seat. Detective Lopez noticed his uneasiness. "I assure you I came alone, Father. Normally, I would have backup in the form of undercover agents, but my instincts told me it would be best to come alone. Sometimes you have to follow your instincts." Detective Lopez spoke without a hint of a Mexican accent. Oliver noticed this and thought he must have either come to the US as a young boy or was born here.

The waitress came to the table. Each of them ordered sweet iced tea. After she left, Oliver handed the brown paper bag to the detective. "I think that is the weapon used to kill Paul Herodias. Don't worry, I did not touch it. Hopefully, you can pull prints from it."

Lopez opened the bag and looked at the contents. "Oh, my. Thank you for bringing this to me. I'll have it dusted. Where did you say you found it?"

"It was in the city trash container across the street from the hair salon." Oliver looked at Regina then back to the detective.

Detective Lopez clasped his hands. Oliver thought he was going to break into prayer. The detective brought his hands to his nose. He seemed to be searching for the right words. "Father Oliver, we met at the hospital a few days ago. I tried to get answers from Mr. Herodias about the incident at your church with a stolen artifact or mask. He was very uncooperative, claimed to be suffering from amnesia. Some of his colleagues thought he might be suffering from schizophrenia. Now he is dead. The telephone I found on his body had each of your numbers stored in memory. Those were the only numbers. I expect even the most unsociable person has more than two phone numbers stored on their phone. My question to you both is why? If you were in my position, this would seem odd and significant." He glanced from Oliver to Regina then back at Oliver.

Oliver noticed a small section of silver chain poking out from the detective's collar. "Detective Lopez, what are you wearing around your neck?"

Lopez's eyebrows went up. He touched his shirt to feel the chain. "It's a small cross. Why do you ask?"

Oliver hinted a smile. "May I see it?"

Detective Lopez reached into his shirt and revealed the small silver cross.

"It's beautiful." Oliver touched the small cross with his finger and then let it go. "Why do you wear it?"

"It's my faith, Father. I'm a Christian. It is our symbol."

Oliver sat back. "Detective, I am glad you're a follower of Jesus. I would like to tell you the rest of the story, but I'm afraid you won't believe me. And, if you do, it could get you killed. It's like the movie about computers taking over the world. You must choose between the blue pill and the red pill. If you take the red pill, there is no going back, and in this case we are not talking about computers, we are talking about evil in its most hideous form."

Detective Lopez leaned back in his chair. "Is that why you insisted I come alone?"

"Yes." Oliver replied.

Detective Lopez thought for a moment. He looked at Regina and then back to Oliver. "Red pill, please."

The waitress brought their drinks and asked if anyone

would like to order lunch. Regina picked up the menu. "I'm starved. Bring me a cheeseburger with fries. Make it medium rare."

Both men looked up at the waitress. "The same."

Oliver raised his hand as the waitress was about to leave the table. "Excuse me. Is there a more private place where we can sit?"

She pointed out the window to a little gazebo, part of their outdoor seating. There were folks eating outside, but the gazebo was empty. "I can seat you at the gazebo outside if you wish."

After they took their seats, Oliver began recounting all that had happened from the time Monty walked into the church office requesting to be baptized, until their close call at Regina's. Detective Lopez listened intently as did Regina. Oliver told them everything he knew about Paul Herodias and Monty McPride. He also described to the detective how he could see evil demonic faces superimposed on people. Lopez nodded periodically as Oliver spoke. Regina also listened. She knew nothing about Monty McPride until now.

Oliver also told them how he had been kicked out of every parish in which he had ever served and how this time it was different. He understood he had a role to play in fighting evil which had found its way into so many crevices of our lives and of our society. He told them about Dr Sinclair and the Council 666, about Monty being welcomed into this very exclusive club, and about the Black Lamia.

"May I see the blade?" asked the Detective.

Oliver reached down his side and produced the short sword. He moved everything on the table to the side and placed the Black Lamia in the middle.

Lopez's eyes lit up. "May I?" He gestured with his hand.

Oliver nodded. "Go ahead."

Detective Lopez slowly picked up the Black Lamia. He handled it like an archeologist might handle a rare anthropological discovery. Very carefully, he removed the sword from its black sheath, producing the brilliant silver blade. He put the sheath on the table and continued to examine the blade. "Extraordinary!" He studied the blade from top to bottom. "There are no markings of any kind. I have seen many blades in my day, but nothing as exquisite as this." He placed the sharp end of the blade against the edge of the table. He dared not touch it with his finger to test its sharpness. As the sharp edge of the blade touched the table it sank a quarter of an inch. Detective Lopez examined the blade at the point it made contact with the table. He thought he noticed a very faint blue glow at the point of contact. It quickly disappeared. It was very subtle.

Lopez looked at Oliver. "You say the witch gave this to Monty. Did he ever say where she got it?

Oliver thought for a moment. "No, Monty never said. I don't think he knew."

Lopez looked around at the planter next to the gazebo. He reached over and picked up one of the bricks that sat loosely in the dirt. It served as decorative edging. "Would you mind if I tried a little experiment?"

Oliver and Regina looked at each other. They were not quite sure what the detective had in mind. Oliver watched as Lopez placed the brick on the table. "So long as it doesn't involve chopping our heads off, go right ahead."

Lopez smiled as he took the sharp end of the blade and placed it against the brick. Again, the blade sank approximately one quarter inch into the brick. He immediately examined the blade at the point of contact with the brick. He saw the same faint blue shimmer. This time it was a bit more pronounced. The detective looked up. "Did you both see that? I cannot explain it, but I suspected as much."

Oliver didn't know what was so exciting to the detective. "What do you mean?"

Lopez pointed to the small gash on the table and the similar cut in the brick. "It doesn't matter. The material doesn't seem to matter. I suspect this knife will cut through just about anything. I have never seen such a lethal blade. Look closely at these two cuts. They are each approximately the same depth, and I applied the lightest touch possible. Yet, the cuts are the same."

Oliver nodded. "Monty mentioned something about intent. The blade seems to know your intent and facilitates it. That's how he helped us escape from Mr. Smith at the rock quarry. He threw it and was able to disarm him. Oliver looked at Lopez. "Literally, Detective." Oliver made a cutting gesture across his wrist.

The detective thought about this for a moment. "Yes, I

wanted to test the sharpness of the blade and also to see if it would cut differently on these two materials. That was my intent. I believe what you have here is something decidedly more sophisticated than a knife or sword. At the point of contact along the blade, I observed a faint blue glow. It was almost imperceptible; I just happened to be focusing on the point of contact. I think this blue glow somehow facilitates the cutting. This is an amazing piece of technology. I would love to analyze it further. I have always been interested in metals. I studied metallurgy at Duke University, but soon discovered I enjoyed investigating humans much more than metals. They are two different types of puzzles." He looked up and smiled at them. "Sorry, I digress. That's just my theory anyway." He was about to put the blade back in its case when he put the sharp edge on the brick and lightly pushed down. They all watched in amazement as the Black Lamia cut the brick like a stick of soft butter. There was a faint blue glow at the point where the blade made contact with the brick as it was being cut. This time, they all noticed it.

Regina's mouth hung open. "What the..."

Oliver picked up one of the pieces of brick. "This is incredible."

Detective Lopez carefully put the blade back into its sheath and handed it to Oliver. "This is no ordinary blade sheath, and that is no ordinary blade. I don't know who on earth would posses this type of technology." He paused. "Maybe it was made by the devil himself."

They all sat quietly for a moment. Then Detective Lopez turned to Regina. "I am sorry about your house being burned down."

She glanced at Oliver. "Yeah, it seems I took that damned red pill without even realizing it."

Oliver turned to Regina. "The only way you will be safe is if we destroy the head. We need to send that evil thing back to hell. Otherwise, it will keep coming for you. Unfortunately, I don't think the same is true for me. After having that meeting with Dr. Sinclair, they need to dispose of me. Their plans for Monty were part of a bigger campaign. Hijacking the souls of the unborn seems to be their preferred method of recruitment. I was the one who helped their prized evil apprentice find Jesus. I baptized him and helped him break free of the evil grip that bound him throughout his entire life as Monty McPride. I also suspect they want this back." He pointed to the Black Lamia.

Lopez leaned forward in his seat. "This head you say is in the trunk of your car. It cannot possibly be alive at this point. What do you plan to do with it?"

Oliver knew it was alive and there was only one way to be rid of the witch. "It has to be burned. Its flesh must be consumed by the fire."

Lopez was still not convinced. "I'm sorry, Father Oliver, but I have a hard time believing a human head can survive on its own after it has been severed from its body. It is simply not possible."

Regina waved her hand. "I don't particularly want to believe it, but that head was very much alive on its own."

"OK, I must see it. Can you show it to me?"

Oliver signaled the waitress. "Check please." He pointed at the detective so she would give him the bill for their lunch. Then he turned to Lopez. "It's worth the price of admission, I promise."

Oliver stood up from his chair. "We'll wait for you at my car."

Oliver and Regina left the restaurant and walked to the car.

Regina took Oliver's hand. He stopped, surprised by her gesture. "I'm sorry I was such a bitch to you. I was very angry. My whole world has been turned upside down. I know I offered to help. Nobody dragged me into this."

Oliver took her hands in both of his and cupped them. "This is difficult for the both of us. I am out of my element, as well. Let's send this thing back to where it came from before it has a chance to summon those goons." He released her hands gently.

Detective Lopez came out and noticed the priest holding the beautiful woman's hands. He cleared his throat as he approached them.

Regina went back inside to use the ladies room.

Oliver looked around the parking lot for demons or anything else that might signal danger. With one hand on the trunk handle, he looked at Detective Lopez. "Are you ready?"

Lopez nodded, but didn't say a word.

Oliver opened the trunk and glanced at the detective. He

pulled the plastic bag closer, untied the knot, and moved back. He kept his arm extended so he could be as far away from it as possible while he showed it to Lopez. He grabbed the hair to steady the head and let the plastic bag drop, revealing the hideous face. It smelled rotten and the detective covered his nose. Its eyes were closed, and no movement.

Detective Lopez observed carefully. He didn't want to get too close to it either. "That is disgusting. The skin seems to be rotting. It sure looks dead to me."

The head was still. Oliver looked at the detective. "Maybe you're right. It was only a matter of time after being separated from its body."

Oliver ripped the tape from its mouth and pulled out the towel.

Mama Crossbones opened her eyes and glared at them. "You can't kill me." Her eyes were bulging. She looked at the detective. He stepped backward and almost fell. He quickly made the sign of the cross on himself. "Dios mio!"

The witch laughed and began shouting obscenities. "I curse you. You can't kill ..." Oliver stuffed the rag back in her mouth and fastened the tape across it. He let the head drop into the bag and quickly tied it.

Detective Lopez got on his phone.

Oliver worried about whom Lopez might be calling. The Detective put up his hand in a just-a-minute gesture as he spoke into his phone.

Regina came out of the restaurant and stood next to Oliver. They both listened to the phone conversation.

"Hello, this is Detective Lopez. I need to use your incinerator for police business. I'm on my way." He paused. "Yes, I understand. This is official business. We won't tie it up very long." He paused again. "No, we are not burning more drugs; it's something more dangerous."

After he ended the call, Detective Lopez took a deep breath and looked at Oliver and Regina. "We need to burn that thing now. I've arranged for the use of an industrial incinerator that we use to destroy illegal drugs. You can follow me in your vehicle. It's about five miles from here."

37

Light My Fire

When they arrived at the incineration facility, Detective Lopez spoke with the attendant. A moment later they were escorted to a large space with a bare concrete floor. In the middle, was a cylindrical incinerator. The door was large enough to fit a casket. An iron flat bed sat on metal rails used to glide items in and out of it. The incinerator was approximately four feet wide and eight feet long.

Detective Lopez opened the furnace door and retrieved the transport table. It was cool to the touch. Nothing had been placed in the incinerator today. "OK, thanks. I'll take it from here. This won't take long."

The facility attendant nodded. "Just make sure to shut everything down before you go. You know the drill, Detective."

"Got it." Lopez knew his way around the equipment. He checked the control panel. "OK, let's do this."

Regina looked on and was a little creeped out by the whole place. She stayed close to Oliver.

Oliver placed the bag containing the head, along with the section of arm and shoulder, on the transport table. He was anxious to get this done. Hopefully, her two wino buddies would not show up with guns blazing. He turned to Detective Lopez. "How long to completely incinerate it?"

"Not long. Five minutes tops."

"Good. Let's get this over with."

Regina reached for Oliver's arm. He did not object.

Lopez pressed a few buttons. A moment later, he glanced at Oliver and Regina. "Ready." He pressed a button and the transport table started to move. The head and arm made their way into the furnace.

Detective Lopez shut the incinerator door once the transport bed was completely inside. They all looked inside at the items on the incinerator table. Then Lopez counted down, "Three, two, one."

Flames shot out of several rows of jets, instantly engulfing the body pieces in an intense wave of fire. There was a high pitched squeal that could be heard over the roaring furnace. The heat radiated from the furnace's walls. The fire was ferocious and lasted for a full two minutes.

Detective Lopez killed the flames. They all looked inside through the small glass window.

Small piles of ashes were all that remained. Detective Lopez let out a sigh of relief. "I'm glad that's done." Oliver and Regina stood quietly as the detective punched a few keys on a control panel. "How are you going to dispose of the ashes?"

Oliver looked up. "It had not occurred to me." He thought for a moment. "Let's put them in a small container and burry it somewhere out of the way."

"How about the landfill on Durant Road?" asked Lopez.

Oliver nodded. "That's perfect. That witch did talk a lot of trash."

Detective Lopez opened the furnace door and retracted the transport table. "What should we use to hold the ashes?"

Regina held her nose and gasped at the stench. The smell caused her to bend over and vomit.

Oliver came running over. "Are you all right?"

Her eyes watered from the muscle cramps, and she vomited again.

Finally, she was able to gain her composure. She looked at him, wiped her mouth and smiled. "You know, being burned alive hurts like hell, but it is very liberating." She stuck her tongue out, licked her lips, grabbed Oliver by the throat with one hand and slapped him across the face several times with the other. Her grip was strong. He could not pull himself free. She roared with raucous laughter and threw him against the wall. His body slammed, almost knocking him unconscious. The Black Lamia fell out of his coat and slid across the floor.

In a flash, she reached him and grabbed him by the throat again. "I will spare your life if you kneel before me priest. Kneel before me and worship me. If not, I will tenderize your meat and have you for dinner."

Lopez hid beneath the transport mechanism. He drew his revolver and took aim at Regina's head. She moved too quickly. He might kill Oliver instead. At seeing the Black Lamia on the floor, he reached for it. He managed to grab it just as the witch grabbed him. But it was too late. She slammed him into the furnace and closed the door. Then she hit a button on the control panel and a 60 second timer counted down to incineration. Lopez's head was bleeding from the impact. He was dizzy and had difficulty focusing.

Oliver crashed onto the floor and gasped for breath. She reached him and stood over him. "I told you. You cannot kill me, priest!" She took a deep breath and stretched her arms, feeling the limberness of her new younger body. You did me a favor, priest. I've been in that old body for nearly two hundred years. It was time for an upgrade. Your little slut's body will do just fine. Maybe if you come to your senses, you and I can have some fun." She picked him up and tossed him in the air. He landed with a crash on top of a desk in the corner of the room. "Or, I can keep slamming your body until it's nice and tender."

Thirty seconds had run down on the timer. Lopez groaned and felt his head. He felt around for his gun. He would shoot the window out. As he felt for the gun, he realized the window was too small. His body would never fit through it. 20 seconds remained on the clock before the burners would ignite. Suddenly, there was a small flame coming out of each nozzle as the incinerator went into pre-ignition mode. Lopez's left hand was in front of one of the nozzles as it pre-ignited.

Oliver tried to get up, but the witch was on top of him in an instant. "What will it be, priest?" She picked him up and held him in the air by his neck. "You righteous, arrogant fool, there have been 666 of my kind roaming this wretched earth, and there will always be 666. Nothing you do can change that. The only one who can cast me into the pit ... well never mind that." She roared again with laughter.

As the timer reached the 10 second mark, Lopez's right hand felt the slender case of the Black Lamia which he had managed to hold onto while he was thrown into the incinerator. He quickly removed the blade from its sheath and hoped against all hope as he sliced the end section of the furnace. He stabbed the end of the furnace and followed its circular outline with the Black Lamia. It cut through the thick incinerator wall as though it was a large stick of soft butter.

Oliver, while in the grip of the witch, could see the blue light making its way around the edge of the furnace.

With 2 seconds left on the clock, the entire end section of the furnace came down in a thunderous crash. Lopez leaped onto the floor as the burners came on. His coat was ablaze, but he quickly shook it off. He ran to the other side to escape the intense heat that was emanating from the open end.

The witch turned. Oliver dropped to the floor gasping for breath. She flashed across the room and grabbed Lopez by the neck. He dropped the blade and tried to free himself, to no avail. She carried him back to the other side of the incinerator. "What's the matter, Detective, a little too hot for you? Well, it's much hotter where you're going." She laughed and then became serious. "Kneel before me and I will let you live." She loosened her grip on his neck.

He was barely able to speak. He struggled to articulate the words, "Put me down."

She put him down, but kept her hand around his neck. "Kneel before me and I will let you live." She ripped the cross from around his neck and tossed it into the flames. "Refuse and you will die." She dragged him closer to the fire.

The witch's eyes grew large with anticipation. Lopez looked into her eyes. "I kneel only before Jesus Christ. You can go to hell!"

Her eyes grew red with rage. She tightened her grip around his neck, then she felt a sting and the room started to spin. Regina's head slid off her body. It hit the floor and came to rest only inches from Oliver's feet.

Detective Lopez struggled to get free as the witch's head began to tumble. The body continued to flail. It ran in front of the open end of the furnace. Fire engulfed the top half of the body as it continued knocking into things.

Oliver stood holding the Black Lamia as he watched Regina's body being consumed by the fire. He picked up the head. It looked at him. "My kind will hunt you down, priest. Make no mistake about it. You cannot hide. You cannot escape. I will see you in hell." Oliver grabbed Detective Lopez's trench coat and stuffed part of the sleeve into its mouth. He wrapped the head in the remainder of the trench coat "I'm so sorry, Regina."

Lopez massaged his throat. He stood up and shut off the incinerator. The roaring fire immediately stopped. He approached Oliver and noticed the bundle containing the head. "Is it dead?"

"I don't think so." He walked over to Regina's charred remains, paused, and looked straight up as if talking directly to God. "I will carry her death with me as long as I live." He wiped his eyes, knelt and prayed over her. He asked for forgiveness of her sins and asked for mercy on her behalf. He remembered the moment he sat in her salon chair. She was a special person, willing to help without really knowing the risk. She was generous, kind and beautiful. Now, the remains of her decapitated charred body lay before him. Oliver bent over, put his face in his hands, and wept.

Lopez waited patiently as Oliver continued kneeling. He picked up the Black Lamia and put it in its sheath. After several moments, Oliver stood up slowly and walked back to join him. Looking at Oliver, Lopez thought of this man who claimed to be a priest but was nothing like the priest he was accustomed to seeing in church. He reminded Lopez more of a gladiator than a priest. The beating he took at the hands of the witch was enough to kill just about any other man. The detective returned Black Lamia.

Oliver took the weapon in his hands and looked at Lopez. "I should have known." He shook his head. "The only one able to send that thing back to hell is God. Evil cannot be destroyed by man. Man can contain it and render it harmless by the power of good, but God is the only one to command it. I'm such a fool. The witch knew all along she could easily invade another body not fully accepting of God. That's why Monty wanted to be baptized. Although he had been in her company prior to being baptized, his heart had already accepted Christ; otherwise he might have served as a host for the demon. He realized the only way to stand a chance against the power of evil was through Jesus. Now Regina is dead. I only hope and pray God grants her mercy and peace."

Oliver held Lopez's gaze. "You must promise me you will pray for her, Detective. She may need our prayers now more than ever. Pray God welcomes her into His kingdom and favors her with his tender mercy."

Lopez nodded in agreement. "I will pray for Miss Regina, I promise you that." Lopez pointed to the bundle containing the head. "What do you plan to do with it?"

38

Durango

Crossing the border was easy. After all, he was a gringo priest. The agent at the gate simply looked at his passport, smiled and waved him on. "Vaya con Dios, Padre."

Oliver smiled as he drove into Mexico. "Gracias."

He had travelled through Mexico before, having spent two years assisting Fr. Antonio at El Monasterio de Jesus near a small village thirty miles north of Durango. Since then, he returned yearly to attend monasterio retreats with fellow priests.

The sun was setting. It cast a warm glow on the surrounding countryside. The day had been a hot one. As twilight turned to evening, the air began to feel more comfortable. Now he was in a different world. Mexico was one of Oliver's favorite places. He loved the people and the food. The sky was turning dark. Night time arrived as Oliver pulled onto the dirt road which led to the monastery.

After two miles on the narrow road, he pulled up to the familiar building. The monastery was an unassuming structure. It looked more like a cheap motel than a religious building. As he got out of the car, he listened to the silence. Aside from an occasional cricket, it was completely quiet.

He grabbed a few things from the car and walked up to the front door. The sound of crunching dirt and gravel beneath his feet broke the night's silence.

Before he could knock on the door, Fr. Antonio opened it.

"Oleever, mi amigo, como estas?"

"Bien, bien." Oliver embraced his friend and patted him on the back.

Fr. Antonio was a slim man whose bald head, beard and angled facial features were reminiscent of a character from an El Greco painting. He was Oliver's senior by ten years or so. Both men had established a strong relationship as fellow priests and as friends. They also shared a love for Asado de bodas, a Mexican dish made with pork, chili pepper sauce and chocolate, traditionally served at weddings. However, that never stopped them from having it without a special occasion.

Once both men were inside, Fr. Antonio's cheerfulness took a serious turn. "You must call Pastor Bob. He calls me many times asking for you."

Oliver held up his hand, "I can't, Antonio. I will explain, but please do not let him know that I'm here."

Antonio was a bit puzzled. "Very well, Oleever." He smiled again. "You must be hungry. No?"

Oliver's stomach grumbled. He had not eaten since lunch. "I must admit, I am starving, Antonio."

"Come, amigo, I have some gorditas which I know you like. They were brought over by Margarita earlier."

"How is Margarita?"

"She is sad woman these days. I think she is angry with God. Her son was killed recently. He got mixed up with a drug cartel. You know, the same old story you hear on the news every day. The poor woman was devastated. She continues to cook for us, and I'm sure seeing you again will lift her spirits. She comes every other day to cook and clean. She left for the day a couple of hours ago."

"I'm sorry to hear that, Antonio. She has been cooking for you for how long, ten years or so?"

"Yes, she is like family." Fr. Antonio gestured toward the kitchen. "Vamos, let us get some food for you before your growling stomach wakes the dead."

Oliver picked up his items and headed for the kitchen.

"Oleever, you can leave your things here for now and take them to your room after you've eaten." He glanced at the item in Oliver's left hand. "Don't tell me you have taken up bowling."

"It's not a bowling ball, and I need to take it with me. It is the reason I'm here."

Fr. Antonio enjoyed a glass of wine as Oliver ate his fill of gorditas and told the story of the visitor who threatened to kill him if he did not perform the sacrament of baptism. He also briefed him on the sequence of events that ensued.

Several glasses of wine later, Oliver finished his tale. Fr. Antonio set down his glass. "My friend, did you stop in the desert and consume peyote today?"

Oliver chuckled at the thought. "No, Antonio, peyote is not involved."

"Oleever, I want to make sure that I understand you. You say that this evil can invade another host given the chance?"

"Yes, I discovered the hard way. That's why I wrapped it up in a black plastic bag and put it in the bowling bag. I figured it came from darkness, best keep it in darkness until a better solution presents itself."

"This is not good, Oleever. Won't someone be looking for this head you say you have, the blade, and maybe the book?" Antonio picked up the little black book and thumbed through its pages. "It has many names and telephone numbers. It even has addresses. They are numbered 1 through 666."

"There's one more thing, Antonio."

"Ay, Oleever! There are names and addresses right here in Mexico."

"Where? How far from here, Antonio?"

"Juarez, Chihuahua, Alcapulco, and Torreón, which is about 2 hours from Durango." Fr. Antonio continued to flip through the little book. "There are others." He put the book down and poured himself a little more wine. He murmured to himself, "Estara loco, mi amigo?"

"What, Antonio?"

"Sorry, I was just thinking. This all sounds crazy. "

Oliver nodded. "I know, but it looks like these people, demons, whatever they are, are distributed strategically around the world. It makes organized crime look like child's play. This is serious, Antonio...and as I was saying, there is one more thing."

"Oleever, you must be kidding, what is it?"

"I don't know if I should tell you. The only two people with whom I have ever confided are dead. It might not be good to share this."

Fr Antonio looked at his dear friend and laughed. "You come in here with, you say, some demon witch's head in a bowling case, you are carrying some kind of devil blade, and a notebook containing the name and phone of the devil's army and you have more to share. But, you are concerned it might get me killed if you tell me? No hombre, creo que Elvis is already gone from building. No?

"Antonio, I can see them."

Fr. Antonio took a sip of his wine. "Who do you see, Oleever?"

"I can see the evil presence in a person. They wear it like a veil or a suit. It is different for everyone. I have been able to see it since I was a young boy. I have learned to live with it. Sometimes it is hard to ignore. The demonic faces are quite hideous."

Antonio sat back with his mouth half open. "Is this why you keep getting into trouble at all those parishes?"

"Yes, but I could not tell anyone of what I could see. They would have thought I was crazy."

Fr. Antonio raised an eyebrow. "You mean, you are not?"

Oliver laughed. "Antonio, I missed you, my friend. I knew if I could trust anybody, it would be you."

"So I take it your Pastor Bob does not know any of this?"

"No, and he can't know. I met an evil man in Raleigh who is trying to corrupt the church, but it would be more dangerous to expose him. If he knew that Pastor Bob knew the truth, he would kill Bob, and I don't know what else he would do. It is best I remain missing. I know there are others from the list in the United States very close to Raleigh. I didn't know where else to go, so I came here."

Both men sat quietly contemplating the implications of what they had just discussed. "You are welcome to stay here as long as you wish." Fr. Antonio raised his wine glass. "My dear amigo, I want you to unburden yourself and rest. While you are here, allow the peace of Christ to fill your mind and heart."

"Thank you Antonio. Who else is here?"

"Right now it is just you and me. Padre Ernesto will be coming to spend time here. He will arrive from Zacateca next week, and Padre Soto will be joining us in a couple of days. He is at the church in Torreón helping Fr. Francisco Jimenez. I don't believe you have met either of them. Padre Ernesto is from Guatemala, and Padre Soto is from Chile. They both speak very good English."

"I will apologize to you ahead of time, Antonio. I am sorry to burden you with this knowledge. I've come to realize that my whole life has been a preparation for this. This weapon, this book and my ability to see evil cannot be a coincidence.

"Come, Oleever, let us bow our heads at this time. Let us pray for guidance and clarity of mind." Both men closed their eyes and bowed their heads as Fr. Antonio prayed. "Please, Lord Jesus, we pray for guidance, wisdom, and strength in this hour of uncertainty. Please pour out your divine grace onto Padre Oliver. Guide him so he may think with a clear mind. And through him, your humble servant, may your will be done. For the glory of our risen Lord Jesus Christ, we ask this as we ask all good things. Amen." Fr. Antonio made the sign of the cross over Fr. Oliver.

Oliver took a deep breath "Thank you, Antonio." He thought for a moment. "I should park my car around back where it will not be seen. It is best to be safe. Perhaps you can arrange to get Mexico plates for it. At least it will blend in as a local vehicle."

"I will ask Manuel for some plates. He works at the garage in town. I am sure he can get them."

"But don't tell him they are for my car."

"Very well."

Oliver moved the car and took the rest of his belongings out of it. He proceeded to a bedroom on the second floor. He fell asleep as soon as his head hit the pillow.

39

Wonderful Chaos

"Find the damned priest! That's our priority, gentlemen" Doctor Sinclair looked around at Mr.Adolfo, Mr. Fredericks, and the twelve other Council 666 members sitting in his conference room. "It pains me to report that Mama Crossbones' host body has expired, which means that the priest must have burned the head."

Mr. Fredericks raised his hand. "What about the body found at the plant. It was headless. Do we know what happened?"

Dr. Sinclair took his seat at the table. "The identity of the corpse found at the incineration facility is unknown at this point. But it must have served as a temporary host. I suspect our benefactor is trapped in it and is waiting to acquire a new host body. I also think it is with the priest."

Mr. Adolfo raised his hand. "Have you talked to his pastor to see if he knows where the priest might be?"

"I've talked to his idiot pastor. The man is truly clueless. He bores me to death. If I didn't know better, I would think he works for us."

Fredericks raised his hand. "Have we informed the rest of the Council what has happened?"

"We have one week to track down this priest. After that, I will have to inform the others. It has been more than one hundred years since one of the Council has been beheaded and burned. We must resolve this matter quickly. Everything was going so well."

Dr. Sinclair rose from his chair and motioned with his

hands as he continued speaking. 'We must continue our assault, my friends. Look at all we have accomplished. We successfully helped cripple the global economy. Mass shootings are no longer isolated events. The wealthiest 4% control 98% of the money in the world. Morality is crumbling. We continue to raise a bunch of worker consumers to feed our wealth. Our reign over the masses is stronger than ever. Society is a mess. Times have never been better. Our nation is obsessed with sex and loves their mind numbing TV shows. They walk around plugged into their little devices. Oh, how they love their entertainment. It is getting easier to control the masses. Now technology allows us to know everything they say and do. Man's inhumanity to man continues to plunge us deeper and deeper into our free fall of evil. Surely, we can find one crazy priest in the midst of our wonderful chaos."

The men around the table nodded in agreement. They smiled at Sinclair's words. It was all true. Evil's agenda was on a fast track.

40

Francis

Oliver spent the following day in his room. He searched for guidance by reading some of his favorite Gospel passages. After his meditation, he worked out in the privacy of his room. Later, he took a walk through the rocky desolate landscape surrounding the building. The monastery was set in a remote area. The nearest town was located several miles south. The monastery functioned as a retreat location and was not a church where villagers came to worship. Oliver was glad for the privacy it offered.

After the large meal at noon, Oliver took a nap. Later, he walked and explored the area for hours. He returned to the monastery late in the afternoon.

Antonio sat in a corner of the patio reading a National Geographic magazine. "Hola, Oleever, did you have a good walk?"

"Yes, I did, Antonio. I remember the area very well, but it is the first time I have explored the surrounding area."

"Si, and did you find anything interesting?"

The sun was setting, and the sky was beginning to reveal its collection of stars. Oliver turned and pointed west. "Over in that direction, I came upon an entrance to what appears to be an abandoned mine. Do you know how long has it been abandoned? I never realized it was there."

"There is a large abandoned silver mine called Mina Del Sol in Durango. It is a big tourist attraction. The little mine here is called Chica Mina Del Sol. It was a small silver mine, older than

Mina Del Sol. It has been abandoned for a very long time. I do not know for how long. I would have to guess at least one hundred years."

"I'd like you to accompany me out there tomorrow, Antonio. I think it may be just the place to hide my bowling bag and its contents. I don't know how that demon is trapped in the head of its host, but I do know, given the chance, it would figure out a way to invade someone else. I just don't want to take a chance. Are you sure you don't want to see it?"

No, thank you, Oliver, but I think this is a good idea. It is best to be rid of the bag. I will go with you tomorrow. We will go early in the morning. I think you will feel better after that."

After a snack of fresh pineapple, Oliver spent the rest of the evening meditating in his room. He examined the bowling bag. It sat exactly where he left it. His phone rang. It was Detective Lopez.

"Hello, Oliver? Did you make it to Mexico safely?"

"Yes, Detective. It was an uneventful trip, thank God."

"I'm calling you from a second cell phone. After what I witnessed, I am not taking any chances. I had to go to great lengths to keep myself from becoming a suspect and a target. In my report, you forced me to let you use the incinerator and threatened to kill me, if I did not. My bruises and burn marks were very helpful, especially the marks on my neck. But my reason for calling is that I have stumbled upon a disturbing pattern."

Oliver was glad Detective Lopez was all right. He did not mind being part of a story to keep him from becoming the next dish du jour for the Council. "Go on, Detective."

"Within the past few weeks, six priests have turned up dead. They were all killed the same way, bullet to the head. The killer has not been apprehended."

"Do they have any suspects?"

"None, but that's not all."

Oliver stood up from his seat in anticipation. "Oh? What else did you find, Detective?"

"They were all named Francis, either first or last name."

"What? Are you sure?"

"Yes. I came upon this as I was investigating the death of Father Francis Jacobs. He was the pastor of Saint Bartholomew's in

Mebane. His body was found in an abandoned warehouse. That's when I learned there had been multiple murders, in different cities, of priests with the name Francis. They were all found murdered the same way. Thus far, we have no leads." Detective Lopez paused. "I thought you'd want to know."

"Yes, Detective. I appreciate it. Thank you for letting me know." Oliver paced the room. His mind was racing.

"I'll call you if I get more information about the case. Knowing what I know, after meeting you, I am inclined to think the Council might be behind these killings."

"OK, Detective. Be careful and thanks for the call."

"Stay safe Fr. Oliver, goodbye."

41

Oliver's Dream

Oliver paced and thought. He prayed. He opened his bible and read. An hour later, he went to bed. Sleep came quickly and with it, a dream of being entangled in large thorny vines. The ground was completely barren, not a trace of greenery anywhere. The large patch of overgrown vines, extended as far as the eye could see. He tried to find a way out of the large thorn patch but could not move very far. The sharp thorns were thick and hard. He accidentally cut himself on one. It stung. He moved and cut himself on another. His range of motion was decreasing. He realized that the thorns were slowly closing in on him. Soon he would be punctured and torn to death by their grip. He was now bleeding from several places. Both hands had been pierced, and his feet were punctured. His side was next as a large thorn ripped into him. He was bleeding profusely and his body stung and pulsed with pain. Then the thorns started to become transparent, and his pain faded. The bleeding stopped. He felt as though he was going up in an elevator, seeing the large thorn patch from above. The view receded as he rose in his invisible elevator. The thorns disappeared. Before him stood a large orchard of trees, except there were no trees, only the stumps remained. Someone had cut all the trees down. They must have been very large judging by the size of the massive stumps. None was less than twenty feet in diameter.

Oliver looked around at the expanse of tree stumps. He

caught sight of a man approaching him. The stranger was holding something in his hand. It was a stick of some sort. As he came closer, Oliver recognized the item in the man's hands. It was an axe. The man stepped up to Oliver and held out the axe. As Oliver took it, the man pointed to the area behind Oliver. Oliver turned. There was a large patch of trees. More of the same large diameter trees, only these had leaves.

Oliver glanced back at the tree stumps then turned to look at the trees with leaves. They were different now. All the leaves were gone. The trees were dead. Large sores on the trunks and patches of peeling bark seemed to indicate the massive trees were rotting from the inside out.

He lifted the axe and examined the fine wooden handle and the blade. He noticed an inscription on the head of the axe. He brought it closer to his eyes in order to make out the print. The words 'None Shall Be Spared' were engraved.

Oliver looked at the man dressed in white. He stood still and looked at Oliver. He raised his hand slowly and pointed to his own ear. Oliver noticed it was red. The man smiled and disappeared. All of a sudden the weight of the axe became very heavy. He did not want to drop it, so he clenched it tightly.

Oliver awoke with hands clenched. "The axe felt real. The dream seemed real." He sat up and prayed.

<div align="center">~~~</div>

Antonio and Oliver reached the entrance to the abandoned mine around mid morning. Antonio cautioned Oliver, "We must be careful. The inside may be not stable."

They entered into the darkness and turned on their flashlights as they followed the descending path. The tunnel appeared to be structurally sound. They passed a storage area on their left. It was littered with pieces of old mining equipment. They continued on the descending path for approximately another 100 yards until they could go no further. Rocks blocked the path. The area appeared to have caved in at some point.

Oliver flashed his light between the rocks to see past the cave in. "This is as far as we can go. But, I think that storage area will serve our purpose."

They headed back and reached the storage space that had been carved into the side of the tunnel. It was about the size of a large bathroom. Oliver turned to Antonio. "This will do just fine, Antonio. Let's bless this space. We will store the bowling bag here. Did you bring the holy water?"

Antonio produced a vial of holy water and flashed his light on it. "Here it is." He removed the cap and began praying and blessing the space. Once the blessing was complete, Oliver entered and placed the bowling bag in the farthest corner and piled rocks on top of it.

They made their way back to the entrance of the mine and stepped into the sunlight. After waiting a few moments until their eyes adjusted to the brightness, they headed back to the monastery.

"Oleever, I am glad it is done. I want you to get some rest these next few days and stop thinking about severed heads and demonic possession. Give yourself some time to unwind."

"Yes, I plan to rest awhile. I hope no one comes out here."

Antonio reassured him. "You don't have to worry about that. This place draws no one. There is no reason to expect a change. This is a good place to leave the past behind. Besides, you and I are the only ones who know where it is hidden. And, you do not have to worry about me bringing up the topic of severed heads and their possible whereabouts at my next social gathering."

42

Soto's Sin

The two men walked through the arid landscape. Their straw hats protected them from the hot sun. Oliver took a last sip from his water bottle as they rounded the final leg of the path leading back to the monastery. Suddenly, he stopped. Antonio turned to him. "You OK, amigo?"

Oliver's gaze was fixed on the monastery entrance. "Who is that?"

Fr. Antonio turned and looked toward the entrance. "That is Fr. Soto. He must have just arrived from Torreón."

"How long have you known him, Antonio?"

"I met him last year during my trip to Peru. He is a very nice man, loves soccer and opera. I think you will like him."

Oliver did not respond. He was unsure whether to reveal to Antonio that Fr. Soto was host to evil. Even from this distance he could see the double exposure on the man's face. *"Perhaps it was the sun and shadow playing tricks,"* Oliver thought as he continued to approach the monastery.

Fr. Antonio waved. "Hola, Padre Soto."

Fr. Soto stopped and looked in their direction. He returned the wave as they approached. "Hola, Antonio."

As they neared Fr. Soto, there was no doubt in Oliver's mind that the priest had compromised his faith in some way and allowed evil to enter. This was the first time Oliver had observed an evil presence in another priest. He was unsure how to react.

Antonio introduced the men to one another. "Padre Soto, meet Padre Oliver. He is a good friend and has joined us for an indefinite stay."

Soto smiled and extended his hand. The demon superimposed across his face was clear. It faded in and out intermittently revealing Fr. Soto's face.

Oliver did his best to ignore the visible evil only he could see. He extended his hand and forced a smile. "Hola, Padre Soto, nice to meet you."

Fr. Soto smiled as he shook hands. "Muy bien. It is nice to meet you too Padre Oliver." The evil on Fr. Soto's face darkened for a moment as it seemed to be observing Oliver. It was a similar look he got from the dark entities in Mama Crossbones and later her sidekicks while in his office. Oliver wondered if the evil presence in Soto suspected something.

Antonio led the way into the monastery. "How was your trip, Padre?"

"Not too bad. I think I returned at a very good time." Soto sniffed the air.

Just then, Margarita stepped out of the kitchen to greet them. "Hola, Padres."

Soto and Antonio spoke in unison. "Hola, Margarita."

Oliver smiled and walked over and gave her a hug. "Margarita, como estas?"

She smiled "Ah, so-so. It is good to see you, Padre Oliver. Long time I no see you."

"Yes, it has been a long time." Oliver held her hand in both of his hands. "I am sorry about your son, Margarita. Padre Antonio told me of his death."

She shrugged her shoulders. "Es la voluntad de Dios."

Oliver continued holding her hand. "Yes, you say it is God's will, but do you really believe that, Margarita?"

"I don't know anymore."

He gently squeezed her shoulder. "You must remain strong in your faith Margarita. We will continue to pray for your son." Oliver looked at Antonio.

Antonio stepped forward. "Si, we pray for Ernesto tonight." Margarita was just over five feet tall. Antonio bent forward to be eye to eye with her. He smiled. "But now, I pray we can enjoy that delicious food you have prepared. My nose is dancing."

She smiled. "Yes, it is time to eat before the food gets cold."

Soto took a deep breath. "Thank the Lord, I am starving so much. I can eat a .., how do you say, me puedo comer un caballo."

Margarita led them into to the dining room. "I hope you are not too disappointed, Padre Soto, but I did not cook a horse."

They sat down. Fr. Antonio said grace and the three priests enjoyed the tasty meal of rice, carne asada and sweet plantains. They ate quietly. After several moments of mouth watering satisfaction, Antonio looked at Soto. "So what is new in Torreón?"

Soto looked up from his dish. "Not very much, but there is a problem in one of the surrounding villages of growing drug use. I met several villagers while I was helping at the Iglesia de la Altagracia in the city."

Antonio nodded. "Yes, and is Padre Franceso Jimenez feeling better? It was good you were able to take over for him while he was recuperating."

"Yes, he has recovered from his appendectomy. He's a tough old bird."

After Oliver's conversation with Detective Lopez, he wondered if Father Francesco Jimenez might be in danger. "Father Soto, does Father Francesco Jimenez go by Fr. Jimenez, Fr. Francesco or by his full name?"

Soto thought for a moment. "Most people refer to him as Fr. Jimenez. Why do you ask, Padre Oliver?"

"I was just curious. Maybe I will have the pleasure of meeting him someday."

"Yes, He is a very interesting fellow. The people of our parish are very fond of him."

Antonio turned to Fr. Soto. "How long will you be staying with us, Padre?"

Soto let out a long sigh. "Well, I am thinking one week. I need to spend time alone with God and reflect. This is a good place to do it."

Oliver finished eating and wiped his mouth with the embroidered napkin. "Padre Soto, did anything unusual happen to you recently, while in Torreón?"

Fr. Antonio and Fr. Soto both looked at Oliver surprised at

the question. Soto smiled. "What do you mean, Padre Oliver?"

"I mean, did anything out of the ordinary happen, anything considered unusual or surprising?"

Soto smiled as his face shifted from man to demon. Oliver watched the double exposure intensify. The demon seemed to glare at him. "No, nothing happened while I was away. Why do you ask?"

"With all the crazy things going on in the world, I was just curious, that's all."

Soto nodded. For a moment the demon face lingered. "Ah, yes there is much craziness in the world."

The men retired to their rooms for siesta, a customary nap after the big meal of the day. It was now 1:30 in the afternoon. Margarita cleaned up the dishes and would be done with her chores by 4:00 pm when her nephew, Felipe, would pick her up in his beat-up taxi. Margarita lived in the town just a few miles from the monastery, not too far out of his way.

Oliver remained in his room until 6:00 pm. He came down to join Fathers Antonio and Soto, who were discussing something over a glass of wine. Antonio looked up at Oliver. "Oleever, come and join us for a glass of wine. We are discussing Vatican II. Fr. Soto and I have differences of opinion over the merit of continuing forward or going back to the pre-Vatican II method of worship. We would like to hear your opinion."

Oliver poured a glass of wine. "I'm a Vatican II man."

Antonio smiled and looked over to Soto. "I think you are outnumbered my friend. Going back to that ritualistic performance we called worship is bad for the faith. We need to encourage and enable participation by all of God's people. Why do you think we are called 'the body of Christ?'"

Soto and his demon face looked back at Antonio. "There was more respect and reverence back in the day. Not so much craziness."

Oliver found it unsettling to hear Padre Soto speak of worship while the evil inside looked out. "We promised Margarita we would pray for Ernesto."

Antonio stood up and poured more wine into his glass. "Yes, I agree. Let us pray for Ernesto. It will give Margarita comfort to know we have done so."

Oliver held up his hand. "Before we pray for Ernesto, I would like to first pray for Padre Soto."

The demon face on Padre Soto surged to become clearly present as Oliver said this. Oliver noticed the reaction and continued. "Yes, I would like to pray for Padre Soto because of the crazy world in which we live, may he be blessed with clarity, truth, and wisdom."

Padre Soto sat up and looked at Oliver. "I don't know what to say. Why do you feel you should pray for me at this time?"

Oliver opened the flask of holy water Antonio used earlier in the day to bless the space in the mine. Soto began to fidget. His knee started to jiggle up and down. Then he put his finger in his collar to loosen it.

Antonio looked on and took notice of Padre Soto's apparent nervousness. He glanced at Oliver, realizing something was wrong. Oliver gave Antonio a very subtle nod. He began to pray, and Padre Antonio soon joined in the Lord's Prayer. "Our father who art in heaven, hallowed be thy name..." Oliver sprinkled holy water on Soto.

Soto put up his hands, almost instinctively, to block the water from splashing on him. Antonio looked at Oliver once again. This time it was clear something was terribly wrong with Padre Soto. The hands tried desperately to block the holy water as they flailed in the air. Oliver noticed the demonic presence darken as it solidified on Soto's face. There was no more Soto, all he could see was the grotesque demonic face where Soto's face should be. A low moan was beginning to emerge from Soto, like that of someone is pain. They continued to pray.

"Thy kingdom come, Thy will be done on earth as it is in heaven. Give us this day our daily bread."

As soon as they said this, Soto vomited his dinner all over the floor.

"And forgive us our trespasses."

Soto's moaning grew louder, dend the tone took on an eerie deepness.

"As we forgive those who trespass against us and lead us not into temptation."

Soto's moaning became a loud wail. He put his hands to his face and shook uncontrollably as his wailing rose to a fever pitch.

"But deliver us from evil, Amen."

When these words were spoken, Oliver saw the demonic presence that had solidified on Soto's face explode into ashes. He watched as each bit of ash hit the floor. They glowed red and disappeared upon contact. Antonio did not see it.

Soto wept in great heaves. His hands were still over his face. He dropped to the floor on his knees and cried out, "Forgive me, Lord, please forgive me." His weeping continued. Antonio and Oliver stood near, allowing him time to compose himself.

Father Antonio glanced at the mess. "I'll get the mop."

Oliver fetched a towel from the bathroom. While Antonio mopped up the vomit, Oliver knelt down next to Fr. Soto and placed one hand on the sobbing man's shoulder. "Here, take this, my friend. Wipe your eyes. I think you are going to be all right."

Father Soto reached for the towel and wiped his face. He managed to compose himself.

Father Antonio handed a glass of water to him. After taking a few sips, he sat hunched over in his seat. His head hung low with shame. "Dear Lord, what have I done?" He shook his head from side to side. "What have I done?"

Oliver gently patted Fr. Soto's shoulder. "Would you like to talk about it?"

Father Soto looked up. His eyes were severely bloodshot. "I am so ashamed, but I am afraid that I must confess my sin and continue to ask for God's forgiveness. I have been a faithful servant of the Lord for almost twenty years. That is, until this past week when I visited Torreón." He shook his head from side to side. He looked up at Antonio then at Oliver then lowered his head. "I was invited to dine at the house of one of the wealthiest men in town, Sr. Angel Molina. The church in Torreón is in need of repairs, and I was there on behalf of Padre Francesco. Although Sr. Molina does not regularly attend Mass, he visits every so often and stays for part of the Mass.

"It was a grand affair. He invited guests from town. During the course of the evening, Sr. Molina and I discussed the church. We continued to talk after all the guests had departed.

"He was very interested in the hierarchy of power, all the way from the Pope to the priests at local parishes. We talked for hours into the night. We drank much wine, perhaps too much. It was getting very late, and I told him I needed to get back to the church. He insisted I stay in their special guest quarters, a separate house next to his grand mansion."

The accommodations were luxurious. The man spared no expense on the beautiful mansion. As I prepared to go to sleep, there was a knock on my door. Before I could get to the door to open it, someone unlocked it from outside. A woman stepped into my room. She closed the door and stood before me. She was beautiful. Before I could ask why she had let herself into my room, she let the robe fall off her body. As she stood before me, completely naked, the small nightlight on the wall delineated the lines of her voluptuous and exquisite body. She approached me, put her hand on my lips and said, "This night is a gift from Sr. Molina." She pushed me back onto the bed, and before I knew it, I broke my vow of celibacy. I knew what I was doing was wrong. I gave into her without much of a fight. Maybe if I had drunk less wine, my mind would have been clearer. Perhaps my will would not have been compromised."

Padre Soto wiped his eyes. "God, I am so ashamed. I thought I could keep it secret, but tonight you reached into my soul and pulled my shame into the open.

Soto looked up with guilt-ridden eyes. "But there is more."

Oliver and Antonio exchanged a quick glance.

Soto continued. "The next morning, as I was preparing to leave, Sr. Molina came down to my room. I hoped I could leave and not have to face him. But that was not possible. He knocked on my door, came in and asked me how I slept. I replied 'fine.' I think he could see the embarrassment and shame on my face. He smiled, put his arm around my shoulder and said, "Now, now, Padre, don't worry. It will be our little secret. She was quite something, hey? And, only fifteen."

Soto's face flushed red with anger and shame as he spoke. "My disgrace was two-fold. I broke my vow of celibacy, and I did so with a minor."

Oliver and Antonio exchanged glances again. This time Fr. Antonio let out a deep breath in frustration. "Fr. Soto, this is very disturbing indeed. You do understand I am forced to send you back to Chile and that I must report this to your bishop, don't you?"

Tears slowly ran down Padre Soto's face. "Yes, I realize

this is what you must do. I have brought this shame upon myself. No one else is to blame. I will arrange my return trip in the morning. I am sorry to you both and I am sorry to my God. Perhaps my faith is not as strong as I thought." Padre Soto slowly arose from the sofa and retired to his room.

Fr. Antonio slapped the side of the sofa in anger. "Como pudo haber sido tan estupido!" Then he looked at Oliver. "Oleever, this is a night of shame, for I am ashamed to admit it, but I almost wish I did not know what Soto has just confessed. What are we going to do?"

"Like you said, Antonio, you must report this to his bishop." Oliver sat and thought about the events of the last few days. Then he stood up, dug through his pockets and pulled out the little black book. "Antonio, didn't you say there was someone from the list in Torreón?" He began to flip through it.

"Si, Oleever, I think so. There was a name. I just remember the city. I think so."

Oliver stopped flipping the pages. "You did. Here it is, Torreón, and the person's name beside it is Mr. Angel Molina. How ironic his name is Angel."

"What are you thinking, Oleever?"

"Tomorrow I will ride with Padre Soto. He can catch a return flight to Chile. The airport is on the way to Torreón, and that's where I'm headed. I would like to check on Fr. Francesco Jimenez, and I need to see Sr. Molina."

"Why do you want to see Sr. Molina? He is not a good man. Why do you think you must check on Fr. Francesco?"
Oliver put the little book into his pocket. "That is where I must go, Antonio."

43

Snakes

Oliver was up bright and early. He took an early morning walk. Upon his return, he noticed Antonio pacing back and forth at the monastery entrance. He was deep in thought, and appeared not to notice Oliver's arrival.

Oliver waited patiently for a moment. "Good morning, Antonio, are you OK?"

He stopped pacing and turned to Oliver. "Fr. Soto is dead."

Oliver did not respond. He wondered if Antonio had spoken correctly. Perhaps he meant to say that Father Soto was still in bed. "What did you say, Antonio?"

"I said Father Soto is dead. He killed himself in the night. The fool slit his wrists." Antonio made the gestures on his own wrist. "I did not think he would contemplate doing such a thing, stupid, stupid man." Antonio began to pace again. "This is terrible, Oleever. I was praying for his soul. He has made his sin worse by this act of cowardice."

Still in shock and at a loss for words, Oliver's mind was spinning as he wondered if he had missed a sign by Soto that might have helped prevent the priest from taking his own life. "I am very sorry, Antonio."

"I have called the police. I must also call the funeral home. They will prepare his body. I will send it to Chile. He would want to be buried there." Antonio paused and pointed into the house. "Come, Oleever, we must pray over him. We must beg for God's mercy on his behalf."

They proceeded up the stairs and into Fr. Soto's room. Once inside, Oliver opened the bathroom door. The dead priest lay in the bathtub. He was fully clothed. There was no water in the tub. Blood stained his black cassock. He was dressed as he would dress for Mass. His arms lay across his chest, and he was holding his bible.

Antonio began to pray. Oliver joined in. They continued to pray. Eventually, the police arrived. They examined the scene and took photos. Then they asked Fr. Antonio a series of questions. Neither priest shared Fr. Soto's confession. Fortunately, it was Margarita's alternate day. She had come yesterday and would return tomorrow to do the monastery's household chores. Fr. Antonio was grateful that she would be spared seeing Fr. Soto like this.

After the body was loaded onto the hearse, Oliver gathered a few items onto a small bag and informed Antonio. "I need to go Torreón."

"Oliver, how long will you be gone?"

He thought for a moment. "I don't know, Antonio. I have no timeline of my own. I'm going where the Lord points me. Right now that is Torreón."

Antonio's gaze fell upon the Black Lamia which Oliver tucked neatly under his jacket. "You're going to kill him aren't you?"

Oliver closed the flap of his jacket, fully concealing the blade. He was surprised by the question. "Antonio, I'm going to remove *it*, not him. The man who was, is no longer. Only the evil remains. It cannot be killed. Temporarily curtail is the best I can do. God may have other plans after that, but I do not know what those plans might be. All I know is I have my instructions, and they are quite clear."

Antonio raised an eyebrow. "What do you mean you have your instructions? Are you saying that God told you to kill Sr. Molina?"

"Not in those words, but He made it quite clear in a dream I had my first night here."

"Oh? How so? What exactly did He say?"

"He didn't say anything, Antonio. The message was

inscribed on an axe he handed to me. It read 'None shall be spared.'"

Antonio's phone rang. He looked at the display. "It's Pastor Bob."

"Tell him you have not seen or heard from me; otherwise, I'm afraid he and you will be in grave danger." Oliver approached Antonio and put his hand on his shoulder. "This is not a time to doubt what I say."

Antonio answered the call and did as Oliver asked. He kept the call short and turned to Oliver after he finished. "My dear friend, I do not doubt what you believe, but are you sure this is what God asks of you? I did not see the thing in your bowling bag. Was it really a live severed head? Just think about it. A head cannot survive by itself. I thought it harmless to help you hide it in the mine, but now you are planning to kill a man over this. You say that you see demons and have relayed a detailed account of all the fantastic things you have survived. I thought perhaps it was your way to provide an excuse to leave the priesthood. Sometimes when we are not honest with ourselves, we can create our own fantastic realities, to justify our desires."

Oliver could not believe what he heard from his trusted friend. "If you doubt, why did you go along with me? Didn't you see Soto's reaction last night?"

"Yes, the poor man was overcome by guilt. I thought, with a little time, things would flush themselves out and you would stop with these fantasies. I was glad you came here, but I cannot let you go kill a man, even if he was responsible for the seduction of Father Soto." Antonio stared at Oliver, waiting for his reaction. He was not sure how to stop Oliver from going, but he could not go along with what might be a delusion caused by a brain tumor, or mental illness.

"Antonio, I'm disappointed. All this time you have been pretending to believe me. But there is one way to prove to you what I say is true. We must go back to the mine so you can see the head. If there is no living head in the bowling bag, I will submit myself to whatever you want me to do. I will gladly see a doctor of your choosing. Perhaps, I am crazy. That might actually be preferable." Oliver started to walk toward the back of the monastery. "We will take my car down the road and go the rest of the way on foot. It will save us the long hike."

Fr. Antonio followed reluctantly. "This is not necessary, Oleever."

Oliver waved him to keep coming, "Oh, yes it is."

Antonio pointed to the lethal blade at Oliver's side. "Must you bring that?"

"I carry it as a precaution."

The two men got into Oliver's car. He started the car and began to back out of the niche where he had parked. Then he stopped the car and engaged the emergency brake. "I'll be right back, Antonio, we need flashlights." In a moment he was back and they were on their way.

Antonio sat quietly. They were getting near the point in the road bringing them closest to the mine. "Oleever, my friend, what will you do if this is something we are about to disprove? It is difficult to believe, I know. What if this whole thing is in your mind? What if it's just in your imagination, made up to avoid some uncomfortable truths in your life? I am afraid how you might react."

Oliver parked the car on the side of the narrow dirt road. He took a deep breath and looked at Antonio. "If I am imagining this, I will give you my blade, and I will do as you say. I won't argue or put up a fight to defend my delusion. I promise."

Oliver opened the door and almost stepped on a snake that was slithering under the car. It kept moving and ignored him. "Are there many snakes around here, Antonio?"

Antonio nodded. "Some, they are not uncommon. There are varieties including poisonous rattlesnakes. Why do you ask?"

Oliver got out and walked up the small bank of rocks and bushes. "I almost stepped on one as I got out of the car."

Antonio followed Oliver up the bank. "Snakes won't bother you unless you bother them."

As they neared the mine, Oliver pointed to a rock pile. "There, see, another snake. I didn't see any when I walked up here before, or when we came to the mine to hide the bag."

Antonio saw the snake as it slithered away. "Yes, you see it is afraid of us. It is probably the time of the day when they find food. Are you surprised to see a couple of snakes? Do you think there is a snake conspiracy of some kind?"

Oliver looked the other way and rolled his eyes. "No, I was just making an observation."

As they reached the entrance to the mine, Oliver spotted four more snakes. They slithered into the mine "Antonio, look at that. Don't tell me that is a coincidence. From the time I got out of the car until now, I've seen six snakes."

Antonio smirked. "Oleever, I don't particularly like snakes, but I am not afraid of them. Like I said, if you leave them alone, they won't bother you." He pointed to the entrance of the mine. "Are you too afraid to go in? It was your idea."

Oliver ignored Antonio's comment. They entered the mine and started their descent. It quickly got dark, and they turned on the flashlights. Oliver panned his light from side to side, and hoped they would not come across any more snakes. Antonio kept his beam on the ground in front of him. He was not concerned with the snakes. He knew they were a natural part of the area's wildlife.

They arrived at the small room carved into the mine where they had concealed the bag. Antonio put his hand up to his nose. "What is that smell? It smells like rotten fish."

Oliver smelled it too. He tried to breathe through his mouth. "OK, this is where we put it. They entered the room. Both men aimed their lights at the pile of rocks in the corner. Oliver hurried closer to it. "This pile has been disturbed." He removed the rocks that were still in place. "It's not here, Antonio." He aimed his light around the room as he stood up and went to the other corners. "I don't understand. The damned thing's not here." He pointed his light onto Antonio's face. "Did you move it?"

Antonio put his hand up to block the light. "No, of course not. Why would I move it?"

"This is not good, Antonio. Whoever took it is in grave danger. We must find it!"

They exited the small room to head back up. Oliver's flashlight came upon something. He turned back to shine the light on it again. "Antonio, there it is!"

Oliver ran to the bag. He picked it up "It's empty, Antonio."

Before Antonio could respond, both men turned to the deeper part of the tunnel that led to the dead end of fallen rocks. "Oleever, what was that sound? Did you hear it? It sounded like something being dragged."

Both men instantly turned toward the top of the tunnel, near the entrance, as they heard a voice cry out. "Padre, are you OK? Are you in here?"

Then the sound of a male voice chorused in. "Padre Oliver, Padre Antonio, estan aqui?"

Antonio recognized the voices. "Si, Felipe, Margarita, we are here."

The female voice yelled out to them again. "I was on my way to the monastery. We saw your car by the side of the road. Do you need medical help?"

Both men quickly turned to face the direction of the dead end. "Antonio grabbed Oliver's arm. Did you hear that? It is getting louder. It sounds very close. They flashed their lights in the direction of the sound. Father Antonio froze when he saw the thing that was approaching. It was the head of a woman supported by a series of snake clusters. One group had fastened itself to it by biting into the neck. Others were fastened to the tail end of the preceding snakes by being partially swallowed. The snakes were fastened to each other in a series of partially swallowed snakes. They made up a squirming mass in the shape approximating a human body. It moved like a person on skis. The feet never left the ground, they just slithered along in large strides.

The snake creature quickly came toward them. The head opened its mouth and licked its face. It looked at Oliver and extended its snake arms. "Miss me, lover boy? Come give Mama Crossbones a kiss." The thing was nearly on top of them. It moved quickly for a large squirming mass.

Oliver grabbed Antonio, who was frozen with fear. He dragged him toward the light. Antonio snapped out of his fright and began to run up the tunnel. Oliver yelled toward the entrance. "Get out, Margarita! Get out, Felipe! You are both in grave danger! Run away hurry!"

Oliver and Antonio reached the portion of the tunnel where there was a small amount of light. It was enough to see without the aid of the flashlight. He pulled Antonio to a stop. "We must face it here. We cannot afford to let it get too close to Margarita or Felipe."

As he turned to face the oncoming creature, he withdrew the Black Lamia and swung it at the snake hands that were wrapping themselves around both of their necks. He cut the snake arm and then cut through the snake bundle that made up the neck. The head fell to the ground, laughing. It said, "Fresh meat, just what I needed." Then it spontaneously combusted.

Oliver ran toward the exit. Antonio freed himself from the limp, entangled snakes. They fell from his neck. He ran after Oliver, but it was too late for Margarita, now possessed by the witch. He arrived to see her hit Felipe and toss him onto the dirt like a rag doll. Felipe was six feet and weight 230 lbs. Margarita was a petite woman. Fr. Antonio looked on as Margarita approached Oliver. She laughed and licked her lips. "Well, lover boy, how about it. You came all the way back! Couldn't stay away from Mama? Oh, how I will enjoy killing you!"

Father Antonio made the sign of the cross and started to pray. He ran to Oliver.

The witch turned and saw Antonio running toward Oliver. "And who's your pathetic friend, another priest? She reached Antonio in a split second, grabbed him by the neck and looked in his eyes. "You disgust me, priest." She spat on his face. Antonio was thrown against the rocks. His body fell to the ground.

Oliver swung the blade, but Margarita was too fast, possessed as she was. She grabbed him and lifted him off the ground. The blade fell out of his hands. Felipe got up and came running "No Tia! No, por favor!" He grabbed the short woman from behind. She dropped Oliver and turned to Felipe. Oliver wasted no time. He picked up the sword and swung as she turned to Felipe. She moved her head just enough for him to miss. After snatching Felipe with one hand, she reached out and took hold of Oliver again. The old woman held each man by the throat as she choked the life out of them.

Father Antonio came up behind her and crashed a large rock onto her head. Blood started to ooze out of the open wound. She laughed with a roar as she continued to choke both of her victims. Oliver's grip weakened as she choked him but he managed to cut off her arm and dropped to the ground. Felipe had stopped struggling. Oliver sprang up still short of breath from her choke hold. He swung the blade slicing her head cleanly off. It tumbled to the ground and rolled toward him. He kicked it out of the way and ran to Felipe. He felt the side of his neck. He slapped Felipe's face a couple of times. "Felipe, come on, snap out of it." Felipe began to stir. "Good. I think you're going to be OK."

Antonio was relieved to see both men were alive. They stood looking at the Margarita's headless body. Felipe was now beginning to sit up.

Suddenly, Margarita's body sprang up and ran toward the severed head. Antonio and Felipe's mouth hung open as they watched the headless body run towards its prize. Oliver grabbed the blade and quartered the body before it could reach the head.

Antonio walked toward the head. He motioned to Oliver to look at it. "What is that thing?"

Oliver coughed to clear his throat. "I think you were right, Antonio. It's probably just my imagination!"

Antonio shook his head. "I cannot believe something so evil can exist. It is a creature from hell which has taken human form. Poor Margarita."

"I hate to tell you this amigo, but welcome to the club." Oliver approached the head. The eyes were completely black. "Why are you trapped in that head? Why can't you just fly around and take over someone else?"

Felipe came up to them as they looked at the severed head. Then a snake slithered over to it as the three men looked on. The snake fastened itself onto the neck by biting it and holding its grip. Oliver and Antonio looked at each other.

"Don't worry, Antonio, snakes won't bother you unless you bother them." Oliver smiled. "Don't tell me you're afraid of snakes, Antonio." He picked up the Black Lamia and cut the snake's head off. The bite loosened, and the snakes head fell away.

Antonio looked at Margarita's head. It was mumbling something. "It is still alive. How can that be?"

Felipe gasped at the sight. "Como puede ser? How can it not be dead?"

Antonio turned to Felipe. "I don't know."

Felipe pointed to Margarita's body. "Lo malo, bad spirit, possess her, make her bad."

Antonio nodded "She was angry at God over the death of her son. Her faith had been weakened to the point she no longer believed in a just and merciful God."

Oliver looked at Felipe. "Antonio is right. That's all evil

needs, a small opening."

Felipe knelt and cried. He removed his shirt and put it over the top of the torso stump. "When I came out of cave I cannot breathe. I think I am going to die. Then I can breathe again. When I look at Margarita, she could not breathe. Then she can breathe, but she look different to me. She smile, not like the Margarita I know and she hit me. I thought she broke my shoulder. I try to stop her from killing Padre Oliver."

Father Antonio put his hand on Felipe's shoulder. "Your faith has saved you, Felipe. Unfortunately, Margarita was not so lucky. We must pray for her now."

Father Antonio led them in prayer and gave Margarita the last rites. After they finished, Oliver stood up and ran back into the mine. He emerged a few minutes later with the bowling bag. "We are going to need something a bit stronger to contain Margarita's head, but for now we can use this." He pointed to Margarita's head. "Somehow, it attracts snakes. So whatever we finally put it in needs to prevent the snakes from getting in, maybe a metal box." He went over to pick up the head. Another snake had already fastened itself to the neck. Oliver cut it off and put the head into the bag and zipped it closed.

Felipe stood up and approached the two men. "I make steel box for that devil head."

Oliver picked up the Black Lamia and put it in its sheath. "That's a good idea, Felipe. We must not let it get out again. It will take over anyone who is not strong in their faith with God. Do you understand?"

Felipe nodded.

Oliver turned to Antonio. He held up the bag. "I must entrust this to you and Felipe. I have to go to Torreón. I think Sr. Molina is one of these demons. That's why his name is in the book." Oliver took a deep breath and let it out slowly. "Fr. Soto and Margarita are dead. Two good people are dead because of this wretched evil. I must carry out what I have been instructed to do." Oliver paused and looked at Antonio "Do you still doubt what I say, Antonio?"

Antonio's eyes met Oliver's "No, no Oleever, my disbelief has been replaced by repulsion. I know evil exists among us every day, but I did not think it could occupy flesh and live so freely among us. It is as though someone has pulled a veil from my eyes. I do not pay much attention to the nonsense of vampires and werewolves or big foot. But this evil, which invades, and is spread to others, it is, in fact, real, and much more terrifying. From your troubles at all of the parishes you served, to your visit here and all the fantastic stories you told me, I thought you were suffering from dementia and paranoia. I see it is all too real. I am sorry to have doubted you, my friend."

"Antonio, you must not tell Pastor Bob you have seen me. Do you understand?"

"Yes, yes, not to worry. I was going to speak with him about your dementia, but now I see the merit of your actions. Don't worry; I will not speak of this thing or of you to him."

"You have two deaths to deal with right now. What will you tell Margarita's family about her death?"

Antonio looked at Felipe. "We must talk." Then he looked at Oliver. "Felipe and I will work through this. I am going to need his full cooperation. This will be difficult and dangerous. We will take care of things while you are in Torreón."

Felipe stepped forward. "I will help Padre Antonio in anything he needs."

Oliver reached for Felipe's hand and shook it. "Thank you, Felipe. I am sorry about Margarita."

Antonio motioned to Margarita's limbs. "We should take the body back to her village so it can be buried there."

They headed back to the side of the road where the vehicles were parked. Felipe and Oliver gently carried Margarita's body parts while Antonio carried the bowling bag containing her head and a rolled up shirt containing the remains of Regina's head. They laid everything in the back seat of Felipe's car.

Oliver turned to Antonio. "Will you call your mechanic friend, and tell him I need a Mexico license plate? It can be an old one. I can stop by on my way through town if you will tell me where he is located."

Felipe held up his hand as he popped open his trunk. "Padre Oliver, I have old plate from my other taxi here. You want to have it? I will put on your car."

After Felipe finished changing the car's plate, he shook Oliver's hand once more. "Vaya con Dios Padre."

"Thanks Felipe, you too." Oliver reached for Antonio's hand and shook it. "Call me if you have any questions. Good luck at the village. I know it will be difficult for the family to accept what has happened to Margarita. She was a good woman."

Antonio sighed as he nodded in agreement. "Yes, it will be difficult, but I promise to take care of Margarita in death. She took good care of us for many years. She will be greatly missed." He lifted his head and placed his hand on Oliver's shoulder. "You be careful, my friend. God has entrusted you with a formidable task. May He be with you at all times."

"Gracias, Antonio. God does not ask us to do anything we cannot handle. The key is to seek His guidance, which I will do constantly. May His will be done. Perhaps, you can call Fr. Jimenez and let him know I will be visiting."

"I will do that." Antonio got into Felipe's taxi, and they headed back toward the village.

Oliver got into his car and headed in the opposite direction, toward Torreón.

44

The Drug Lord

It had been a while since Oliver attended Mass in Spanish. He walked into the church and sat toward the back as the first reading was about to take place. It was Friday daily Mass. The church was half full. Oliver listened to the homily. His Spanish was good, he understood all that was said.

After Mass, Oliver waited patiently until the congregation exited the church building. Then he went over and introduced himself.

Fr. Francesco Jimenez greeted him with a warm smile. He was a frail gentleman in his early seventies. He looked a bit pale, like someone who did not spend much time in the sun. "So, you are a friend of Fr. Antonio, I understand. He called me and told me that you would be paying me a visit, something about you and your special mission."

Oliver wondered how much Antonio had revealed. "Is that, right? What kind of mission did he say that I was undertaking?"

"He only said he felt you were serving God in your own special way and I should help where possible. He thinks very well of you."

Oliver smiled and nodded. "Yes, he is a good friend, and I guess that is true of all of us. We are all serving God in our own special way, through the lives we have chosen."

"Yes, as was Fr. Soto." Fr. Francesco Jimenez's face became drawn. "His death is a terrible tragedy. I've known the man for over ten years and would never have suspected he was suffering from depression or any emotional issues. I am saddened at the news. He was a big help during my convalescence. Fr. Antonio is making arrangements for the body to be transported to Peru."

The old priest motioned to Oliver to follow him. "Come, let us go to the rectory. I will show you your room." They walked out of the church through the side entrance and across the church grounds and into the rectory. The house was a three bedroom, two story home that connected to the church via a covered walkway. Upon entering the rectory, Oliver noticed that it was furnished modestly but had exquisite works of art hanging throughout the house. "Later, you can join me upstairs, and we can chat." He pointed to the stairs leading to the second floor where the old priest's bedroom was located. It was adjacent to a large outdoor patio. "The kitchen is over there. If you are hungry, help yourself." He pointed down the hall where the bedrooms were located. "Your room is the second door on the right."

Oliver washed up, helped himself to a few tortillas from the refrigerator, and poured himself a glass of wine. After having his fill, he made his way up to the second floor. The stairs opened onto a short hall leading to Fr. Jimenez' bedroom on one side and the outdoor patio on the other. The patio used the space above the kitchen and dining room.

As he stepped onto the patio, Oliver caught sight of Fr. Jimenez. The old priest stood looking into the eyepiece of a telescope positioned on a tripod. It was aimed at the heavens. "It's an old man's addiction." He motioned with his hand for Oliver to come closer. He did so without taking his eye away from the eyepiece.

As Oliver got within a step of the telescope, Fr. Jimenez moved his head away from it. "Go ahead, have a look."

Oliver looked through the eyepiece. "It's beautiful."

"It will be easier to look at the stars when it becomes completely dark."

Oliver continued to focus his eyes. "I've always wanted to look through one of these." After a few moments of looking at the moon, he pulled away and turned to Fr. Jimenez. "Antonio didn't tell me you were a star gazer."

"Ah yes, ever since I was a child, I have been fascinated by the planets and stars. They are wondrous. If I was not a priest, I would like to have been an astronaut."

Oliver could see the sparkle in Fr. Jimenez's eyes as he talked about his passion. "I'm surprised that someone with a passion for science wound up becoming a priest. They are often mutually exclusive."

Fr. Jimenez walked over to the outdoor table and chairs and took a seat. "They are, but only to those who are threatened by the presence of God."

Oliver took a seat across from him. "Perhaps you're right."

"I am right. If people acknowledge God, they cannot themselves be gods. It's quite a blow to the ego. Complete self-determinism cannot permit such a belief. Their hearts are hardened under the mask of logic. While they might exhibit kindness, generosity and love, it is done through a veil of individual and self righteous pride. It's self-denial of the highest order. If you deny God, you deny yourself. But don't get me started."

Oliver was intrigued by the feisty old priest. He listened intently.

"There are those whose embrace of this belief has led them to great monetary wealth and influence. Coming to church is no more than an exercise in appearances, a social nicety. It is a narrow mind that clings to self-deification, when the overwhelming evidence of God's presence is all around us, here and up there." Fr. Jimenez pointed toward the sky. "Some people never bother to look up." He looked at his watch. "It will be dark in an hour. On a clear night like this, I can spend all night out here. But enough of my rant, Fr. Oliver. What of your visit? What kind of mission have you undertaken and how can I assist you?"

Oliver expected Fr. Jimenez to be quiet and tired. His countenance did not match his personality. He was a passionate little spitfire. "My mission involves the study of persistent evil. I guess you can say that the mission found me. I don't fully understand it myself."

"Then why do you persist in this mission which you did not seek and don't fully understand?" The old priest looked at Oliver with an expression of eager anticipation.

Oliver thought for a moment. "I persist because I feel I must. It's a road God has placed before me, and I am sure He expects me to stay the course."

Fr. Jimenez laughed loudly. It caught Oliver by surprise. He studied the old man to see if any demons were superimposed on his face. He saw just the old priest with a wide smile on his face.

Fr. Jimenez took a deep breath and looked up at the sky. "A man on a mission which he does not care for, or fully understand; if not for God, then why? That is my point. You are not forced, your will is your own, is it not? But yet, as you say, you must stay the course. I call that faith. Faith is remarkable and beautiful, even more so than the splendid sky above us." Fr. Jimenez paused. "But, there I go. Well, if your mission is the study of persistent evil, you came to the right place. It is all around us in drugs, greed and pornography. Welcome to Torreón."

"Yes, drugs are a big problem in the US, but here it's a major industry, isn't it?" Oliver noticed the evening sky gradually growing darker. Lights were starting to come on in the houses on the hills.

Fr. Jimenez pointed to the east. "One of the biggest drug lords lives over there. Do you see the big mansion on the hill? You can just barely see the lights. Even from here you can see the place is huge. It is the home of Angel Molina. He controls the flow of drugs through much of northern Mexico. Anyone who stands in his way either disappears or is found dead. The police look the other way. There is a constant turf war. If it's not the Sinaloa or Los Zetas, there is some other drug cartel battling for dominance. We are fighting a losing battle when it comes to the drug trade. Because of the money, many have come to depend on drug trafficking as their main source of income. They have chosen mammon over God."

"I understand Fr. Soto met with Sr. Molina."

"Yes, he thought he could convince Molina to donate money to help us with repairs and a new addition to the church. I told him about Molina's involvement with drugs. I wanted no part of his dirty money. He justified it by saying that the money could be used for evil, or for the kingdom of God. Better to use it for good, regardless of where it came. The damage was already done. I reluctantly agreed. He said the meeting went well and he would revisit Sr. Molina. But then he changed his mind and decided to head back to the monastery."

In the distance gun shots could be heard, several rounds then several more. Both men looked in the direction of the gunfire. The old priest shook his head. "Drug related killings are all too common."

"Fr. Jimenez, can you tell me why Fr. Soto thought a drug lord would even consider donating money to the church? That seems a bit foolish to me."

"Many of these drug dealers and murderers act as though they are doing nothing God would disapprove. Many go to church and contribute to charities. It's hard for me to say whether it is out of pride or guilt they do this. No matter, Angel Molina is one of these men. He enjoys the recognition of being a benefactor to the Church and other charities. Aside from murder, drug trafficking and money laundering, Sr. Molina would make a fine Christian. He shows up about once a month for Mass. He is like a celebrity with his entourage. When he does show up, he gets more attention than I do."

"When do you think he will make his next appearance at Mass?"

Fr. Jimenez thought for a moment. "It's been almost two months since I saw him. He is due to make an appearance. Perhaps he will grace us with his presence this coming Sunday. It is all show. He never stays for the entire Mass. In fact, he is out of here by the time we begin the Gospel reading. There is always some emergency that comes up, without fail."

<div align="center">~~~</div>

As on any typical Sunday, parishioners were dressed in their Sunday best. Families filed into the church. Volunteers were busy preparing for the 11:00 am Mass. Of the four Masses held on Sundays, it was typically the most heavily attended. Among the influx of parishioners, Oliver noticed the occasional demon double exposed on someone's face. Throughout his life and after recent events, Oliver came to classify three types of superimposed shadows. The first could be best described as a shadow on an individual's face. There was no demonic face along with the shadow. It was as though someone stepped out of the bright sun and into a darkened room. The person's face would tend to shift back and forth without any change in the ambient lighting. Oliver understood this to be the visible manifestation of a serious sin, but did not signify demonic possession.

The second was similar, but within the shadow a second face could be seen. Such a person was deeper into serious sin. They had attracted a demonic presence which had attached itself to them. This was what Oliver saw in his uncle when he was a young boy, and most recently with Fr. Soto. Occasionally, more than one demon had been drawn and could be seen intermittently as the demon faces faded in and out.

The third was what he had recently encountered with Mama Crossbones. The person was gone and had relinquished all control to the demon. The face of the demonic presence was always prominent. The underlying person was nowhere to be found because they had completely surrendered to evil. The shadowed presence extended beyond the person as it cast a shadowy haze around the person's entire body. This was the most disturbing to see.

On this particular Sunday the influx of parishioners was interrupted by a commotion outside. Oliver stepped to the entrance to see what was happening. He saw the demonic entourage of Angel Molina approaching the door. He was accompanied by five men. Three walked ahead, and two walked behind the demonic creature as it made its way to the church entrance. People recognized him. Many stopped to shake his hand. Angel Molina and his henchmen were all dressed in white suits. They looked like a Las Vegas lounge act.

They all took their seats. A few minutes later, Fr. Jimenez began Mass. Like clockwork, as the Gospel reading was about to begin, Molina and his five bodyguards rose and prepared to leave. Oliver met them as they were about to exit the building. He stood blocking the door as the men and their demon leader approached. "Saludos, mi amigos. My name is Father Oliver." The men stopped as Oliver extended his hand to make his introduction. They looked at Molina who then stepped forward. Oliver did his best to appear cordial and unaware of the demonic face. It was difficult not to gaze into those black eyes.

Angel Molina slowly reached for Oliver's hand. As he took it, Oliver felt temporarily weak, to the point where his knees shook for an instant. Oliver did his best to remain calm. "Hola, I'm Father Oliver. I hope everything is all right. We are just starting the Gospel reading. Are you sure you cannot stay?"

The demon let go Oliver's hand and smiled, exposing black gums and jagged teeth "I am Angel Molina. No, we cannot stay. I have important business. You are new here are you not, Padre?"

Oliver noticed the large eyes bulge in the demon's head as he asked the question. "Yes, I am here helping Fr. Francesco for a while."

The demon tilted its head and examined Oliver. "Where is the other priest?"

Oliver played along. "You mean Father Soto?"

The demon moved closer to Oliver. "Si, Father Soto."

"He's dead." Oliver replied, curious how the demon might react to the news.

The area below the demons eyes wrinkled as his smile became broad. It was as though this was delightful news. "Oh? What happened to the good Padre?"

Oliver sidetracked the question. "Perhaps we can talk more at leisure when you have time. I wanted to speak to you in private about a few matters of the church. Father Soto mentioned he met with you and that you were a most kind host."

The demon eyes were bright with pleasure at the news of Father Soto's death and now an opportunity to corrupt and bring down another member of the enemy's army. "You may visit with me the day after tomorrow, 6:00 pm, 999 Camino Grande, up on Chavez Hill. We will drink, we will talk, and we will have a special feast." The demon did not wait for Oliver to respond. He immediately left with his entourage.

45

The lord's Last Supper

Two armed guards stationed at the entrance to the property wore green military style uniforms. Each brandished a high capacity machine gun. Oliver drove up to the gate which featured large wrought iron numbers, 999, painted in gold. The guards did not open the gate. As Oliver's car came to a stop, one of the guards pointed his machine gun at Oliver from behind the gate. The other opened a door within the framework of a section of the left gate. It was a small door, just large enough to allow a person to pass through without having to open the larger sections.

The guard walked up to the driver side of the vehicle and looked at Oliver dressed in traditional priest garb. Then he poked his head in the car, looked back at the other guard and yelled. "Es un padre."

Oliver smiled as the guard turned toward him again. "Yes, I am a priest. My name is Father Oliver. I was invited by Sr. Molina."

The guard made his way back to the gate. He passed through the small door. Shortly thereafter the other guard lowered his machine gun and disappeared into the small room at the side of the gate.

There was a loud click, then the sound of a motor. The gates slowly opened, and the guard waved Oliver through. As he pulled his car onto the property, the second guard signaled him to stop. Then he signaled him to get out of the car.

"Sorry, padre, but we cannot take any chances. I'm sure you understand," he said as he patted Oliver down searching for a concealed weapon, then scanned him with a metal detector.

Oliver nodded and smiled as he complied in the search. "I understand, no problem."

The other guard opened the driver side door, looked in the car, then released the trunk latch to examine the contents of the trunk.

"Esta bien, Padre." The guard signaled him to get back in the car. He pointed at the long driveway. "Sr. Molina is waiting for you."

"Gracias," Oliver replied as he drove up the hill to the main entrance. He pulled into one of the parking spaces. The mansion was constructed of stone and looked like a castle. He made his way up the series of grand stairs to the large double door entry and rang the melodic door chime. A moment later a guard opened the door and signaled Oliver to enter. This guard was also armed with a pistol which sat in a holster on his side.

Oliver followed the guard toward the sound of chatter. The corridor from the foyer was decorated with Italian Renaissance art. The furniture featured ornate swirls and intricate designs. As he entered the great hall, Oliver found himself in the company of approximately twenty demonic figures. Demonic faced men and women held glasses of wine as they talked. In the middle of the group was the largest of the demonic figures. Angel Molina was surrounded by guests.

Oliver had never seen such a gathering. He closed his eyes for a moment and prayed for God's grace. *Lord, guide me through this house of darkness.*

"Hola, Padre Oliver." The booming voice of Angel Molina rang out. He approached, with hand extended. The handshake creeped out Oliver, but he hid his emotion and maintained a cordial smile. "You come to my house. Now you drink with us and celebrate." The demon raised his arm and a waiter quickly came over with a tray of drinks. Molina waited as Oliver took one of the Swarovski crystal wine glasses. "Here's to our new friend and special dinner guest, Padre Oliver." The rest of the demon guests raised their glasses. Molina winked at Oliver. "What happens en mi casa stays en mi casa, hey Padre?" Then he guzzled his wine, and everyone one else did the same. Oliver took a small sip.

Molina pulled over one of his guests. "This is Carlos Figueroa, my compadre. You two talk now, and we talk later, hey padre? I must speak with a few business associates now."

Figueroa turned to Oliver as Molina walked over to the other guests. "Well, Father, how do you like Mexico?" His eyes shifted quickly from left to right. His demon face reminded Oliver of a cross between a goat and a snake. His voice was raspy, and his words seemed to drag.

"I like it very much." Oliver took another sip of his wine as he looked around the room. The only human beings he could see were the support staff. All the guests were fully demons. There was no trace of the humans who once occupied those bodies. He glanced back at Carlos Figueroa and tried to see past the demon and find the person inside, but he could not. Oliver did not realize he was staring at the Carlos demon.

"Father, Father, is there sumting hrong?"

"Oh, I'm sorry, Carlos. I didn't mean to stare. It's because you remind me of someone."

"Yes, I know. I have been told I look like Antonio Banderas."

Oliver smiled and held up his glass. "Yes, very nice, but it's not who I had in mind." Oliver paused as another demon approached and shook his hand. This one did not speak English and began jabbering at Carlos. It spoke quickly in a staccato fashion which Oliver found irritating.

Oliver interrupted the annoying demon. "Excuse me, where is the bathroom?"

Carlos pointed toward the archway leading to the large hallway. It ran down the middle of the mansion. "It is the third door on the left."

Oliver nodded and headed toward the restroom. Once he was past the archway and out of view of the guests, he stopped and waved to one of the servants. The Deman came over quickly. "Si Padre?"

Oliver pointed his fingers in the shape of a gun. "How many men have guns?"

The servant looked past Oliver in the direction leading to the guests. "All of them have weapons, Padre."

Oliver figured there would be guards with guns, but he did not expect all the guests to be armed, especially after undergoing a thorough search. He thought for a moment then turned to the servant. "Thank you, Señor."

"De nada, Padre."

Oliver entered the restroom. It was dimly lit. Gold plated hardware adorned the sink and toilets. There were three stalls and three sinks. A full-length mirror hung on the wall closest to the entrance door. The mirrors over the sinks were in ornate frames. There was dark green marble tile throughout. The sinks were black, and each held its own set of soap and towels.

Oliver approached the sink and looked into the mirror. *"What am I supposed to do with all of these things? How can God allow such evil to roam free?"*

The evening was hot and muggy. He leaned into the sink and splashed water on his face. The cold water felt good on his clammy face.

He reached for a towel, but was startled into his Wing Chun fighting stance. He suddenly realized there was someone standing a few feet away near the full-length mirror. At first he thought it was his reflection. He stood there with hands at the ready. The man did not look familiar. Oliver waited for the stranger to attack, none came.

"It's me, Fr. Oliver. It's Monty."

A moment later he lowered his hands. "Monty, is that really you? I did not recognize you. You no longer look like Paul. Is this your original appearance?"

Monty stood tall and straight. He was dressed in a comfortable jumpsuit. He looked straight at Oliver. "Spare no demon. Remember God is with you."

Oliver slowly approached the apparition. "But, how could..."

"You were right. It is never too late to seek God's forgiveness if you really want it."

Oliver held his hand up slowly to touch Monty.

Monty smiled. "I had no idea, Oliver. I had no idea."

As Oliver was about to touch the figure of Monty, it disappeared. Oliver was barely able make out the last few words as Monty vanished.

"Thank you, Fr. Oliver. Trust God. He is with you."

Oliver remained where he stood and thought about all the events that had transpired since a crazy man walked into his office at St. Ignatius back in Raleigh, North Carolina. *So much has happened. So much has changed.* He could not help feeling responsible for Regina's and Margarita's death. He prayed for their souls. Everyone who stood in the way of this evil was either dead or in danger of being a target. Now it seemed he was tasked with doing a bit of divine cleaning up. *"Was my whole life in preparation for this?"* He thought and remembered how he would play priest when he was in the second and third grade.

Before going to bed, he would stand on his mattress and face the wall. There was a small plastic wall mounted holy water dish which held a few ounces. He would take the holy water from church when no one was looking and fill up the small dish. At night he would stand on his bed, face the little ornament, and make the sign of the cross while pretending to be conducting Mass. He would kneel and rise, kneel and rise, jumping up and down on his mattress as he had observed the priest doing many times at Mass. Young Oliver would speak gibberish, just like the priest's Latin during Mass. He did not understand what the priest said, but it sounded holy. The little holy water receptacle was his altar. Oliver's pretend Mass would last a few minutes and end with a few sprinkles directed at his make believe congregation.

Oliver leaned over the sink, splashed more cold water on his face and prayed. He dried his face, left the restroom and signaled the servant once again.

The man came over quickly. "Si, Padre?"

Oliver put his hand on the man's shoulder. "You must leave this house right away. Tell all the other servants they must leave if they want to live. Only the servants, understand?"

The man looked puzzled. Oliver tightened his grip on the man's shoulder. "Es muy importante. Tienes que salir de aqui ahora mismo. Lo malo esta aqui. Do you understand? You must leave here now. Evil is here. All the servants must leave, only the servants." Oliver held up his cross for the man to see.

Oliver let go of his grip on the man's shoulder. The servant walked away slowly at first, then in rapid steps. Once the servant had gone into the service area, Oliver made his way to the front door. He smiled at the guard. "I need to get my bible from the car."

The guard nodded as Oliver let himself out. He walked down the series of steps and opened the driver side door. He maneuvered his body to block the view of the front door of the house.

The piece of cloth draped over the side of the seat didn't look out of place. It blended well with the inside of the vehicle and did not draw attention. Oliver quickly removed it. The small gash on the side of the seat looked like a simple tear, but it was just wide enough to insert the Black Lamia into the seatback. He stuck his finger into the small gash and felt the weapon. He slide the Black Lamia out of its hiding place. Oliver tucked the weapon under his cassock, grabbed his bible, and headed back into the house.

He opened the front door and held up his bible as he re-entered. The guard looked up and nodded. Oliver continued past the foyer making his way back to Angel Molina and his group of demon guests. The noise level was dramatically higher than when he left to go to the bathroom.

Servants were still pouring the wine and tending guests. Oliver figured his warning was not taken seriously. Carlos Figueroa approached him. "Father, where have you been? Sr. Molina is about to start dinner. He led the way and the guests started to move to the adjoining dining room.

Oliver noticed the large painted portrait hanging on one of the walls. It was framed in an ornate gold frame. "Who is that?" Oliver asked as he pointed to the painting.

Carlos Figueroa turned to look at Oliver with a contorted demonic expression Oliver guessed to be surprise. "That is Mr. Angel Molina. Do you not see the resemblance?" The man in the painting had short black hair combed straight back. His mustache was formidable as was his nose. He had brown eyes and was dressed like a matador.

Oliver had never seen Molina's real face. Whatever remained had been completely consumed by the evil which possessed him. It was a voluntary consumption. Oliver continued to look at the painting. "I guess I'm not very good with faces. It is a very nice painting though."

As they entered the dining room, Oliver was taken aback at

the beauty of the place. The long table was set for twenty. The china and table decorations complemented one another. Finely polished silver candelabras were set at three points on the table. Guests took their seats.

"You will sit there, Padre," instructed the Carlos demon.

Oliver took his seat. "Thank you." He was careful not to reveal what was under his priestly garment.

Angel Molina stood at the head of the table and waited for everyone to be seated. He then held up his wine glass. "Amigos, we will begin our sumptuous dinner feast soon. Our meal this evening will be prepared by the illustrious Chef Rodrigo." He pointed at the side of the room where Chef Rodrigo waved at the guests. Everyone applauded as Chef Rodrigo bowed. "But, first I have a short presentation you all are invited to enjoy." As he spoke, he pressed the buttons on his remote control and a large screen came down from the ceiling. The sound of a telephone connection could be heard. There was a flicker on the screen, and the image coming into view was crystal clear. "Hola, Dr. Sinclair and how are things in Raleigh?"

Oliver froze in his seat as the image of Sinclair loomed large on the screen. This was a live two way transmission. Fortunately, it was dark enough in the room his face would not be seen by Sinclair. He took no chances and kept his head at a slight downward angle so he could not be recognized.

Dr. Sinclair was in his office. "Doing well, amigo. And, how is our business in Mexico?"

"Better than ever. We've assembled our twenty Mexican Council members as was requested and I assure you, we will find Mama Crossbones soon." Molina replied in a roar of a voice. "It's a shame that you could not be down here to join us for our feast. I would have had Chef Rodrigo prepare some greets for you."

Dr. Sinclair laughed. "That's grits, Angel, not greets. And you must try it sometime."

Molina roared with laughter. "Yes, yes, another time perhaps. I suppose you would like to say hello to your old friend?"

Oliver felt beads of sweat form on his brow when he heard Sinclair. "Hello, Father Oliver. It is so nice to see you again. We thought you might have gone overseas to live among the monks of Tibet. No one has heard or seen you in weeks. But here you are among friends, and in fine health I see."

Oliver looked up at the screen and saw Dr. Sinclair's large demonic head looking back at him. He did not respond. Several demon guests rose from their places and surrounded Oliver from behind.

Sinclair turned his attention to Molina. "How will you be preparing him?"

"Chef Rodrigo will be preparing the padre in a chili sauce, but not too strong, as that would mask the taste of the meat."

Sinclair nodded. "Hmm, yes, sounds wonderful. You must tell me how it all turns out. After you are done with our holy nuisance, retrieve Mama Crossbones and kill Fr. Francesco. We must eradicate all priests by the name of Francis. We do not know which one of them will fulfill the prophecy. Best kill them all and take no chances." Sinclair paused and glanced in Oliver's direction. "And, Molina, make sure you feed his remains to the dogs." The screen went dark and retracted back into the ceiling. Oliver rose slowly to his feet as he clutched the handle of the Black Lamia.

Chef Rodrigo rolled a large food preparation table out from an adjacent alcove. The table was roughly three feet by eight feet. "My friends you are in for a treat. Our meat for tonight's feast will be fresh, and Chef Rodrigo will prepare it before your very eyes." Molina turned to Oliver. "Well, Padre, thank you for accepting my dinner invitation. Now, if you don't mind..." Molina pointed at the food preparation table. "We are getting hungry."

As the demons surrounding Oliver closed in, he withdrew the Black Lamia. Several of those closest to him attempted to draw their guns. Before they could get off a shot, demon claws fell to the floor with guns in hand. Oliver swung his body around as he made slice after slice. Everything seemed to be moving in slow motion for him. He picked off his targets easily. The thuds of flesh hitting the floor continued as heads and limbs were cleanly sliced from demon after demon. He cleared his way down the table in a ballet-like flurry of graceful moves taking the demon party guests by surprise. Everyone scrambled but could not get away from the crazy priest. By the time bullets started to fly, Oliver had made his way to the end of the table and started to come up the other side. Hands, arms, and heads continued to drop.

"Get that son of a bitch!" Angel Molina roared, his face

contorted with anger. The sides of his mouth drooled. He pounded the solid mahogany table so hard the wood cracked under his fist. He made his way toward Oliver, pushing a few of the other demons out of his way.

Bullets were zinging past Oliver, many of them hit the blade and ricocheted off. Oliver focused on mowing down the demon guests. The Black Lamia seemed to have a mind of its own as it managed to get in front of a flurry of otherwise deadly bullets. Oliver realized he was not completely in control of the blade. He remembered what Monty said about intent and how the blade somehow knew it. He felt his hand was being guided by something more agile and powerful than himself. Bullets could not get through as long as the blade was between them. Oliver proceeded to slice and dice between gun volleys.

One of the demons crept from behind and rushed to tackle him. Oliver's senses were in overdrive. He knew where each body stood or had dropped. His every move was a masterpiece of efficiency as he simultaneously attacked and defended against the dwindling demon guests. He saw Angel Molina coming closer, and he saw Chef Rodrigo pick up a meat cleaver and throw it. He knew the demon from behind had full confidence he would put an end to Oliver's onslaught. As the demon lunged to surprise Oliver, the buzzing of the approaching meat cleaver grew rapidly louder. Oliver rolled his body to one side, leaning over as far as he could to avoid it. The attacker from behind received the full impact of the cleaver as it tore through its head. Angel Molina grabbed Oliver as he dodged the cleaver, lifted him up by his left shoulder preparing to slam his other fist into the annoying priest's face. Molina heard a swoosh and felt a cold sting as the blade cut through his bulging demonic arm.

Oliver dropped to the ground. The powerful demon swung with his remaining arm. It, too, dropped to the ground with a loud thud. With his next shift from the waist, Oliver took Angel Molina's head off. The torso and legs continued to move. Oliver sliced them apart so that no part of Angel Molina could stand.

In a loud outburst, Chef Rodrigo rushed Oliver waving another meat cleaver. Oliver side-stepped the attack and shifted as he swung the Black Lamia, cutting Chef Rodrigo in half just below the chest.

Several headless bodies ran toward him. He sliced them down to the individual limbs. Torsos, arms, and legs were everywhere. He became aware of his own breathing. It was smooth and relaxed. He felt light and ready. His senses maintained a high alert and he stood motionless. The room was quiet. Something was wrong. He had accounted for all but two of the demons. He remained completely still and listened. "None shall be spared." The words appeared fresh in his mind's eye. Then he heard Molina's booming voice coming from the severed head. "Get him you fools! Get that scum! Make him pay!"

Two demons lunged from across the room. They landed in front of Oliver but out of reach of his blade. They studied him as they paced from side-to-side, waiting for just the right time to attack. One picked up a gun and fired a few rounds. Oliver picked them off with the blade. It felt natural. He did not have to think about it. The blade did most of the work.

The demon threw the gun down in disgust and looked at the other demon. The second demon nodded as he glanced at the end of the table. They both looked at Oliver. With a loud roar, the two demons headed for the ends of the table. They toppled everything over as they lifted it off the ground. The food, plates and candles came clamoring to the floor. They flipped the tabletop side toward Oliver and rushed him.

Angel Molina's severed head laughed. "That's right, squash the pathetic priest to death. He has nowhere to run."

The demons closed in on Oliver. The large mahogany table top was approaching fast. He had just a few feet between him and the wall. He stood his ground and held the blade ready. As the table was within a couple of feet of flattening him, he sliced through its top as though it was a loaf of bread. A faint blue glow could be seen as the table was sliced in half. The two sections fell to the ground, inches in front of where he stood. The demons did not realize what happened until they felt the thump of their table section hitting the floor.

Oliver did not hesitate. He rushed to his left and surprised the demon still holding the end of the table with a crew cut just above the neck. He took out the legs and arms with fast strokes of the blade. The look of surprise was still on his face as his head hit the ground. The second demon ran toward the exit.

Again Oliver saw the words "None shall be spared" emblazoned on his mind. *"No way to catch him."* He hurled the Black Lamia across the room as the demon reached the exit. The front door guard made his way into the dining room at the very moment the force of the Black Lamia knocked the demon creature into the wall, where it was impaled through the chest.

The guard fumbled his gun. The demon howled and grabbed the handle of the blade in an attempt to free himself. Oliver rushed the demon. As he did so, he grabbed one of the meat cleavers, courtesy of Chef Rodrigo. The demon pulled the blade partially out. He howled again. The guard continued to fumble for his gun and then caught sight of Oliver approaching with a cleaver in hand. Oliver reached the impaled demon beast and struck it with the cleaver as it was in mid howl. The head rolled off and into the arms of the guard.

Oliver removed the Black Lamia and quartered the beast. The pieces dropped to the ground. The guard also dropped as he fainted. Oliver was amazed at how little blood was shed, though the insides of these once human creatures were filled with a thick black jelly.

Oliver turned to the guard and raised his blade. As he was about to behead the guard, he stopped the blade a fraction of an inch from the guard's neck. Oliver realized that the guard was human. No demon was permanently affixed to his face. He let the guard live.

He turned and faced the carnage. The heads were all spewing obscenities in Spanish. Oliver walked over to Angel Molina's head. "Sorry to ruin your dinner, but I didn't like the menu."

The demon spit at him. "Te voy a matar. Hijo de puta!"

Oliver searched the mess for the remote control. The candles were still burning in the middle of the marble floor. He looked for something in which to put Angel Molina's head. He glanced at the food preparation table and saw a large box of aluminum foil. He grabbed it and rolled each of the heads in foil. He was not interested in preserving their freshness. He wanted to keep them in the dark and unable to reach another host. He sliced several sections of the curtain and used it as a sling to carry five heads at a time. He took two bundles at a time and threw them in the trunk of his car. After all the heads were packed, he closed the trunk's lid and went back into the mansion.

He stacked all the body parts in the center of the room. Oliver grabbed a bottle of cooking oil from the food preparation table and walked over to the spot where the screen had been lowered earlier. He pressed the remote control and down came the screen. Oliver stood directly behind the screen, out of camera range.

There was a flicker and, a moment later, the image of Dr. Sinclair loomed on the screen. "Molina? What's going on?" The doctor's eyes widened. He stood up from his seat and looked closely into his computer screen. His mouth hung open as he surveyed the carnage. Torsos and limbs stacked in a heaping pile. "Molina, are you there? What the hell happened? Who did this?"

"Sinclair, shut up and listen." Oliver knew that Sinclair could record what was on the screen, so it was best to stay out of camera range.

"Who's there? Is that you, priest? What have you done, you murdering bastard?"

"Sinclair, I must be running along now. But I just want you to know I'll come and pay you a personal visit if anyone I know is hurt, anyone!"

Oliver walked toward the entrance to the dining hall.

"We'll find you, priest!" The voice boomed from the screen. All the doctor could see was the back of a figure walking across the room. As he walked, he poured something onto the pile of body parts. Then he dipped a piece of cloth on one of the burning candles to let the fire catch. He then threw it to set the body pile ablaze. The fire grew instantly. The figure on the screen made it to the dining room entrance, leaning over and dragging someone out of the room with him.

Once outside the dining hall, Oliver slapped the guard to wake him. The guard opened his eyes and immediately tried to get away. Oliver held him by the front of his shirt. "Take it easy. I'm not going to hurt you." Oliver pointed at the dining hall. "Fire, we have to go. Vamonos!"

Oliver held the guard's revolver and signaled him to get into the car. They drove down the long driveway to the gate. Oliver pointed the gun at the guard. "You stay with me. Tell them that Sr.

Molina has sent us on an errand.

The guard nodded.

When they reached the gate, the car pulled to a stop. One of the guards came out and approached the passenger side window. He spoke to the guard in the car. "Que pasa?"

Oliver's passenger responded with a hand wave pointing up to the mansion. "Senor Molina nos mando a buscar algo." He repeated for Oliver's benefit. "We must go get something for Sr. Molina."

The guard signaled to the second guard to open the gates. There was a familiar click, and then the motors began to pull open the gates. "I see you later."

As Oliver began to drive past the guard post he looked in his rear view mirror and caught sight of the mansion in the distance with flames shooting out of the dining hall windows. He drove on. A moment later he turned to the guard. "What is your name?"

"Arturo, me llamo Arturo." The guard pointed to the rear of the car. "Why you kill those people?"

Oliver took a deep breath. He was glad to have put distance between himself and Angel Molina's drug palace. "They were not people."

Arturo glanced at the gun in Oliver's left hand. "Why you not kill me?"

Oliver looked straight ahead and continued to drive. "Because you are a person."

"No comprendo." The guard searched for the right English words. "I not understand."

"Do you believe in God, Arturo?"

"Si, of course, Padre!" He examined Oliver for a moment. "Are you really a padre? You no look like a padre to me. You work for one of the cartels?"

Oliver had been asked whether he was really a priest so many times, he sometimes pretended to be other people. Depending on where he was traveling and the person asking the question, he might pretend to be a pilot, a race car driver, or some other exotic personality. People were always fascinated. It was one of the ways he amused himself and also avoided being asked the question. He would assume some made up name, to go along with his new persona. If Pastor Bob ever found out, he'd have a cow.

"Yes, I am really a padre. I serve God, not a cartel."

Oliver pulled the car over a few blocks from the center of town. "Arturo, you can go."

The guard began to grasp the door handle to let himself out. Oliver grabbed him by the shoulder. "Forget what you saw today. Comprende?"

Arturo nodded and started to open the car door.

Oliver did not let go of his shoulder. Arturo looked at Oliver and wondered if the priest might be a little loco. Oliver relaxed his grip and handed him his revolver. "Find another job. A guard that faints is apt to have a short career."

Arturo smiled as though he understood. Oliver knew he did not. The guard that faints got out of the car and walked toward the center of town.

Oliver sat in the car for a few moments before continuing. He took out his phone and called Antonio.

46

Moving On

It was dark by the time Oliver returned to the rectory. He ran inside, retrieved his belongings, then jotted down a name and address from the little black book. Once that was done, he made his way upstairs.

Father Jimenez was at the telescope. "Hello Oliver. How was your meeting with Sr. Molina?"

"It was cut short. The chef lost control of the food, and it started a fire."

Fr. Jimenez continued looking through the telescope. "I'm sorry to hear that. Was anyone hurt?"

"No people were hurt." The old priest continued to star gaze. "I need to leave tonight, Father Jimenez. I'm all packed up."

Father Jimenez shifted his attention away from the telescope. "What is the rush? Are you going back to Antonio's?"

Oliver looked up at the night sky. "I don't know. I haven't decided yet, but I know it is time to go."

"I am sorry that you will be going so soon, my unusual friend. And what has triggered this hasty departure?" The feisty old priest approached him. He looked into Oliver's eyes. "Does this have to do with your study of persistent evil?"

Oliver looked at the chiseled face of Fr. Jimenez. "I'm afraid it does."

Fr. Jimenez nodded. "Well then, please make sure to come back when you can. I have enjoyed your company, brief as it has been."

"Thank you. I enjoyed the astronomy lesson." Oliver shook the old priest's hand. "It is best if you do not go by Francesco-Jimenez. Continue using Jimenez only, at least until we have a new Pope."

The old priest's eyebrows went up. "Why? What do you mean? We don't need a new Pope. We have Pope Benedict. Why should I not use my full name?"

"Your life will be in danger if you use it. As far as the Pope goes, it is something that has gotten the attention of hell and its minions."

"Your mission frightens me, Father Oliver. You have not shared much about it, yet I sense there is great peril in it."

Oliver nodded. "There is a war raging between good and evil. But this time it's different. The Lord has allowed me to see the enemy clearly. Please bear that in mind when you listen to the news tomorrow." Oliver glanced at the telescope. "Perhaps I'll get one of those someday and take up a little star gazing of my own."

Father Jimenez smiled. "May the Lord guide you and watch over you."

Oliver bowed his head as Fr. Jimenez blessed him with the sign of the cross. "Thank you, Padre Jimenez."

"Go in peace, Oliver."

47

Emergency Meeting

"I regret having to call this meeting and take you away from important business, but the situation has deteriorated. I will turn the meeting over to Bill Droper in New York, our highest ranking Council member. I'm sure with his leadership we will bring this situation under control." Dr. Sinclair's image on all the screens was replaced by that of Bill Droper.

Bill looked noticeably irritated. "My golf game was interrupted yesterday by news that there is a problem bringing drugs into the United States from Mexico. As ridiculous as it sounds, it's true. Aside from the money we are losing, it's a major pain in my ass.

"As some of you may have heard by now, a rogue priest took it upon himself to kidnap Mama Crossbones. He then proceeded to take out the leaders of our Mexico cartels. The twenty Council members who ran ninety percent of the drug business in Mexico are missing. Their heads have not been recovered. We don't think they were burned in the fire.

"Shortly thereafter, the body of the leader of our Western Mexico cartel was found in the bathroom of a restaurant without the head. I happen to know the food in that particular establishment is not that bad as to cause one of our own to lose his head.

"Our Mexican worker bees are running scared. They think God has sent an army to punish them. Drug imports from Mexico have all but ceased, all because of one crazy ass priest who has

275

decided to go Rambo. He has systematically captured Council members and has managed to keep them from resurfacing in new host bodies.

"We must find this bastard priest and eliminate him. We can't afford to let him take us away from profits and the important business of preventing the one called Francis from becoming pope. We are continuing with the systematic elimination of any priest named Francis.

"Let's find this son of a bitch quickly and get our comrades back from wherever he is holding them."

48

Guillermo

As Oliver drove toward Margarita's village, he wondered how all of this would end. *"As far as I know, there is no way to get rid of these demons for good. One was bad enough; now I have a trunk load of them."* The road was dusty and full of holes; he had to drive slowly. Antonio and Felipe would meet him in La Chole, under the sign at the entrance of the hacienda La Soledad. From there, they would drive out together to the place where the heads were to be stored.

Oliver approached the rendezvous point. He saw a pickup truck parked under the large sign. Antonio waved from the passenger side. Felipe started the engine. They headed north along a stretch of road for a couple of miles, then off road through sparsely vegetated landscape. Oliver drove close behind Felipe. The pickup's cargo banged around in the back making a loud racket every time they hit a small hole or bump.

The dwindling light from the setting sun began to reveal a few stars overhead. Oliver followed Felipe's lead as they made their way to a dot on the horizon. As they approached, Oliver saw what appeared to be a small structure; a shack. Felipe drove past it and looped around in a large circle. Nothing grew inside the circle which was edged by rocks piled to about eighteen inches. Small bushes and cacti dotted the landscape, which seemed to go on for miles outside the circle. Felipe stuck his arm out the window and pointed to the center of the circle.

Oliver looked where Felipe pointed and saw the box. It was silver, and there were a few snakes squirming alongside it. Both vehicles circled back and pulled up in front of the small shack in the middle on this particular nowhere.

Oliver opened his door, got out, and stretched. Antonio came over to greet him. "You look like hell, Oliver, welcome back."

"Thanks, Antonio, it's good to see you, and you too, Felipe."

Felipe stepped forward. "We tried burying the metal box containing Margarita's head, but the snakes kept digging it up. All we could think to do was to put the box in a remote location and let the snakes have at it. There is no way they can open the metal box."

Oliver looked around at the barren expanse. "What is this place, Antonio? Where are we?"

Antonio did not answer the question. His face was solemn. He had a more pressing question of his own. "Did you really bring twenty more of those things with you?"

"Twenty one, it is the way it had to be." Oliver looked at the cargo in the back of Felipe's pickup truck. "How did you round up all these metal boxes so quickly? We spoke only a few hours ago by phone."

"Yes, I know," replied Antonio. "But, Guillermo told us we would need at least twenty more after we brought Margarita's head here."

Oliver picked up one of the boxes and examined it, then he put it back in the truck. "Who is Guillermo?"

Antonio motioned to the shack. "This is the home of Guillermo. He has become the self-appointed guardian of the demon head."

Oliver smiled in disbelief. "You mean somebody lives here?"

Antonio nodded. "Yes, after we brought Margarita's body back to the village. He was the person who took charge of explaining to the villagers what had happened. He is the town's elder. The people respect him. They come to him seeking advice. We did not tell him what actually happened because he already knew. He told the villagers he had foreseen this day, even as a young man. He warned them not to speak of it and to stay away from this place. He made them understand it is not Margarita but a demon that is locked up in the box and placed where it can do no harm. We buried Margarita's body in the cemetery after a Mass was held for her sendoff to God. We prayed she would be with Him and He would be merciful. We also prayed she would be made whole by His grace."

Antonio patted Oliver on the back as he walked toward the shack's crooked front door. "Yes, come. I want to introduce you."

They entered the one-room shack. In the corner sat a skinny old man with a grey beard. His head was bald. His skin was dark, and his eyes were white. He was sitting on a scrawny chair, one of four in the square shaped room. The only other pieces of furniture were a table, a small dresser, and a cot with a thin mattress against one side of the room. Light from the setting sun leaked in through the many slits in the wood planks that made up the exterior walls. The old man turned toward them as they entered. "Buenas noches, amigos."

Felipe and Antonio responded in unison. "Buenas noches, Guillermo."

Guillermo motioned to them to take a seat. "Por favor."

Antonio and Felipe sat down. Oliver remained standing. The old man turned to him. "Is this him?"

"This is Padre Oliver." Antonio replied. "He has just returned from Torreón."

Guillermo stood up slowly. He used his walking stick for support and approached Oliver. He stood quietly facing the priest. Then he extended his hand and Oliver reached for it. As they shook hands, the old man's eyes widened. "So, at last I meet you." Guillermo's voice was raspy and low. "I have been waiting for you, Padre." The old man gently tightened his grip on Oliver's hand. "Si, I have been waiting a long time." A hint of a smile crossed Guillermo's face, but it faded as he turned toward the door. "And I've waited for them as well."

Oliver looked toward Antonio, then back to Guillermo. "How do you know of me and all of this?"

Guillermo walked back to his chair and slowly sat down. "Sit, Padre."

Oliver took a seat and watched as the interior of the shack

continued to darken.

"When I was a young man I had a very strange encounter. A man dressed in a beautiful white suit approached me as I was on my way to our little church. He asked me my name and if I could give him directions to the church. I told him I was on my way there and would be happy to show him the way. As we walked, he asked me why I was on my way to church. It was not a Sunday. I told him I just felt I wanted to go. He then asked me if I would not prefer to see the wonders of the world instead of the inside of a rinky-dink church. 'After all, you are young. No sense wasting your time on such superstitious nonsense,' he said. I told him one day I would see the world, but I needed God in order to have a clear perspective of what I saw in the world.

"He stopped walking and turned to me. I noticed he had a large stack of money in his hands. 'You mean to tell me you would prefer going to some old church instead of going on an adventure where you can make so much money you could have anything you wanted?' I stopped. My eyes were fixated on all that money in his hands."

"'I need someone to help me with an important project,' he said. 'Do you think you would like to help me and earn all this money?' He slowly flipped through the bills and raised them up to his nose as he took a deep breath. All the while he looked at me and smiled."

"What is your project," I asked.

"To show everyone my truth," he said.

I did not understand. "What do you mean, your truth? What is your truth?"

"That your god is a liar. Only I can help mankind see true prosperity." He held out the money to me as his smile intensified. I think he was sure I was going to take it, but I backed away realizing who he was. He became angry when I did not take the money. Then he stepped close to me and smiled again. "Guillermo, you are a peasant living in poverty. You want to see the world. I am giving you the opportunity to see it. It is an opportunity you do not want to pass up. You will have everything you want, including women, beautiful women. Think of how wonderful your life could be. You don't want to kick yourself in the future by passing up this incredible gift I am offering you. I have chosen you because you are special. Now, I'll ask you one more time: whose truth would you rather see? That god of yours who hides in a broken down church and doesn't know you exist, or my truth, filled with joy, laughter, and money, lots of money?"

I backed away and said, "God's truth is the only truth I need to see."

His eyes became red as he said, "Very well, you young fool, as you wish."

With that, he was gone, and so was my sight. I was blinded instantly. I have been blind ever since. The only thing I see is God's truth. In that truth, I see you, Padre, and I see what you have done in the name of the Lord. I witnessed this day before it happened and I foresee God's hammer falling on this evil in His due time."

There was silence. Then Guillermo continued. "Where are my manners? There are candles and matches in the top left dresser drawer. I do not need them, but perhaps you would like to light one. It must be dark by know."

Felipe made his way to the dresser. "I will light the candle. It is dark, but there is a full moon outside."

When Felipe finished lighting the candle, Oliver turned to Guillermo. "Do you know why these demons are trapped in the heads of the hosts they occupy? Why don't they just fly around and find another person to inhabit?"

"They cannot. Unless there is a willing host nearby, they remain bound to the part of the flesh they inhabited. That is the head because this is where the senses are located. Once the demon vacates the flesh, if it does not find a suitable host, it is plunged back to hell and another takes its place upon this earth. Once it leaves the decapitated head, it cannot return to it. As you can well imagine, there is no shortage of demons wanting to take their place among us. While those who make up the 666 are here, they are not enduring the agonies of hell. Their torment is turned to pleasure as long as they do evil's bidding. Who would not want a vacation from hell?

"Those lucky enough to be here have an unspoken pact to help keep their comrades with them. It is not often they go missing. Those present on earth will do anything to stay here. You could not ask for a more highly motivated workforce. Once every hundred years or so, one of them loses their head and cannot find a host. Myth has it they can occupy an animal like a snake or a cat and live in that host until they can locate a suitable faithless human. This is not true. They can influence a snake. That is all. Once out of their human host they must locate another human host. If they leave the decapitated head, they would be unable to return to it. But as long as they remain there, they cannot be cast back into hell."

Oliver thought about this for a moment. "What about the others? From what I have seen, there is no way there are only 666 of these things out there. I have seen their numbers grow over the years. There must be thousands, if not hundreds of thousands, throughout the world."

Guillermo gave him a subtle nod. "Yes, the 666 are Satan's hand-picked army. Much of the foul stench of hell makes its way here through acts of everyday evil done by the living. There has always been a direct connection between here and heaven, just as there has been between here and hell. Our world has invited much of the stench that seeps out of the cracks of hell. As a result, evil lurks in dark corners everywhere. It patiently waits for an invitation. Direct, implied or unintentional, it does not matter. You are right, Padre. They are everywhere. That is why your work is so important. The expansion of evil must be halted. It is like a runaway train."

Oliver glanced at Antonio and Felipe. Both were listening intently. "How can this spreading tide be halted? Do you know what will happen?"

"What I know, Padre, is they fear a man named Francis. He is the tide changer. They think he might be Pope one day. But it is not clear when or how. Evil's number one agenda was to find this man. Nowadays you are their number one agenda. You are too great a threat. Not only are you hampering their search for this man, they fear you could end their vacations from hell. None is eager to return."

"Guillermo, do you know anything of this blade which came into my possession?"

The old man stood up again. He walked to the entrance of the shack. "A great truth will be revealed through it, but I cannot say what or when. It will be made known to you in God's time.

Now come, let us tend to the business at hand."

The men exited the shack. The night was clear and the moon provided ample light. Oliver placed each of the severed heads into one of the metal boxes. Then they transported them to the circle's edge. The men made several trips carrying the boxes to the center of the circle. Oliver was amazed at how easily Guillermo was able to navigate his way around. The blind man knew where every rock and pebble lay. "Did you make this circle, Guillermo?"

"Yes, I worked on it for the past five years," he replied.

Such a large circle seemed like overkill to Oliver. "Why is it so large, and why did you put rocks all along the perimeter?"

"If a demon cannot find a host by the time it gets from the edge of the smaller circle in the center, to the edge of this exterior circle, it will be cast back into hell."

"How do you know that, Guillermo?"

"I just know this, Padre, in the same way you know the blade at your side will do precisely as you intend."

Oliver looked at the old man's blank white eyes. "You see very well for a blind man, Guillermo."

"I see what I need to see according to God's will," he replied.

Felipe finished carrying the last of the metal boxes. They were stacked in the form of a small pyramid, three layers high, placed inside the boundary of the smaller circle in the center. "That's it. They are all in the center."

Antonio suggested they pray before disbanding. The four men stood side by side at the edge. The moon cast their shadows into the circle as Antonio and Oliver took turns praying. When Oliver finished, they stood silently for a moment.

Guillermo turned and grabbed Oliver by the arm. The old man's grip was firm. It surprised Oliver, and he turned to look at the strange blind man. "Padre, you must be very careful. These next few weeks will not be easy for you. You are a most wanted man. Things will happen that cannot be explained. Trust your instincts and trust God. The tide changer is almost here. You must see to it he is safe." Guillermo released his grip.

"Who is this tide changer, Guillermo? How will I know him?"

"I believe him to be Pope Benedict's successor. You will

know him, Padre. Before the entire world knows him, you will know him, and you must protect him. I do not know the exact time when all this is to occur. I only know that it must occur sooner rather than later."

"I will trust what you have said, Guillermo. Thank you."

"Padre, there is one more thing. You must also play the role of ambassador."

Oliver smiled, *"That sure beats being the official head remover."* He was about to ask Guillermo what he meant.

Antonio interrupted his thoughts. "We should get going, Oliver. It is getting late. I will ride with you in your car back to the monastery so Felipe can go home from here."

Guillermo headed back to his shack.

"Adios, Guillermo."

"Adios, Padre."

Oliver and Antonio climbed into the vehicle.

Felipe climbed into his pickup truck. "Adios, Padre Oliver, Padre Antonio."

49

All Points Bulletin

Father Francesco Jimenez peered through his telescope. The night was perfect for stargazing. He stepped back and looked up at the splendidly clear night sky. As he was about to put his eye back to the telescope, he caught sight of a shooting star. He could not keep from smiling. He saw another, then another. It was an active stargazer's night. He pointed the telescope at the moon and examined its chalky surface. Suddenly, he heard banging at the front door. The banging continued. It seemed urgent.

He raced down to the first level, careful not to trip and fall. The pounding continued. He finally reached the door and opened it. Four police cars with flashing lights were parked in front of the rectory. He had been so focused on the stars he didn't notice the lights flashing below. Two policemen were at the door. The others remained further back. Their guns were drawn and pointed at him.

The policeman at the front door kept his hand on the butt of his gun. "What is your name?"

"I am Padre Jimenez. What has happened?"

"Where is the other priest?"

"What other priest?"

"We are looking for a Padre Oliver. Where is he?"

"I do not know where he is. He left earlier this evening. He did not tell me where he was going. Why are you looking for him?"

"He is wanted for murder. He was positively identified by

one of the guards at the Molina Mansion, and one of the wait staff also identified him. He massacred Sr. Molina and all of his guests today, then he set fire to the bodies. We must find him. He is a dangerous criminal." The policeman waved at the others behind him. "Do you mind if we have a look around?"

Before Father Jimenez could reply, several policemen stormed the house and began searching it. The officer at the door continued his questioning. "How do you know this priest? Where did he come from?"

Father Jimenez thought carefully about how he might answer questions about Oliver. "He is from the states. He said he was traveling through Mexico and came to spend a few days."

"Had you ever met him before?"

"No, he came about a week ago. That was the first time I met him."

"Did you know about his visit to Angel Molina's house?"

Father Jimenez nodded. "Yes, he told me he had been invited to visit, and I understand that is where he went today."

"Do you know of any reason why this priest would kill all these people? Did he say anything about this to you?"

"No, when I last saw him, he mentioned there had been a fire, but that is all he said. Then he left."

"Padre Jimenez, I hope you realize if you are hiding this man or lying about anything you know, you could be arrested and charged as his accomplice."

He looked at the officer's badge. "Officer Padilla, this old priest has told you everything he knows. I am not hiding him, and I do not know his whereabouts. You are free to search the house, but you will not find him here. It is all as I have told you."

"Do you make it a habit of admitting anyone who claims to be a priest into your church? How did you know he was really a priest?"

"I didn't ask him for ID. No one has ever come to the rectory impersonating clergy. As far as I know, he really is a priest."

"Are you sure you do not know where he went?"

"No, when I asked him where he was going, he said he was not sure. That is all I got from him."

"Are there any other priests here? Is there anyone else here with you, a priest that goes by the name of Francis?"

Father Jimenez shook his head. "No, Officer Padilla. I am the only one here."

The police who stormed the house came pouring out. "He's gone. There's nothing here."

Officer Padilla looked at Padre Jimenez. "If you hear from him, call the police immediately. I think there may be a sizable reward on his head, and I'm sure the church could use the money."

"Thank you, Officer Padilla. I will keep that in mind should he turn up here again."

Officer Padilla joined his partner in the police car. They pulled away and turned off their flashing lights.

50

Under a Shimmering Cloud

Oliver and Antonio pulled onto the narrow road leading to the monastery. From a distance, they could see the bright lights of several police vehicles parked at the entrance. Oliver stopped the car. "Antonio, you must drive up to the monastery alone. I cannot risk coming with you in case they're looking for me. Hurry, before they see that we've stopped the car."

Antonio slid into the driver's seat as Oliver took his few possessions out of the vehicle.

"If they ask you about my vehicle, tell them we had a fight and you escaped in my car."

Antonio smirked. "Oliver they will never believe me. Do I look like I've been in a fight?"

"Sorry, Antonio but you are right." Oliver punched Antonio in the face with a glancing blow, just hard enough to cause his lip to bleed. Then he messed up his hair. "There, now they'll believe you. Sorry, but this will protect you. Now go!" Oliver stepped away from the vehicle as Antonio sat in shock having been punched in the face by his friend. "Go, Antonio!"

Antonio drove to the entrance of the monastery. Oliver gathered his things and walked. He took a wide approach so he could arrive at the monastery from the side. He watched as Antonio arrived and later was close enough to hear some of the conversation. It was all in Spanish. He was able to understand they bought Antonio's story, however, one of the officers would stay behind in case the crazy priest returned. In fact, they would keep a Police Officer at the monastery on rotation until the murdering priest was apprehended.

Unable to return to the monastery, Oliver walked in the direction of the abandoned mine. A few moments later, he received a text from Antonio.

"Do not come to monastery. They are looking for you. They will be waiting for you for many days. I will text Felipe to pic u up."

Oliver texted back.

"OK I will be by the side of the road - near the turn off. Sorry about the lip."

Oliver used his crumpled jacket for padding. He sat on a large rock waiting for Felipe. He was glad at least he would not have to spend the night in the abandoned mine. Just about any other place would be preferable. He listened to the quiet and looked up, captivated by a few shooting stars and the shimmering silver cloud in the sky. The night was warm.

An hour later he received another text from Antonio.

"Felipe cannot come. Police are checking cars on all roads. Hide wherever you can until morning."

Oliver picked up his jacket, dusted himself off and walked toward the abandoned mine. Forty-five minutes later, he reached the entrance. He picked up a rock and threw it in, to see if an animal might be inside for the night. He did it several times. Nothing seemed to be inside. However, with the moon so full and the sky so full of stars, Oliver decided to lie outside and look up at the heavenly wonders. He remembered the special properties of the blade which he had in his possession. He walked over to a large boulder sticking out of the side of the mine's entrance. With several easy strokes, he sliced the boulder into sections roughly two inches thick. The blade's blue glimmer lit up the area around him as he cut the stone into pieces. The pieces were smooth, and he butted them together flat on the ground to make an even resting place. He lied down on his makeshift bed of rock using his knapsack and jacket as pillows.

He lay looking up at the stars. The silver shimmering cloud had drifted closer, almost directly above him. He realized he was quite tired. Just then, his phone rang. His battery was almost dead.

It was Detective Lopez.

"Hello Oliver, It's Detective Lopez."

"Hello Detective, what's up. My phone is about to die, with no way to charge it."

"Have you heard the news?"

"What news?"

"Pope Benedict has resigned from the papacy. It's been six hundred…"

Oliver's phone went dead. He lay still. All was quiet. He looked up at the sky and prayed.

"Here I am, Lord. I will go where you lead me. Guide me as you must, as only you can. May your will be done. I am yours."

A few minutes later, the demon slayer fell asleep under a shimmering silver cloud floating in the star-filled, moonlit sky.

Epilogue

When is it too late to ask for forgiveness? The human lens through which we try to understand God's love falls short of grasping a love so large and encompassing that it could forgive someone after they've committed an atrocity. This leads to the question: Why do we do what we do? Monty's free will was compromised before he was born. Is our free will compromised without us even realizing what's going on? Perhaps not as obvious, but equally dangerous is our overriding denial of the impact the media has on our behavior. Reality TV, gratuitous violence, self mutilation, aggressive secularism, plummeting standards of what is deemed acceptable in our society, violent video games, all have a dramatic impact on our free will.

Like Mama Crossbones held Monty's free will captive, are we allowing ourselves to be held captive by mind-numbing entertainment programs, hatred, and an over dependency on technology? These are our crossbones. But, how can one see clearly past all the clutter and noise? How can we deprogram ourselves and know we are on the right track? How can we know that we are truly being ourselves, and that our free will is our own?

We can all find answers to these questions in the same place Monty found answers: in God. God's will is that we should love one another and find happiness and eternal life through Christ. The delusion of God, or the conviction in God, depending on your point of view, is the only way to find true happiness and purpose.

If you enjoyed *Persistent Evil, The Demon Slayer*, please take a minute to write a review and post it on Amazon.

Thank you for taking the time to read my book.

The story continues with *The Francis Conspiracy* up next.

Questions to Consider

Should someone who has done horrific things be forgiven if they are truly sorry for what they've done?

When is it too late to ask for forgiveness?

Are there people in your life who need the gift of forgiveness from you?

Have you forgiven yourself for things in your past which may be holding you up and filling your heart with guilt?

What are the crossbones in your life?

Are you exercising your free will or is it the will of someone or something else (TV, abusive partner, guilt, video game, warped self image, low self-esteem, envy)?

Have you really allowed God to work in your life, or are you waiting for proof before you fully open your heart?

For Those Who Are Searching

The Bible promises that when you sincerely ask God for forgiveness and trust in Jesus, you will experience new life in Christ.

That if you confess with your mouth, "Jesus is Lord," and believe in your heart that God raised him from the dead, you will be saved. — Romans 10:9

Today, with all your heart, surrender your life to Jesus Christ. Confess your sins. Ask God to forgive you. Say that you'll trust in Jesus. And thank Him for the gift of everlasting life. Pray now:

"Father, I know that I have sinned against You. Please forgive me. Wash me clean. I promise to trust in Jesus, Your Son. I believe that He died for me — He took my sin upon Himself when He died on the cross. I believe that He was raised from the dead. I surrender my life to Jesus today.

"Thank You, Father, for Your gift of forgiveness and eternal life. Please help me to live for you. In Jesus' name, Amen."

There is nothing magical about the words you use. It is the attitude of your heart that God cares about.

I put this page in my first book and received some criticism over it. My response to that is: All my gifts come from God. Not taking the opportunity to reach even that one person who may be searching, would be shame on me. If that one person happens to be you, then it's worth the criticism and bad reviews. If that person *is* you, please share your story of conversion with me. Email: diogenesruiz@live.com

Peace and all good. - DR

Acknowledgements

Thank you, Jesus, for everything!

Thank you, Father William McConville, aka Fr. Bill, aka "The most interesting man in the world," for your tremendous good humor and equally large ego. Your amazing stories helped me with character development and your life of service to God has inspired me, and many others, along our faith journeys. Thanks for inspiring the character of Fr. Oliver. He would not have been possible without you. Also, thank you for your moving homilies, for treating your flaws like they are old buddies, for being real and approachable, and for making it cool to be a priest. You're like a combination of James Bond and Billy Graham. (Father Bill is the only priest when entering a premise while wearing a short sleeve shirt is told that no weapons are allowed. His arms could be mistaken for rocket launchers.)

Thank you, Fr. David McBriar, Pat Kowite, and Trina Sugrue for beta reading and providing valuable feedback.

Thank you, Charlie Felix and Tricia Downs for beta reading and proof reading, and providing such helpful editorial mark ups. Special thanks to Tricia for her good spirit and help during the age of dry toast.

Thanks to, Nancy Stout for her line-by-line editing as she lay in a hospital bed with *Elements of Style,* by Strunk and White at her side. If you found a typo in the book, it wasn't that Nancy didn't catch it, most likely it got lost in a sea of red and yellow marks and I missed it.

Thanks to my family and friends for their support, especially to my wonderful wife, Karin.

Thanks to everyone who purchased A Rabbit's Tale, An Easter Story. Your comments and encouragement gave me the confidence to write this book.

About the Author

Diogenes Ruiz is a Christian fiction author. He was born in the Dominican Republic and grew up in New York City's Washington Heights. A lover of all things sic-fi, he specializes in fiction with spiritual insight. His debut novel *A Rabbit's Tale, An Easter Story*, has received overwhelming praise.

"A terrific, fast-paced little fantasy with the most realistic message of love and Life in Christ. I think God must be smiling."

"For a new author, Diogenes Ruiz has produced a wonderful tale that has many well defined characters you can truly relate to as well as a well structured story line that is easy to follow even through the many twists the story takes! I honestly couldn't put it down the closer I got to the end! Not a story for young ones, A Rabbit's Tale is for those of us who reminisce about Easter from our younger days! Bravo!!"

"I really enjoyed this story. It is a real inspiration to me to try and live a better life for Christ. Even though I am not of the same Faith, we all serve the same God."

"I started reading thinking this would be a quick read to fill-time but instead it was much more. I loved the characters but much more enjoyed how the story of Christ and His love for us was woven into the story. Recommend this to anyone searching for a fiction piece with spiritual insight."

"I enjoy writing stories that highlight the struggle between good and evil, and the implications of the choices we make. My life has been filled with the Divine manifested through the insignificant. I am grateful for the opportunity to entertain and make an impact on the lives of people who read what I write."

To My Readers

Thank you for reading *Persistent Evil, The Demon Slayer*. If you enjoyed it, I hope you will like *The Francis Conspiracy*, the next book in the series.

The Francis Conspiracy:

The Conclave is about to gather to elect a new pope. Fr. Oliver has his work cut out for him. He is supposed to protect someone, but he doesn't know who.

Once a priest, at a large parish community, he is now hunted by the Council, a large and powerful global network of organized evil. If they find him, they will kill him. They will do anything to prevent the prophesized election of a new pope by the name of Francis from being fulfilled. *The Francis Conspiracy* is scheduled to be released in the spring of 2016. Look for it on Amazon.

Don't forget to leave a review on Amazon. My goal is to write novels full time. I pray that God will hear my prayer and I want to thank you from the bottom of my heart for purchasing this book and helping me fulfill that dream.

May all your hopes and dreams come true.
Thank you! God's bless you and your family. – D. Ruiz

Stay in touch, write and let me know your thoughts.
If you've had a conversion experience, please share your story with me.

Email: diogenesruiz@live.com
Website: http://www.diogenesruiz.com
Facebook: www.facebook.com/DiogenesRuizAuthor